DOVISCH IN THE WILDERNESS AND OTHER STORIES

BY HERBERT WILNER:

ALL THE LITTLE HEROES

DOVISCH IN THE WILDERNESS AND OTHER STORIES

HERBERT WILNER

The Bobbs-Merrill Company, Inc.
A Subsidiary of Howard W. Sams & Co., Inc., Publishers
Indianapolis · Kansas City · New York

CONTENTS

for
STEVEN
SARAH
and
AMY

DOVISCH IN THE WILDERNESS

Call me Dovisch, another wanderer survived to tell a story.

I mean it. Since I saw you last Wednesday, I had an American misadventure. I find myself obligated to share it with you, a class in American Literature, Early Period. Yes, I know what you are here for: because I announced last week this hour is set aside to talk with you about your final examination. Thus come all the bright faces at eight in the morning at the end of May in yet another spring in a part of California that has only weather and no climate, thus no season, hence no time. Except finals time. What kind of questions will Dovisch ask on his final exam? A short route to a high grade to know beforehand the kind of questions. So no one is absent today. Perfect attendance for the first time in how many weeks? Let it be so.

Nevertheless, I shall share this experience with you. I promise it will be preparation enough for your finals. I share it with you fresh and unrehearsed because it didn't end till two o'clock this very morning. Six hours ago. No, that's not right. Today is for a flyer, but it is also for facts. My colleagues would remind me: dates, figures, facts—toughness. At the bottom of all knowledge and every wisdom, a fact. It is the gossip of the corridors, what my colleagues accuse me of. And some of you have heard it in the corridors, or over coffee, or in your other classes. I know how they accuse me, leavening it with an intolerable affection: Dovisch, the rainbow-maker. So the hard fact of it is that my misadventure did not come to its end at two this morning. It continues still, because I am obligated to share it with you, and I am going to share it with you, delicacies notwithstanding. And you will not learn from it because you will not see the immediate profit to yourselves, because you will not imagine it can have anything to do with your final exam. You begin already to put down the ballpoints, to close the notebooks, and on some of your faces I see that smile reserved for moments like this when you know I am about to go the long way around. There goes Dovisch again, the rainbow-maker on another flyer. Students of Early American Literature, Section 2, listen to me. Take notes. My little misadventure *is* your finals. And thus I begin, Dovisch fashion, learned from Emerson, accented by way of the Bronx, inflected not a little by a history somewhat older than the American, accent and inflection slightly more exaggerated this morning.

I went last week to Pyramid Lake. I went alone after my last class on Wednesday. I went in my car. I curse cars every day of my life, but I went to Pyramid Lake to be alone, to hold conversations with no one, so the car was a matter of free choice. For those of you not from this part of the country, know that Pyramid Lake is thirty miles north and slightly east of Reno. It is thirty miles long and ten miles wide. I went to Pyramid Lake to test myself in the experience of solitude, and to know at first hand the distinctions to be made between solitude and isolation. I had four whole days to spend there. It will come to some of you as no surprise that I had never in all my life sustained a period, however brief, of true solitude. Isolation yes—isolation always—but not solitude. So the four days, seized from my work and my family, seemed time enough for a deliberate test. I took a sleeping bag which I preferred to buy for the occasion rather than borrow from a colleague. I knew too well not their unwillingness to lend but their looks upon lending. Dovisch in a sleeping bag? I took a sweater, a flannel shirt, changes of socks, and so forth, also canned fruits and a can opener, and boxes of zwieback borrowed from my daughter. I have a credit card, so I needed no money even for gas. I took fifty cents for bridge tolls, and no more. And my checkbook. I must explain this.

I did not start out intending to make things difficult. I wanted, if possible, to experience joy in my solitude, not hardship. Thus my food arrangement. I was not going to test self-reliance in the form of survival. That's not what Emerson meant. Thoreau either. I was going to test solitude, in which self-reliance was a mere consequence. I can't fish, I have never in my life gone fishing. And if I did fish and caught a fish, I could not trust myself to build a fire. And if I caught a fish and built a fire, I would have had to have brought along the fishing equipment. Also a pot for cooking. No, I was altogether less encumbered with the canned fruits, and I admit a fondness for sweet syrups and a distaste for fish. I must insist upon the fact that I went responsibly to Pyramid Lake for pleasure, not hardship. I left out money not because I sneer at it. I am Puritan enough to know its grace. But in my wallet it would remind me always of purchase, and that would imply some other person who sells; and though he might through all my stay be absent, the money in my wallet would be an emblem of his implication in my life and a diminishment of my solitude. I took the checkbook because solitude is the essence of responsibility and has nothing in common with thoughtlessness. I have a wife and four little children. There are emergencies in such a world. I will come soon to tell you of some of them.

Be advised also that I took no books, magazines or newspapers. I took no paper and no writing implements. I must correct again the easy assumption some of you begin to make that I went to Pyramid Lake on a merely literary impulse borrowed from those very books I refused to take. "Life is our dictionary," Emerson said, *American Scholar*, 1837, and you imagine I set aside books the better to experience real life. It is not what Emerson meant. It is not what I intended. He wanted us to possess and not be possessed by what we read. Reading was an extension of the active life by which he challenged all Americans. For my own part, I disavowed books because they implicate a voice roaring at me, a diminishment of solitude. I disavowed writing. It implicates my untalented efforts to roar at someone else. Another diminishment. You see—I tried to be practical in everything.

So, directly to it. The time goes. This is our last meeting. I must get it all in. I tell you, I see America now. I can open my fist and watch it dance. Rainbows, Dovisch, rainbows. Facts, dates . . .

I arrived at Pyramid Lake on Wednesday at five-thirty in the evening, having traveled east to find the West. I went through Reno and then north. Motels, restaurants, gas stations, domiciles for the divorced, the divorcing, the gamblers. Scarlet letters in every face, branded in the flesh. The un-epic frontier of our present time. Then northward through the desert mountains. Sagebrush and female slopes and hollows. Late sunlight shifting. Mountains shifting in the light. The windshield dances. A curve in the road, a descent, and there to the right, below the lowering line of the desert mountain, Pyramid Lake. Brilliant even for a polished stone. Water polished by water. A table top in a naked world. Not a tree. Not a cloud. The whole lake in one turn of the head. A great belt of not quite water under a balloon of sky. Into which enters, into that universe of silence, the *phtt-phtt* of the old Plymouth, inside of which, Dovisch, Professor of American Literature. Specialist in Emerson; seminars offered also, for a touch of the old country, in Dostoievski. Inside of Dovisch, before this naked world all in silence, the heart empties with a gush, a roar reaching into the corners of *our* Promised Land.

Terrifying landscape. Perfection for solitude. I must impress you with it through *my* eyes, but I have no power for such description. From where would I get it? Born forty-two years ago in the Bronx, Simon Dovisch, second son to Morris and Esther Dovisch, immigrants from Russia, that Eastern world tilting off Europe; related also to uncles of Oriental countenance to make a boy wonder from which angle the wanderers first began to wander, to cohabit with what strange ancestors along the way. Raised on the fourth floor rear, sharing his brother's room with a view opening to other windows on the fourth floor with coal-smoked bricks between, and raised in the streets, down there on the dark concrete bottom of what *your* Whitman called the clefts of streets, raised to games of ball, at which he was inept, and among the squealings and the yawpings of those to whom solitude would be death and for whom isolation was a way of life. Who learned sex on the corners under lampposts and fumbled at its practice in night-time backyards and on tenement roofs, filled with it by a guilt the whole tribe of Mathers could not have endured because it derived from the shame of poverty and not from a mere redemptive sin. So with much to prove through the years, and with books already the only means of his demonstrations. Immersed then, drowning in the vivid American history: splashed and drenched with Pilgrims and Puritans and Quakers, Revolutionists and Rationalists and opportunists, inventors and fur trappers and Indians too, Natty Bumppos and millionaires and Abolitionists and poets and novelists and cowboys and presidents, prairies and mountains and deserts and oceans, gleaned, all of it, from black type on a white page, millions of pages by a light bulb on the fourth floor rear in the Bronx. Later in libraries. Here now on the Western shore, a Professor of American Literature.

That literature beginning, as I have told you, in a bitter romance with God for the possession by His grace of an endless wealth of wilderness to be ravished in love, goaded into the love of primitive instincts, and shamed by those instincts into savagery itself, which is the worship of the thing. So they found emblems of it everywhere, the thing: witches, kites, and keys, scarlet letters, a whale, a ferry, a river, things celebrated by the very prophets who saw the doom in them. And all the while even the most ignorant of them learning in their blood what Dovisch from the Bronx, professing American literature, cannot infuse into the blood, melt down the books how he will.

Things, things, things. To fish, to hunt, to build a house, to farm, to conduct a business, to repair a car, to predict a season. To name a tree, to name a flower, to name a fish, a bird, to control a single practical art—to build, say, a fire. To repair, say, a car, a damned, cursed old Plymouth. Things, things, things. In them resides the power of all description. Dovisch alone at Pyramid Lake, in a naked world of silence, seeking solitude, testing whether he can so late in life experience it at all, in order to understand by experience one of the conditions of what he teaches.

Students, I take pride in telling you I remained at the lake all my allotted time. You must understand what it was for me if you are to share my experience of what came to pass at the end of it. That first night. Arrivals are stunning. Impressions are immediate. You never know again all that lives in the first encounter. And now, a mere four days, I cannot recover those first minutes of coming upon the lake. Because none of what followed...

Look. I did this the first day. I arrived in the evening at five-thirty. I drove on. I did not want to stay where the highway came directly to the lake. There was something like a diner there. Hot dogs, soda, so forth. Closed and deserted, it could nevertheless be a point of gathering. I follow the lake road some miles farther. The sun glaring. Barren everywhere. I park the car. I open a can of stewed pears, a box of zwieback, and I have my supper at the lake. I sit and stare. Dovisch alone. Later, the sun going down. A dish of flame. Thoughts of my family in our Metropolitan Life Housing Project. Thoughts of my students, of you. Thoughts of America. Then a chill, the sudden cold. I put on my flannel shirt, my sweater. The growing darkness. I prepare the sleeping bag. Ah, that first night of trying to sleep in that wretched sack. Smile all you want, but one thing all of you can learn from the Bronx is the nature of a true mattress. Here at the lake, rocks and stones underneath. And I told them in the shop where I purchased the sleeping bag. Look at me, I told them. A tall man, feet like canoes. Ample room, ample room, he assured me. American entrepreneurs. The human contact gone, the cash register everything. I was too big for the bag, the bag too small for me. In physical discomfort begins the wilderness of imaginings. The enemy of sleep.

In the total darkness, in the universe of silence, what else, what vast night life crawls and slithers here? Snakes? Rattlers? Spiders? Tarantulas? Calm yourself, Dovisch! Achieve solitude. I ransack such knowledge as I have of flora and fauna. Miserable knowledge. I could have written all that I knew on a part of one zweiback and have made a supper of the part remaining. So I confess. The first night was full of imagined horrors. I have from a cockroach childhood on the fourth floor a loathing of crawling things.

You can imagine, then, the depths of my self-contempt when I commenced to believe I would not even make it through the first night. Not only the lumps and clumps of stones beneath me, but the wretched sleeping bag too small. Not only the stones and the sleeping bag, but my eyeglasses too. If the stones and the bedding should keep me awake, I should at least enjoy the stars. When in his life did Dovisch sleep with the stars? But with his eyeglasses off, who could see the stars? With his eyeglasses on, how sleep at all? And if the stones and the sleeping bag and the eyeglasses were not enough, comes now the wild imaginings of crawling things. Thoughts, then, of retreating to the car. It was not that much of a cheat on my idea of solitude, but something in me argued against it as a mere disguise for an early withdrawal. Besides, what if a crawling thing had made its way into the car while I had unloaded? Wouldn't the thing then seek artificial revenge on me, whereas in the open space, with a whole Western desert in which to conduct its slithering life, might it not merely crawl away from me as a nuisance to be avoided?

Ultimately, I resigned myself. In the middle of the night I offered myself the following proposition. If it was my fate to succumb to a venomous bite, if a snake or a spider with thousands of square barren miles to crawl in chooses the few inches of my exposed face, then God's will be done. I surrendered. I can report to you I overcame my imaginings. Ultimately, I slept.

Came then the first of my pink dawns at the lake. Morning is when I am awake and there is a dawn in me, said Thoreau, echoes Dovisch now, who ordinarily, by old Bronx habit and by way of avoiding noisy children in the morning, leads the Dostoievskian life of the underground world after the midnight hour when the soul, losing God, finds the psychiatrist. Let me summarize those blessed days. Let me give you the light and the tone and the angle. You squirm. You ask yourselves, of what relevance? Is there at least a story? But the story is also the arrangements to be made. Didn't Hawthorne arrange? Didn't Melville?

Know then that I sat for long hours in sun-bright places at the other side of the lake. That I walked for miles along the rim of the water, my pants rolled, feet naked, naked head to the naked sun. My eyes grew accustomed to naked distance. My mind thereafter sought relief from panoramic registrations. It ordered my eyes to closer recognitions. I forced myself to look for long uninterrupted sequences at nearer things. At pebbles, rocks, pools of water, boulders that were porous, at the pores of boulders, at brush, at silence itself I looked and listened. I spent a whole hour tossing one pebble into shallow water, retrieving it each time. I spent a whole hour watching a large bird flying high in great circles—watching me, perhaps. Crow, eagle, hawk, falcon—who am I to know the names of birds? For a whole hour we were hundreds of feet apart, but eyeball to eyeball. And I knew its great power of sight compared to my weakness of vision. Easy then to make factual what I have told you again and again as mere surmise: the object seen is in the image of the eyes, not the object. Never again ask me, where is it—the Oversoul? Of what size, what shape? Know then what I mean when I ask in turn: of what size and shape is your eye?

Look—picture my days at Lake Pyramid this way. Know that my days were symmetrical. Know that I lived inside them with great precision. Picture me there from up close as a tall, gross-featured, big-footed, clumsy man, alien to where he stood and

what he gazed at, reddening in the sun, his hidden heart slipping
into the thrill of un-isolation. Picture him there from afar as
but another sparrow in the great void, not without a little grace,
a small addition of human design against the barren mountains
overlooking the blue and stony water under the height of the
sky. Hear me whistling Mozart melodies into the Nevada air.

Students, in this landscape so strange to me, I learned how I
loved the great, secret, mythical history of my country. Yes, *my*
country too. Removed by the solitude itself from all isolation, I
would have laid down my life for my country's secret heart. Yes,
Dovisch on a flyer, but fly with me if you can. Solitude is the
experience of the idea itself. It is the racial nostalgia reducing
the baggage of our life's factuality—even the fourth floor rear
and its crazy summons to books. But in the thingness of time, the
idea vanishes. It had to be lost. Long before cars and jets and
bombs and rockets. Lost even as far back as whaling time, as
Walden time, as *Leaves of Grass* time. But history is the aspiration as well as the loss.

The idea and the fact and the emblem between. I could not
wait to get back to share some of this with you in the beginning
of this hour, to give you a particle of my new feeling. But how
would I say it, since it was itself only another idea? More Dovisch rainbows. But fate waited. Nothing is wasted. My misadventure waited. The facts themselves waited. So—the arrangements
made and the story at last.

My time was up and I threw my litter into the car. I left not
one trace of my presence there. The bird who had watched me
was long since gone. Would its eyes in their future remember
Dovisch? Who knows? It was Sunday. It was yesterday. It was
two in the afternoon. I was exuberant. I had stayed out my time.
I had learned. Which of you cannot by now picture Dovisch in
his exuberance? I almost could not find my keys. Trembling
fingers fumbling in pockets. The beginning of panic. Voluntary
solitude is one thing, but who am I to confront an enforced one?
Calm, calm, I urged myself. There were the keys in the glove

17

compartment where I had with good forethought left them. The return home then.

I turn the key. I press the pedal. Nothing. A little *erk-erk* noise in the big silence, and then nothing. Calm, calm, I urge myself. First the fuel. But how should it be the fuel when I had filled up in Truckee with just such a precaution in mind? I am almost afraid to look. If there was a leak and in three days it all ran out, where should I walk now for gas? I turn the key and look. Plenty of fuel. The needle almost to the three-quarters. It was a mistake. A clumsiness of the fingers. My excitement to get home. To see you here this morning, to tell you. Again, then on the pedal. Again nothing. *Erk-erk-erk,* and nothing more. In the middle of nowhere with a car that won't start on a Sunday afternoon with a lecture class to meet on the next morning, having promised, given my word to review for the finals, not to mention a devoted family, the oldest child only seven, but who knows already how to worry. Calm yourself. A voice into the panic, into the silence, into another *erk-erk,* another and another. I ransack such facts as I have gathered of cars that will not start. Another zwieback full. Gathered from the general mechanic atmosphere and previous car catastrophes, like old people in hospitals who know their organs in proportion to the number of survived diseases therein. So a car that won't start: wet spark plugs? How could that be in a desert? Once with an old Studebaker there was trouble with the vacuum advance. A vacuum advance. Who could remember what it was? Where in the engine would I find it? Once with an old Ford there was trouble with a voltage regulator. Again, who knows where such a thing is to be found in an engine? Would you believe me when I confess I do not even know what voltage is? I would tell you back what you tell me of the Oversoul. I can't see it, so why should I believe in it? Is a voltage regulator something to believe in? Tinker Toys for children. Apparatus. But if the ignorance derived from a lack of faith should cost you your life in the desert? or attendance at your job? or the peace of mind of your family? There's the rub.

So smile at me and my car pickle. Do you pause ever to count up all the things to which you have delivered faith and are ignorant of? Girls here who drive cars to campus. Do you know what makes them go? Gasoline. Is that an answer? Then food alone would keep alive a dying man. Do you know, when you press a button, why the elevator should close a door and go up or down to the designated floor and not through the top of the building, or through the bottom of the cellar? Do you know why an airplane should fly? Why these senseless tubes in the ceiling should light up when I press a button? Not to mention computers. Or X-rays. Or a radio. Or television. Listen—our Benjamin Franklin, whom I treated so scantily in the first semester. Sandwiched between Puritans and Emerson, who could afford to pause there? But who would deny he was one of those who lived with his feet on the ground? That I despise the man is another story.

The battery. Of course I thought of the battery. Three days and I had not once used the car. But the battery was only three months old and the guarantee was for eighteen. So go cash in a guarantee at Lake Pyramid. A million eighteen-month batteries, and Dovisch gets the lemon. Another old story. The question was a push. Where could I find another car to push me in that sand and sage where I had pulled off the road? Calm. Calm. Perhaps not the whole battery. A cable connection, perhaps. I too had heard of such things. For luck I try once more. *Erk-erk*, and then nothing. I open the hood. I see the battery and the cables thereto, one with the plus and one with the minus. What all that means, I never knew. Gingerly, I touch the wires. My heart leaps. Indeed, one seems loose. I turn a little, and it tightens. I rush back to the car, turn the ignition. *Erk-erk*, nothing more. I go out again. Again with the cables—pinching, stroking, prodding, pushing, punching at last, punching the senseless cable, the stupid battery, and for good measure the hot fender. *Erk-erk*.

Listen—the hour flies. To make it short: I need a push and the solitude is over for me, but not for where I am. To walk then and return in a car with help. I take the keys. I walk. I walk and walk. At last a sign. Four miles to Nixon. It is already an hour since I first tried to start the car. Three o'clock now and who ever heard of Nixon? A community, a hamlet, and people nevertheless. Nixon in an hour, I assure myself, and perhaps a car I can flag down along the way before then. I am a good walker, an old Manhattan tramper. A deep breath for fortitude, and off I go, driven by hatred of cars, hurried by my anxiety about driving at night on highways.

There is no time to give you the hike in the hot desert sun. Fill in as you will. All history is incomplete. Only imagine the anger, the distress, the reasonable panic. A cool head, says Melville, betrays an icy heart. The sweat, the dust. The beginning of trees, an oasis. The sight at last of a car on the highway. I get out in the lane. Exultant, I wave my arms. How lucky that I so soon see a car! Would you believe it that they nearly ran me down? A gang of boys, maybe college boys, car-tinkerers. Maybe any one of them could have helped me. Am I innocent to believe any one of them would have if I had had the opportunity to explain to him what it was all about? But can I make a speech to a rocket? Seventy, eighty miles an hour they went past me, swerving into the other lane in the last minute, and at the same time I leaped into a thicket of sage on my side. One of them had the gall to stick a head out the window and shake a fist at me.

I brushed myself off and resumed walking. Only then did I think for the first time of the appearance I presented to others. Since the Wednesday morning of my departure, I had not shaved. My nose and forehead, I knew from old experience, would be shining like a McIntosh apple—sunburn. My khaki pants were some other color now, and no end of wrinkles everywhere from struggles with the undersized sleeping bag. My T-shirt smeared from where I leaned under the hood of the car, and my hands all dirt and grease from playing with the battery cable. What sort of welcome could I expect at the first house I came to? Bedraggled and begrimed, how would I be received on someone's property, uninvited on a Sunday afternoon?

Came then the first house. Not a house, a shack. Albeit under a few trees and with a porch, and before the porch not one but three cars. Not a person in sight. Behind the dwelling place, on a small slope, cows, cattle—it was not then the time to discriminate. But on the other side of the road, another shack, and only one car. I decide for that one. Three cars on a Sunday before such a small dwelling place means company, visitors. Not, it seemed to me, an encouraging atmosphere for a plea of distress, a call for help. I crossed the road, noticing the newness of the car. A shack to live in, but a new car for leaving and returning. Another small porch. Three, four steps, the wood answering back to my feet. Good, I tell myself: for the door to the right of the steps is half open, and the noise of my approach forewarns them I don't come in stealth. Outside, the brilliant sun; inside, all dark. And already a foul odor. Better that way, I encourage myself. Poverty and even filth will be less offended by my own appearance. I knock, not timidly, not too loudly. Good luck to you here, Dovisch, I announce to myself, implore. Then I tell myself at once: ask only to use the telephone, to call the nearest service station.

There is no answer to my knocking. I knock again, somewhat louder. I wait. No answer. There is the odor, definitely foul, reminiscent for me of dark corners in schoolyards, of relief stations on certain desolate subway stops. Also sounds—a chair scraping, perhaps. But no footsteps, no speech. I call out, "Anyone at home?" And that, in four days' time, is the first spoken language I have addressed to a listener. Do you know the experience of separation from your own voice? Do you know how it accounts in Thoreau for the initial acid of his Walden tones, the isolation invading solitude? But yesterday at that moment I was not looking for insights into Thoreau. I thought: should I push the door open the rest of the way or knock again? I push. Not vigorously—politely. The light from outside floods in. They are standing there blinking at the light, watching me.

A man and a woman. Puerto Ricans, I tell myself. No, Mexicans. What would Puerto Ricans be doing there? Short and thick and swarthy, wide foreheads, wide noses, like Gauguins—but no

21

sparkle: sullen, suspicious. They keep blinking at the light. They look at me, and they look at each other. Dark black hair, both of them. The man in a sort of crew cut, but not cut down enough. The hairs standing up like quills, and greasy. The woman's, too, but lank, uncombed. He wears dungarees and one of those faded blue worker's-farmer's shirts, also denim. She is bare-armed in a dress that merely hangs from her, that needs a belt, a collar, a something. Will they even understand English, I wonder, as I begin my introduction, my explanation, my need.

Students, I am not a good reporter, not a good observer to begin with. Furniture I am blind to. I can stare at stuff in the house of a stranger or friend and not remember the very next day what was there. But did you need to be Henry James or even Dreiser to stand where I stood yesterday afternoon on the threshold of that shack (no one had yet invited me in) and not know at once as you tried to explain your predicament that there could be no telephone in such a place? Perhaps there was not even electricity. Between the two of them, where they stood, there was a little table on skinny legs—a bridge table—piled with dishes and beer cans, and on the table was a thick, half-burned candle. So you see how I had to shift my explanation toward a plea for direct help. What I do remember is a pot-bellied stove with a tilted flue, clothes on hooks on one of the walls, and in a corner by itself, nothing near it, like a museum piece, a single contour chair on those pipe legs. Sears Roebuck modern. Red yet.

So—were they in all those exchanges of looks between them understanding a word of what I said about my car, my plight, my explanation and apology for my ragged appearance? I must confess I said nothing of my professional occupation. Instinctively I imagined it would make no impression, or it would actually run a risk. Anywhere in Europe it would have been my first announcement. Put that in your notebooks and make of it what you will. I ended with a mention of my children and my wife, and the worry my certain absence from dinner tonight would cause them until I could get the car started and find a telephone. Did they under-

stand? Another exchange of looks between the two of them.
Then at last the man speaks. One word.

"Sunday."

No accent, least of all a Mexican accent. But with spitefulness.
That haughtiness of the permanently deprived addressing the
temporarily deprived.

"Yes, Sunday," I say. "My wife alone on a Sunday and worrying that something has happened to me. The accidents on highways these days." I look toward the woman. I have, you noticed,
dropped the plea of children. I get the impression this is a child-
less place. Who can guess what resentment it causes? Again the
exchange of looks between them. Except for the turning of their
heads and the blinking of their eyes, they remain all the while
motionless. And I am still only on the threshold. He talks again.
Two words now.

"How much?" he says.

"How much what?" I ask him. I look again at the woman. I
am forced to say she was ugly. That stoop, that arch and thick-
ness between the shoulder blades. The filthy hair. That sullenness, that stupefaction of face. She looks again at the man.

"Sunday," he repeats. "You pay how much?"

"How much do you want?" I say.

"How much do you give?" he asks.

"How much do you get paid an hour?" I ask him.

No response. Like wood. Nevertheless, in fairness, in fact,
though I am but a poor businessman, I do admit the bargain is on
his side, and, humanity apart, the right too. I cannot conceive of
what I intruded upon between those two, but I am the intruder,
and in need.

"Ten dollars if you get the car to start," I tell him.

Again the looks back and forth. This time a little perceptible
heightening of effect. The impact of ten dollars in this place, in
these lives.

"Fifteen," he says. "Fifteen for the car to start."

I smile to him. I shrug. All this from the threshold still. The

23

smile and shrug of my people for centuries with their backs against the wall. "It will take you," I tell him, "ten minutes to get there, two minutes to push, ten minutes to get back. But all right, fifteen."

"Ten anyway," he says.

"Fifteen is all right," I say. "I made a bargain. I gave my word."

"Ten anyway," he repeats. The woman moves now for the first time. She scratches.

"Anyway what?" I ask him.

"If the car don't start, ten dollars anyway."

Bitter money-sucking pessimist! Go romanticize peasants. What could I do? I agree. I refuse to contemplate the possibility that the car should not start. What could it be after bringing me all this way here without incident and sitting there undisturbed for four days, what else but a battery?

And so then to his car, the key for which he removes from a chain around his neck inside his shirt. Can you imagine? And though it was parked right outside his shack, the doors were locked. Well, I do not make much of it. Who is really to blame him? A brand new Chevy with red leather seats. What efforts it took to buy it, the labors now to keep paying for it. Did he come all the way from Mexico—under what hardships?—to live here—in what alienation?—and not have some chrome glitter of our ways rub off on him? So let Professor Dovisch sweat blood with the old Plymouth that won't start and let the laborer of the shack have his firebox that he was driving now at a wild seventy miles an hour. Compensation, Emerson called it. It was also a source of reassurance. When they drive like maniacs, they know all about cars.

He had nothing to say to me. We sat the first minute in silence. There was almost a foot between us in height—the advantage on my side. I must say it helped me to contemplate with a little less anxiety the financial arrangement I had made—the fact that I would have to pay with a check, and somewhere find a pen, and commence with identifications. And what would he make of such identifications? American Association of University Professors, Modern Language Association, New England Historical Society. He would have to settle for the gasoline credit card.

I mentioned at the beginning of the hour that I would tell my misadventure despite certain indelicacies. Let me say, then, that in the man's car on the way back to the lake and to my own car, whether from understandable tension, or from the unrelieved diet of stewed fruits, whatever it was, my stomach commenced now to emit noises. To cover the awkwardness, though I had determined I could be as sullenly silent as my companion, I began to speak.

"My name is Simon Dovisch," I say to him.

He nods. No handshake. Nothing.

"Any your name is . . . ?" I ask.

"Mike," he says.

"Mike what?" I press him. Why should I alone be the vulnerable one? Why should I have given away everything and he nothing?

"Mike," he repeats. Nothing more, and stares straight ahead. A profile, I am forced to say, that looks as if it got finished off with a bang from a flat shovel.

"This is an impressive country," I remark. I confess a twinge for the stuffy ambiguity of the word I chose. "A beautiful country," I correct myself. No answer. I try again. "The kind of country," I observe, "in which, for four days, you might say, we were almost neighbors." Like a stone he sits behind the wheel, not even a blink of the eyes. An elbow on his door where the window is open, the arm up, the fingers drumming on the roof. With one hand, seventy miles an hour, seventy-five. What else can I try with him in this simple way that's demanded of decent human exchange? Can I offer a hint of what I was doing at the lake? How would he understand it? From where do human connections come anyway? Must language always fail except among the limited few who have formed a corporation to study from it, but also without connection and only until finals time, and then the corporation dissolved, finished? Am I committed forever to my alienation? Is it my fault, or the other's? Who was alien in the car that I should talk and he shouldn't answer and that ten inches between us should be a whole Mississippi? Do I make mistakes not knowing country ways? Is there a right subject for conversation with him that I have not the instinct for? The colors on the hills? Or even Reno: gambling? Or something personal—a compliment to his car? Or something more manly, albeit speculative, about the common labor before us of starting my car, and by which, if he would respond, I could sneakily test his air of authority over such matters as batteries and vacuum advances? Or something historical, as, for instance, not too long ago Indians had lived here?

Indians!

I had no sooner shaped the word in my head when my eyes gave it back again, in type, recollected all at once from the road map I had used on the way up. Near Pyramid Lake, Nixon. Printed next to Nixon, each word under the other inside the lines designating borders of the allotted land, the words: Pyramid Lake Piute Indian Reservation. An Indian! Not a Puerto Rican, not a Mexican—a Piute Indian. Simon Dovisch in a car in the Far West with an American Indian.

"You're an Indian!" I exclaimed.

Students of American Literature, Early Period, I call on you to appreciate that moment. I am not one of those who hide their faults. I leave myself open. I do not hedge on the personal if it will but throw a particle of light on the common subject. But I call on you now to admit with me, would I, could I, am I the one to shout out "You're an Indian!" and mean it as a curse? What was it if not plain and unchecked Dovisch enthusiasm? A joy for an unexpected enthusiasm, this embodied experience, new at least to me, of meeting and traveling and about to labor with, an American Indian—Piute. Could I have meant anything but a form of my own congratulation for his identity? Did he have to at seventy-five miles an hour slam on the brakes? Did he have to nearly kill us both, the car screaming and squealing and twisting on the highway and not stopping till I had jammed one hand on my side of the dash trying to brace myself and skinned an elbow on the door handle? Did he have to turn on me then and show his teeth for the first time in a snarl God meant only for creatures of the jungle who go on four feet with heads turned down? He holds out his hand to me.

"Five dollars till here," he says.

"What's the matter?" I plead. "What did you do that for?"

"Five dollars till here," he repeats.

I can feel the heat of his eyes, and though I have done nothing I dare not look at them.

"You could have killed us," I say, and thought to say, do you run a taxi, the mileage and fare and destination based on unfounded resentments along the way? Bending my wrist, rubbing the elbow on my thigh, I try to explain. But how? But how? Can I bring him into the exuberance out of which I spoke. Can I tell him that, on the contrary, I love Indians. How shall I love Indians? I never met an Indian before. And if he who sat there snarling at me with his hand out was a prototype of his race, or even his tribe, why should I pretend to love them?

To make it short, I apologized. I had said nothing for which I had to be guilty, but there was no other way. On top of the apology, I offered five dollars more. Twenty now to get the car started. Thus Dovisch, the rainbow-maker, is also a man of bribes. That flicker appeared in his eye again. We resumed. This time I chose silence. Dovisch, I told myself, let the facts stand for themselves, their own essence toward their own emblem.

Come we at last to my car, there as I had left it, hood up, no one else in sight, a forlorn object: a machine which doesn't work. Immediately, then, another disagreement. I want him to push. He wants to look. I explain how it could be nothing but the battery. He looks under the hood. I look with him. He orders me into the car.

"Start it," he says.

What do I know of cars to quarrel with him? Perhaps he is a man of craft, after all. But if I could start it, would I have walked all those miles to find him, Indian or not? Into the car then, the hood up before my vision like a metal wing. My head out the window to hear signals from a body I no longer see. "Start it," he says. Again, *erk-erk*. "Stop it," he says. "The battery?" I suggest. "A push?" I plead. "Start it," he says. And this time a variation, an *erk-erk* with a gasp at the end, an asthma. Nevertheless, a slight improvement, a promise. I can see him now come past my side of the car on the way to his. His face, as he passes, a mask of sullenness and resentment. I get out to follow.

"You know now what it is?" I ask him. "Is it the battery? Are you going to push?"

He stops with his hand on the door of the trunk and looks up at me. If it was not a hostile look, then call me Natty Bumppo. If it is the way of his people, then too bad they learned no written language. They would have left us a great literature, for they are melancholy enough. If it was merely his own way, then my heart goes out to the woman, ugly or not, he lives with in the shack.

"Fix," he says to me, leaning over the trunk. Nothing else. Then opens the trunk and rummages inside and walks off, going around me without another word, holding in his hand some kind of tool that I tell you did not inspire confidence. Too big to be a scissors, too small to be a shears, not a screwdriver, not a wrench, but almost a pliers. I follow him. I try to summon control and decency, also a little command, and yet a degree of deference for the unhappy incident on the way here with him. Helplessness for my ignorance and plight—that, I didn't need to summon.

"Would you mind telling me what's wrong with my car and what you are going to do now?"

Delicacy set aside, the last part of my question was addressed not to his ear but to his behind. He was already gone, altogether under the hood, his body draped over its insides like a dungaree rag. Should such a man inspire confidence in the ignorant and dependent? Who's to say? Doctors also will probe and prod with gadgets on your own body and tell you nothing. But I must confess I had no confidence. Call it the prejudice of a provincial man. God knows I regard mechanical work as toy-tinkering, a skill on the idiot level of man's capacity. But to each his own, and from each, nevertheless, a kind of evidence, an emanation, manifesting the essence of the work itself, the man at or in his work. Thus a professor of sociology, say, shall be known by his bow tie and pipe, and the smack of brightness in his face, like an insult. And the true professor of literature, by the weariness of spirit. And so with auto mechanics. Also an essence. Was it that he lacked the boyish gleam of the eyes you see in the born mechanic let loose before an automobile, a refrigerator, a clock, an anything in need of repair? Was it his sullenness alone? Was it the strange implement he carried as a tool? Was it merely, finally— face it, Dovisch—my own bigoted preconception that an Indian and an engine make for no better combination than Dovisch and an engine do, admitting, as I face it, that I hold myself above such a combination and hold him not up to it? And on top of it an Indian who might be bent on spite for what he ineradicably regarded as name-calling?

I squatted down to see better what he was up to. It was already four o'clock. The instrument he had carried, I could see now. He had placed it on top of the engine. All covered with rust, between a wire cutter and a pliers. He was head down into the engine, grunting, his hands, both of them, pulling at something, yanking. Was this a part of a skillful operation?

"What are you doing?" I shouted. "What are you pulling on like that?"

You must understand I was still not used to talking. How much opportunity had he given me? It was the unmodulated sound of my sudden voice that frightened him into snapping his head back. He banged it against the hood. Then he turned his head toward me, a side of his face against the engine, his eyes all white, with terror, or anger—who knows? But his hands kept

29

on pulling. And then I heard something snap. It was as clear as a bone fracture in total silence. He began inching out of the engine, his arms working now, hauling, the way a sailor pulls in rope, a housewife a clothesline. And coming out after him, draping over the engine and then coiling on the desert floor, was half the insides of my car. Who knew a car had such insides? Bowels, I tell you. A regular vascular system. Wires and wires, black ones and red ones, and then a piece of tubing, and a piece of hose, and more wires, and some sort of chain. And he kept on hauling it all out, backing off farther and farther from the car and hauling on it, his own face now a picture of surprise. You can imagine the horror with which I regarded this performance. From where could I find voice and words to tell him what I felt?

"Madman!" I cried. "Spiteful lunatic! You have ruined my car. Look at what you did to my car! You have pulled out all the insides. It is all there on the ground. My car will never go again."

Let me not make it a big thing, the feelings I endured. Suffice it to say I wanted to punch him. Instead, I pulled at my hair. You see, it was more than my car he destroyed. It was the whole sense of my experience, of belonging—all that I had fought for in my solitude in those terrified nights, the silent days. What recourse now? Salvage what? Was it for the car alone that there passed now, at last, some expression on his face? He glanced at me and then looked at the heap of car guts at his feet, his small eyes widening and his heavy mouth falling open in an uncomplicated look of—what shall I call it—astonishment?

Students, listen—you are free to leave. I can't keep you, those of you due for another fifty-minute injection somewhere else— Geology, Speech for the Classroom Teacher, Spinoza. I have used up all my time, a lecturer and not a storyteller. Some could go directly in, but for Dovisch, layer by layer. Because aliveness itself is the crisis. But you know the end of the story. Here I am, I got back. Go, those who need to; stay, those who can. If I haven't come yet to that last layer which opens on at least the conditions of your final exam, then add up consequences as you

will. Not a threat, not a bribe—another fact. Facts are facts. Leave your term papers here, those who go.

So then—half of you gone. More than half. Let it be so. I will not for all that change my style. A picture is also a picture, and a picture we made then, Dovisch and Mike the Piute. It's hard to believe it happened only yesterday. The time for it seems to have been histories ago. The two of us, soon to become three, and then four, and five if I may count that passive Cleopatra whose description you can relay to your fellow students who walked out.

See us then on the highway, car chained to car, Dovisch in the old Plymouth pulled by the Indian in the new Chevy, having removed a chain from his trunk and lashed us bumper to bumper. Crawling now on the highway toward Reno that follows the Truckee River along the valley in the desert through the purple-shifting hills in the growing twilight. Fancy diction, but we were on our way by my command to find an open gas station. The guts of my car stuffed back under the hood. And me staring with constant hot and maybe tearing eyes at the constant backside of the head in front that belongs to him who pulls. Always twenty feet away. And Dovisch ponders. And now I say a curse upon the analytic mind. That it kept me from resigning myself to my recognition. Which spoke this way to me, the recognition —which is the beginning of all compassion. Said to me then: wherefore not peace in this peaceful place, albeit you are being hauled? The man who hauls you, is it not a labor for him as felt with pain as it would be if he hauled you with his back instead of an engine? Regard the slope of his shoulder that crowns his back. Heaped with humility which is born out of his very anger and spite. Born also out of remorse for the harm he did me that might have been done to revenge a mere word I spoke that he imagined as a name I called him. All the old stuff: pride and defeat and foolishness and sorrow, and damage too. From Russia to the Bronx, and from God knows where to Indian Reservation, Nixon, Nevada—an old story. A shack and slop jars and beer cans, a sputtered candle and a contour chair—red. And a woman to live with made ugly not by nature (what woman is ever by nature ugly?) but by deprivation, designation, contamination. But then is it my fault, I plead? A Simon-come-lately to this total land, and a stranger altogether to this specific place. But for him who calls himself Mike, how shall it not be in some part my fault? For if Dovisch is a rainbow-maker, why shouldn't the mind of the other have some license to abstract? So resign then, Dovisch, to this moment given to you as a gift, and feel for him who pulls you in the desert as though he pulled you on his back. The aspiration and the loss. But comes then the needling analytic fact. A question. Does he pull me for the money? Not as we are stretched and held as men across the rack of his chain, but for twenty dollars? And if it is for money, do I owe him money who wrecked my car? And if my car is wrecked and I need some other way of getting home, does he owe me? And if he owes me, is it money? Can I collect?

With such questions the sweet elegy of dependent journey is done with, finished. Arrive we then, after miles, at the gas station, my mouth sour, the time now almost five. In two seconds flat my benefactor is out the door, has the cars unchained, and with two words justifies all the cruelty of my analysis. His hand out and his back to the station: "Fifteen dollars." See what he was up to. Because I had raised from fifteen to twenty the amount I would pay him for starting the car, he raises from ten to fifteen the amount I should pay him for not only *not* starting the car, but for destroying it. "At least wait," I reply acidly. "At least see what happens here." No answer. A glance toward the station, and a nervousness of face. His wide mouth twitches a little. He shifts from foot to foot, a thick, arrogant body. He holds the chain, the main length of it coiling on the asphalt, and a foot or two of it hanging from his hands. Like a weapon. This I need now to cap my quiet intention—bloody violence.

There is only one attendant I can see at this small station, a Negro. Yes, a Negro. Am I responsible for the racial distribution of Nevada? He is watching us as soon as we arrive, and he is still watching, leaning against the window of the office—whatever you call it where they keep the money and the oil. He wears one of those one piece things from the Army. His arms are folded on his chest. I said he looks at *us*. He looks at the Chevy, and he looks at the back of the Indian. There is a charge, a tension to how he looks. Even from where I stand, I can feel its current. This, too, I need: petty anthropological animosities. He gives no sign, the attendant, that he will come to us. He leans there, arms folded, glaring.

"Listen," I say to the Indian. "I solicited your help. What you did, I invited, I understand that. What your motives were, that's for a debating society. Some other time. Now, whether I pay you ten dollars or fifteen, I need first to get squared away. Surely you can wait five minutes, since, as a result of your help, I might have to wait until tomorrow. Now let me pass."

I walked around him. I walk to the attendant. I summarize the situation. I ask him finally for the use of his phone for a long distance call, collect. I need to eliminate my own anxiety for what will soon be a worried wife. I need to have the time and latitude to do whatever has to be done. There is the nagging problem of money. Not only that I don't have cash and I might confront skepticism about a check. But the checking account itself now at the end of the month will take just so much for the repair of a cursed car. Know then that all the time I told my story and endured my fears, the attendant never once looked at me. He looked always at the other one. At his back because the Indian hadn't turned. I repeated my immediate need. I raised my voice to repeat it. "May I use your phone? It's an emergency. Can't you people see that? My wife . . ." Then the Indian turned. Then the attendant moved. He came off the window. He dropped his arms to his sides. Over his breast pocket in red embroidery, the name Wilbur. A lean man with a sharp moustache and ears back on his head as though they had been sewed. A little pointed also. A regular Donatello. Not a word to me. Once a glance. A slightest turning of the head and a shot with the eyes. He takes two steps forward.

"You gonna get off? You gonna beat it?" Not to me. To the Indian. The Indian looks back at him.

"I got money now," the Indian says. "I got fifteen dollars from him."

The attendant takes two more steps. "The boss says *you* come back here, even if you have fifteen *hundred* dollars, I keep you off. You gettin' offa here?"

"No boss here now," says the Indian.

"Piute, me and you together makes me boss."

I run up to him. "Wilbur, I told you. My wife. I need to use your phone."

Now he spins on me. Movements like a boxer. "I call you Mister, you call me same. You don't hear me callin' you first-name basis."

Another one. In the middle of nowhere Dovisch flushes out these advocates of niceties. That I'm the one in the human crisis, that they ignore.

"Look . . ."

"I already looked. I see a Piute haulin' a tramp in here that . . ."

"Now just you wait a minute."

"—ain't too smart either. 'Cause you hired a guy to fix your car that went and wrecked your car that likely pulled a wire on it in the first place some night you were snorin' away out there and now you got to pay him for it."

"Liar!"

Not the Indian's protest. Mine. If the Indian at that moment took himself to be insulted, I can't report. He merely stood there, his back almost on the door of his car, the chain still hanging from his hands. Once he turned his head to look down the road. Otherwise he looked at the attendant. Not yet with plain hatred. Something worse. His face, his whole body pinched with watching and waiting. And the Negro, arrested from his walking toward the other one by what he had stopped to tell me, was arrested still by the epithet I had impulsively flung out at him. I had to. I didn't intend by it to take sides in whatever miserable history the two of them had made together. How, anyway, could I have been on the side of the one who had done me so much harm? But to believe that the harm had been done even before I saw it? To believe that it had been done so that I couldn't see it? While I slept and dreamt, overcoming fears of animals and crawling things? While I made blueprints for an architecture of ideas about my country? It was more than I could bear. Picture now the Negro himself frozen to the spot. Confused for the moment. Confronting suddenly a second enemy. Diverted from the one idea of the Indian which was obviously all his mind could hold from the first moment he saw the cars.

So I apologized. Why not? What pride did I have at stake here? I asked once more for the use of the telephone. I called him Mister. I told him he could call me Simon. I told him all right, he could forget the telephone. Would he at least look at my car? Would he try to repair my car?

"This ain't no mechanic place," he says. "On Sunday I pump gas," he says. "I don't need no lookin' in your car," he says. "He got his hands on it; you can send it back to Detroit. Take it to a dump. Maybe you get somethin' for the tires."

"To a dump? Listen, let me call my wife. Let me . . ."

"Boss says nobody use the phone."

"But this is an emer . . ."

Enter once more the Indian. Hear again the voice of love. Two words spoken with a flatness you cannot make out of speech with two such words. Not on the spot. It takes centuries. Spoken with the mouth, it goes along the ground the way a snake moves.

"Cotton picker," he says.

Goodbye Negro attendant. Like a track star, like a shot: back to the office and in the door and then out the door with a yard of iron bar in his hands they use for tires, running with it over his shoulder behind his head. Good God, murder! I say to myself as

35

he runs past me, and I see the Indian turn sideways and brace his legs and let out two more feet of the chain and raise it to the height of his shoulder and almost close his eyes, as if he prepared himself to lash out when his hearing told him to and not his vision. Or else thinking of it as a kind of foregone conclusion, a suicide, and who wants to greet his own death with wide-open eyes? They will murder each other, I say to myself, or out loud—who knows?—and begin to close my own eyes and raise my hands to my ears to keep out the sounds of iron and bone. I raise my shoulders and lower my head and almost turn away— waiting, waiting. Nothing. The attendant has stopped in his tracks a little better than the chain length away. His iron bar is still raised. They confront each other, their chests heaving as though they had already fought. Their faces twisted with fear and hatred—nostrils and lips. Dark skin and darker skin. A madness here.

What goes through my mind, frozen there? I turn lunatic myself. I analyze: What did the Indian mean? Why did he choose that time to fling his curse? Was he on my side? Was I back again to his remorse for my plight that made him empty his sack of venom at the attendant's refusal to allow me the telephone? Or was it the mere overflow of hatred that drowned his need, his claim, his greed—whatever you want to call his idea of the fifteen, the ten dollars he could get from me? Because what he chose to say he must surely have known would provoke what it did.

So picture us. Make the tableau. It was not there for me then, but I see it now. Off the highway a little gas station with two yellow pumps and a small office. A dot in a desert country. One way with the road is back to the lake and the Indian Reservation. The other way is to Reno. The dry, tough land—Bible land—and the shifting, shimmering mountains and the miraculous stony water. Sunday at 5 p.m. When even solitude itself ceases to have value and all men past thirty should be home—shack, palace, Metropolitan Life Project—in the tumultuous retreat of family. Picture, then, that neighbor of a bird I had looking down with hawk vision at that spot of a gas station in that vast empty land, seeing three alien specks of men inside that spot on the vast land, all of them motionless, waiting, not for the consolations of an alien man to a more alien man to the most alien of men, but for murder.

Come down from there and the bird and see it with Dovisch, who, lugging the Bronx with him, thus Europe too, finds in man himself all the universe. Dovisch looking at the other two, also men, poised with implements of murder. The hatred in their faces, which is the willingness to murder, dreadful to see. And dreadful to see, also, the fear in each face for his own murder, which is all that holds them back. Muscles in the hands and faces, too tight to be too long held back. Dovisch saying to himself : outsider, alien—did you start this? Did you bring it on? But a moment for panic, not questions. Finished with analyzing. In panic, to the drowning man the pictures, the fantasies. Picture Dovisch, then, picturing salvation. To be out of there. To be back with family, with books, back here in this classroom with you. Then cries out to himself : to hell with books! To give it all, his whole kingdom, for one skill : to repair a car. Picture him staring in dread at the two men who begin at last to put the slightest pinwheel of motion into the tableau, making half circles about each other across the diameter they still fear to diminish, the weapons poised. And see Dovisch making fantasy as he looks, seeing himself in a Disney rescue, rushing to the car, opening the hood, the flash of Ben Franklin hands and the restoration of wires, tubes, hoses, chains, and in an instant in the car, the car starting, and Dovisch, all in the same timeless Disney instant, lowering the window and calling out : I don't understand you. I never understood you. The lake was a lie. Gentlemen, goodbye !

Picture finally what I did do, a madman equal to them. Between an iron bar and an iron chain, and between the savage intentions born out of the heartache of their own isolations, strides Dovisch. In dirty clothes, in a four days' beard, off a diet of zwieback and stewed fruits, and in a celebration of or recoil from the hot blood of abstract insights, with his arms outstretched, one for each of them so that they could have fractured his wrists at a single impulse, offering for peace what he has taken from his wallet: identification cards. And a brief illustrating lecture that must have gone something like this.

"Madmen, what are you doing? You are going to kill each other. For what? Listen, I am no tramp. That I don't belong here, I grant you. But not a tramp. Are you Russians that you tell everything from a man's clothing? See—here. Take the cards. Look. Identification. I'm Simon Dovisch, Professor of American Literature. See this one—The New England Historical Society. And this one—The Modern Language Association. This one too, from my university—Simon Dovisch, Ph.D. That's Doctor of Philosophy. Take them. Read them. Put away the chain. Put down the bar. I only came here to recover something I lost that I never had! Take them, please! Read! Study! Peace!"

I have returned to tell you they put down their weapons. They looked at me as though I alone were the one madman, and they looked at the cards I held out the way I would have looked at tarantulas held out to me. But they took them. And they looked at them. And they looked at each other. And then at the cards again, turning them this way and that. And then they spoke to me. The Negro says, "I ain't afraid of him." The Indian says, "I pulled you. You pay fifteen dollars."

Nobody heard the new car come until it parked behind my Plymouth. I ran to it.

"You have to help me!" I begged to the window.

Right then, on the spot, I didn't notice, but now I can tell you. A Cadillac, white like the whale itself, and as long, and with fins and flukes too. Behind the wheel, lowering the window so he could hear me, this—what shall I call him? What is the term I have heard you people use against yourselves—WASP? White-Anglo-Saxon-Protestant? Well, I have never used it. I deplore it.

It is your own form of Bronx snobbery injected from behind. I use it now as a shortcut from your own shorthand. I would say, rather, that he was a papermonger. Insurance, banking, credit, stocks, even publishing, even a registrar in a college—except for the Cadillac. Anything by which the management of the entity itself, people or things, is accomplished by the avoidance of the person or the thing. The paper accomplishes. So I say a papermonger to describe a face. And if you say to me a man's work does not describe his face, I say to you it is because you haven't begun to work. In his fifties he was, with silver hair, a Palm Springs sunburn, a straight nose, like a knifeblade, a tight mouth, a light-grey suit. Later I would notice the transparent film of nail polish. But much before that—indeed a moment after I noticed him—I would notice who sat beside him, the Cleopatra I promised some while back to describe to you for the envy of your fellow students who have abandoned us.

I asked him to help me. What I then, at the first moment of his arrival, like salvation itself (yes, I confess, I was grateful at once that it came in all the pompous authority of a Cadillac)—what I then told him I can't now recall. It would have had such phrases in it as "destroyed," "my wife will be frantic," "murdering each other," "Professor of American Literature," "only my checkbook," "four days at the lake," "fruits and zwieback," "excuse my appearance"—and so forth. He looked at me once while I was talking, the look of a long moment, of taking someone in. Then he never looked at me again. Dovisch summarized. But his face was alert and firm, and I must confess my heart went to calmness, rubbed and soothed by this stranger's—who in all other circumstances would have been so inimical to me—by his Cadillacs of certainty. Came then the gas station attendant to the car. Edges me from the window. Makes at-your-service smile.

"Fill 'er up?"

"Just a minute," says the stranger, like a slap across the face. And turns to the Cleopatra beside him and says, "Go ahead. Use

39

it, now that we've stopped." She makes a reply I can't hear, and he says, "Yes, here. It won't kill you." Her door opens and she walks to the office.

I promised a description. Say only that she was no older than some of you here. Say also that she could not have been his daughter. Even a blind man could sense that right away—an essence. And let me say her hair was beautiful, and her own color, blond, like sunlight. And almost no make-up, make-up only on the eyes, but a quality in the face of something between good health and a frost that made the face more blatant than all the sticks and paints and rouges in Woolworth's could have. She wore a white dress—bare arms, bare back, bare shoulders—and was tanned as he was. Listen—we are, what is left of us, a mixed group here. Propriety is a value. Furthermore, my place here before the room and behind the desk is a position of trust. A prig is a bore, but a libertine is a coward. Suffice it to say that what she wore she filled; what she filled she wore. And say also that her walk to the office and whatever rest room she would find there was a short parade under the desert sky. The attendant watched her, the Indian watched her, I watched her. Only the stranger himself did not watch her.

When she disappeared, I edged at the attendant, nudged him from the window, and began again with the stranger on my baggage of miserable phrases.

"Yes," he said, and cut me off. He opened the door and got out. A trim man. Squash and swimming twice a week at the athletic club. Also a wedding ring. You may wonder that I notice it after my admission of my incapacity to observe. I say then, given the *mise en scène*, wait till you are forty-two. He addresses the attendant.

"Fill it with super. The oil's all right. Check the water." Then to me: "I'll take you as far as Sacramento. You can get a bus there. I'll give you the fare."

I am broken by his kindness; also with my own resentment. I

mention my car, a badge of ruined shame beside his great white whale.

"You have no choice. It's Sunday." He turns to the attendant, who is already pumping gas, wiping windows. "You have this man's car towed to a mechanic tomorrow. Leave it here overnight."

"I can't do that. My boss..."

"Tell your boss a letter from my office will cancel his franchise. Tell him I can have this place closed in twenty-four hours."

So—an oil man.

The attendant stares at him, wipes the windows. End of debate. God in his wisdom, seeing my troubles, sends me not an Emerson, not a Thoreau, not even a Franklin, but a regular James Bond—or his father. Comes then the Indian, not to me, but to the stranger, and still dragging his length of chain.

"He owes me fifteen dollars," he says.

I looked once to the attendant. Will he go again for his iron bar that he had placed against the pump with the arrival of the Cadillac? No. He stops his cleaning of the windows to watch the outcome. His face is full of pleasure and deliverance. The stranger turns to me. He inquires of details. I give him details. You understand that the moral situation behind my business arrangement with the Indian is now complex. Yes, I hired him to start the car. But I stipulated for a push. The surgery was his idea. In sum, my answer to the stranger is yes and no. Shakes his head, then, the silver-haired stranger. Obviously ambiguities are outside his territory. He turns to the Indian. One sentence. A question.

"What's the name of the Indian Commissioner here?"

Exit the Indian, trailing the length of his chain. Smile on the face of the attendant as wide as vengeance. The Indian, my so-to-speak neighbor of four days, tearing off in a lamentable assertion from his exhaust pipe and a shouted obscenity one can barely hear. But for me, before he shut the door of his car, he reserved a special look: accusation, betrayal, or some secret shared—who knows? Re-enters now from the Palace of Fine Arts, Miss America. Another parade. Dovisch rejoins the staring. A polite walking aside by the stranger and his possession. Hushed conference. Looks from her toward me. Dovisch shrugs. And now a look for me from the attendant, even a laying on of hands, at least a finger on the shoulder, a warm smile. But for what?

So now a trio in the car, myself in the back, the deep black leather seats of a Cadillac. Another first for Dovisch. The stranger starts the car. No *erk-erk* here. The power of God's chosen continent in the turn of a key. Which he turns off again.

"You want to make that call home?" he asks. She turns and regards me. That mere flesh could hurl such a challenge. Another old story.

"No need now," I reply.

Off then to Sacramento. Goodbye old Plymouth. Dovisch from the rear murmurs gratitudes. Stranger from the front in brief disclaimers. Pays respects to higher education and learning. "They ought to raise salaries," he concludes. Dovisch deeper into the corner, arms over chest, bottom lip out. A long and uneventful journey back, if you exclude from eventfulness the growing frequency of exchanges of hot glances in the front seat, the sliding of thighs. Dovisch stares out the window. An intruder, yes, an isolate always, but not yet a *voyeur*.

The misadventures, then, almost at an end, but not quite. I said at the beginning that I did not get home until 2 A.M. Wherefore, then, you should ask, all the consumed time? Departing a little past 5 P.M. yesterday, it is not nine hours to home. Know, then, that two hours were spent in Sacramento waiting for the bus. Know that two hours before that were spent in front of a motel. Dovisch pacing like a patrolman, waiting for the two of them to get done with the business that is now the national pastime all the way from the Bronx to where we were now on the Western side of the Sierras. A factory of Hester Prynnes sewing night and day couldn't keep up with the scarlet letters needed here. It was also, from the stranger—let me credit him with his deservings—a gesture as well as a need. The need for him, with her; the gesture for me. Having rescued, having saved, having as much as said to me: aren't you lucky that I came along instead of another Professor of American Literature? He says now: so eat a little crow. Do I need to spell it out? Can't you see the rainbow finished now? Poor thingless Dovisch is the emblem itself.

In Sacramento, after long silence in the car, the beauty asleep and the stranger quiet, and even Dovisch in a surfeit of his own, speaks now the stranger, out of nowhere addressing me.

"I took a course in Lit. once. Never knew what he was talking about."

Pronounced, of course, before the bus station, when there is time for Dovisch to retort with nothing more than another "Thanks" because the stranger turns now to put in my hand the money that is the bus fare home. Dovisch closing the door lightly not to wake the dozing Cleopatra. Goodbye Prince of the Silver Hair and Master of All Situations. Then to the bus and the wooden bench in this midnight depository of transportation and breakage. Home then to keep up his wife all night in a rehearsal of what I have told you now. Checking with her wise soul the relevance of it all for your final exams. When I make rainbows and take my flyers, she is there, bless her days, like a shining thing. And checking with her all night, too, on remaining ambiguities. Today's schedule, for instance, for the return to that American Bible landscape to retrieve my car. And my identification cards. Which means, this afternoon, another visit to that shack and the Indian. Or to let it go. Let him paste the one I gave him on the wall somewhere. Paste it over the red chair. Whichever one I gave him, let him be an honorary member of the society. And let it suffice, too, for my own resignation. Enough can be too much. And even too much is inadequate. Endure, endure—and not the least of it now, I confess frankly, is that half of you should walk out in the middle of all this Dovisch vulnerability, prior commitments notwithstanding. Well, I am not altogether drowned. I have my own survival weapons. Ishmael and his floating coffin, Dovisch and his final exam.

Listen, leave me your term papers on the way out. Your final exam? Only this. A critical appraisal of my original intention and of what befell me. Include a moral estimate of the characters involved. Answer to the question of lawful and human guilt. Discuss deprivation. Also rescue. And don't neglect the car. Support all your assessments with liberal references to as many of the works we have studied this semester as will shed particles of light on such dark problems. References to be factual (God bless all my colleagues) and ideational (you know, rainbows).

That's all. Dovisch is finished. I'll see you at our finals.

THE BANDAGED MAN

After a week Manny was finally getting used to the smell of carbolic and ether. At times he even waited for the odor, inhaling it deeply with the mysterious pleasures of convalescence. It reminded him of how the leg, which no longer pained, had been so badly hurt. Then the Italian, bandaged like a mummy, was put in the bed next to him. The cops came in three shifts through the day and night to sit at the foot of the Italian's bed, and the hospital began to smell again for Manny like a place where people with sickness inside them came to have the infested places looked at, and to die.

He was certain something bad was happening again inside his leg. The doctors didn't know because they never looked under the bandage anymore. During the night he would die. It shamed him to admit it, but he wanted his mother to be there. He felt weakened with sorrow, and if he did not bite his lip against it, he knew he could cry. Even biting his lip, he felt the welling of his eyes. He blamed all of this on the Italian in the next bed, but he did not know why. He turned his head to look at him again, but the afternoon sun coming through the open window cut through the aisle between the four beds of the alcove and fell upon the chest of the cop. He was sitting on the chair reading from a magazine. The light made the silver of his badge glitter. Manny lay still.

After a while he raised the blanket and sheet. His bandage

went from thigh to shin. The leg had been painted with iodine, and now the skin was peeling in small orange flakes. He pulled at one of the strips and it came loose. He rubbed it between his fingers, then he let it fall on the bed. He started to think ahead to after supper, because Matty had said he would try to come again tonight and maybe bring Flip or Dox with him. It was a good hour when any of the fellows came. They always wanted to look at the leg and they talked about how he had gotten hurt. They talked of how they knew something was going to happen as soon as they saw Styrass jumping to pile on, and Manny lying there with his knee already on the ground and the rest of the leg in the air. They said they saw the leg twist. They said it would have broken off if Manny hadn't turned that little bit when Styrass dove. He wanted to laugh when they said this, so he would turn his face away and smile and say he wasn't sore when they told him Styrass was afraid to come and visit him. Then they would look around the ward as if they wanted to leave. The last time Flip did that Manny told him to look through the glass partition behind his bed. He watched Flip as he looked, then saw him pale and rear away.

"God! How do you stand it here?"

"Get used to it." He winced a little, as though with a new pain. Flip turned away.

Tonight the fellows would see the cop first, and then they would look at the Italian and not see anything else. It was that way for the whole hospital as soon as they had brought the Italian down from the operating room last night and a cop followed after them and sat down in a chair before the bed. The patients tried always to look at him, and they were all talking of him this morning. Even the nurses, as they hurried by, turned their heads, and the doctors had stood at the foot of the bed after breakfast talking in whispers. When they came to Manny's bed they looked at the chart and then went away, some of them turning to glance at the Italian once more.

The man's whole head was bandaged. There was a narrow slot

for the eyes to show, and two others, smaller, for the bottom of the nose and the mouth. But whenever, now, Manny turned toward him, he would look only at the eyes which had opened for the first time after lunch. They always stared straight ahead, somewhere into the cop sitting on the chair at the foot of the bed reading from a magazine. It was the eyes that confused Manny about the smells of the hospital, made him feel as he followed their empty stare toward the cop that he himself would never get better anymore, he would not get home. Sometimes the eyes would blink closed, not with sleep, but as though the Italian could not any longer hold the weight of them. Soon they would open again to stare at the cop, who never looked back at him. An hour ago, when the nurse had come to give Manny his shot and he moved to his right side, the eyes of the man turned on him, big, bulging, the pupils far in the corners because he had not moved his head at all. Manny felt his face go warm. He bit his lip and could not think of smiling as he always did when the nurse called the place she was going to put the needle in his hip. When he looked again, the eyes were staring past his bed toward the window beside it. Then they blinked and opened on the cop again.

That was the last time Manny had looked at the Italian. Now he wanted to look once more. He thought he would close his eyes and turn his head on the pillow and then open his eyes again. In that way he would not see the cop. But he did not turn his head far enough, and when he opened his eyes, he saw only the man's hand. It was bandaged across the knuckles and there were brownish stains on the white gauze. The middle finger was bandaged too, and against the splint it looked like white decoration on a little box. All the other fingers showed, and the one next to the splint rubbed slowly against the gauze. Manny watched the fingers move, then turned his head away, closing his eyes. The detached motion of one finger teased him, like pulling at the skin of his own leg.

He wondered what the Italian's face was like. He wondered if it was like a face at all anymore, and if he would recognize him because the cop had said he was from Van Sicklen, or if Dox would know him because his older brother had gone with Italians for a while, if Dox would know him just by the eyes and the part of the lip that showed beneath the small slit in the bandage. But the Italian might be as old as his father. The cop hadn't said anything about how old he was.

That morning, after the doctors had come and while the Italian had not yet opened his eyes, some of the patients who moved about the ward on wheel chairs and crutches had gathered around the cop, making him look up from his magazine. They tried to keep their voices low, but they talked all at once while they looked over their shoulders at the bandaged man. The two men in the beds opposite Manny leaned forward to hear, and even the old one who had the thing that looked like scissors handles stuck through the bandage around his stomach, even he tried talking to the cop. But when Manny leaned forward, something in the knee pulled. He fell back against the pillow again, listening.

"What happened to that guy?"

"Who fixed him like that?"

"What you cops sittin' around watchin' him for? He ain't goin' nowhere."

"Go on! Get back to your beds. Excitement ain't good for sick people." The cop tried to read the magazine again. He was fat and his face was very red. Like blood, Manny thought.

"Come on. Tell us."

"What he do, get in a fight with somebody?"

"He walked into a bus." The cop looked up from the magazine and smiled. He looked like a clown, Manny thought, with the dark blue, almost black of his shirt, the silver badge, the very red face, and the crooked teeth of his smile.

"Yeah, sure. I broke this leg kicking statues. Come on, tell."

"He killed a cop, the sonofabitch!" He brought the magazine

down to his lap, then raised it again, pointing it toward the bandaged man.

They all turned toward the bed.

"Yeah. We picked him up at his old lady's house on Van Sicklen. She was laying there in bed howling like a cat. The bastard was trying to hide behind her bed with half his ass sticking up. We could've blown it into the next street."

"It don't look like it was his ass you shot at."

"What happened to his head?"

"He try to run away?"

"That's right. He tried to run away." He looked down at the magazine again, then raised his eyes toward the bed where the others were still staring. "Wop bastard!"

"Hey, why you call him Wop all the time, Mick cop?"

"What'd you say?"

"I say don't call him Wop." It was the old man with the scissors in his stomach.

"I'll call him what I call him. Don't say Mick to me 'cause you're an old man sick in bed. Now all of you, outa here. Let me read. I don't want to catch nothin' from you."

"This is a hospital. You ain't no boss here."

Then the nurses came, and a doctor too, and they hurried everyone away. Manny saw the doctor look at the cop, but he was already reading his magazine. He supposed another cop would come at four to take his place. It was strange how careful they were about a man who couldn't move. It made the eyes—always peering now at the cop from the white and faceless head—even more terrifying. Manny knew that if the Italian died, the eyes would still be open. He imagined what the cops with their clubs must have done to the face. Under the bandage it was wet with blood, and the eyes stayed open and stared, afraid to close, afraid to become a part of the face and the leaking blood.

At four o'clock the other cop came. He took the magazine from the blood-faced one and they stood whispering for a minute while they looked toward the bed where the Italian stared back at them. Then the nurse came and hung another bottle from the pole at the side of the Italian's bed. It was after she left that Manny heard him moan for the first time.

He tried, without looking, to listen to the sound. It was different from the other hospital cries. He listened for a long time, and then he knew the sounds had nothing to do with pain. They came from far away, as though, behind the bandages, the Italian remembered a word and was trying to say it now, but could only moan. Manny thought he heard something like Mahyeea, or Mahmeeya. Then he knew it was Mamamia the Italian groaned, and he knew they all did that and it was their religion, but they could say it other times too—like Jesus or Christ—and it would not be religion.

He was afraid of the Italians and did not like them. They came down the Parkway in gangs, from Avenue U and beyond, from Lake and Van Sicklen. They would start fights for little reasons, and only Dox had kept them once from jumping Whistle. They said that Whistle, with the sick voice he had, was making fun of them. He heard the Italian moan again, a little louder now. He stopped thinking of the gangs. He wondered if the Italian was speaking the Mamamia, or really praying. He would turn his head again and see. But first he wanted to look quickly at the new cop to know if he too heard the moaning and watched.

But the cop, like the other one, was reading from the magazine, almost with his eyes closed. The light fell on the white gun handle and the black holster. The holster hung loosely, almost on his thigh, so that it lay partly on the seat of the chair. Manny stared at it. Slowly he realized that the bandaged Italian had killed a cop. He would go to the electric chair. He felt his skin dampen under the sheet, and he began to listen to the moaning. He turned his head to the window. He looked down at the leaves that had turned with the late October and were swirling on the pavement.

That night, during visiting hours, none of the fellows came, but his parents did. They looked in disbelief between the still-reading cop and the faceless, motionless, still-peering Italian, who had no visitors. They tried to ask Manny questions, but he could not tell the story clearly, though he knew he could have told it to the fellows. His father went finally to talk with the cop, and Manny tried not to look there, or at his mother either. She kept glancing at the Italian. His father came back to the bed and whispered.

"He's a murderer. That man's a murderer."

"Please." She put her hand on the lapel of his jacket.

"I tell you he's a murderer. He killed a policeman yesterday. He's one of those Italian gangsters."

"Sh."

"What shush? A murderer is in the bed next to your son." Manny turned his face away and bit his lip when his father pointed to the next bed.

"The leg hurts you, doesn't it, Manny?" His mother moved closer to the bed, her lips pursed, her head moving slowly from side to side.

He nodded.

"Well, thank God for that anyway. No more ball."

"Listen, I talk one thing and you talk another. I don't want my son in bed next to a gangster, a murderer. I'll find the head nurse."

"Dad, for Chrissake."

"Listen, he can have a gun under the pillow. There can be shooting in here." He leaned over Manny's bed, whispering dramatically.

"The man is dying," his mother said.

"You know that? Who told you? The policeman said he's like a bull."

"Manny, why are you crying? Does it hurt so much? Should we call the doctor?" She put her hand on his shoulder and was rubbing it, her fingers reaching to his neck.

"No." He turned his face toward the window.

Before they left his mother told him the doctor said he would go home soon. He said nothing, but he did not believe her. He did not try, before they put the lights out, to look again at the Italian. He was certain he had heard everything and was staring at him now from out of the bandages with those terrible eyes. When the lights went out Manny turned slowly toward him, but he could not see his eyes. He saw the blanket rise and fall, and the light color of the bandage. He could not hear the moaning anymore. He saw the cop, sitting now on the other side of the Italian's bed, his chair tilted back against the edge of the partition. He was reading from the small light above him. Manny tried again to look hard at the bandages, then, suddenly alarmed, thinking the Italian was staring back at him in the darkness, he let his head fall quickly on the pillow. He tried to think of school and all the work he would have to make up. He wondered when he would be able to play ball again. He tried, in the darkness, looking up at the ceiling, to worry about it, but he couldn't for long. He woke during the night many times with the noises of the hospital. Each time he thought he might look at the Italian again, but he never dared.

The tinny rattling of the wash basins woke him in the morning. He saw immediately that another cop was back in the aisle at the foot of the bed, his eyes closed, his chin on his chest, the magazine in the hand that hung below the seat of his chair. The eyes of the Italian stared at the cop. He was moaning again. The Mama-mia was very plain now.

They did not bring the Italian any food at breakfast, and after it the doctors came and stood at the side of his bed, nodding their heads and looking at the chart. The fat, blood-faced cop of yesterday who came after breakfast looked up from his magazine to watch them. The Italian stopped his moaning and his eyes went up to the ceiling. Then one of the doctors picked at a corner of the bandage below the eyes. Manny turned away. A stretcher-wagon came, and he heard them put the Italian on it. When he turned again he saw the cop get up to follow them, saying, "I can't do nothing about orders."

It was about an hour when he heard the stretcher again. The two orderlies got him into the bed while the one doctor watched. The cop sat down in his chair and said, "What keeps the Wop alive?" The doctor, without looking at the cop, said, "Hate, maybe." As soon as they left, the Italian, looking now not at the cop but at the ceiling, started to moan again. The bandage was whiter, and Manny knew they had taken the other one off to do something to what was underneath. He wondered if the face hurt as much as his leg had when Styrass jumped on it, and if all the skin behind the bandage was the same color his knee had been when Flip had pulled away the elastic of the football pants—red-blue-purple, like fish scales. But he knew the Italian's was worse than that. It was open and hanging and the red was the color of beef. Some of the bones might even be showing. He wondered what they could do to fix bones broken in a face. If he had to look at it he would be sick, and he knew again he did not want to be a doctor anymore. He knew that even before the Italian came, when he had sat up and turned around last week to look through the glass of the partition behind him. The head he saw through the glass was bald. On the top of it there was a big, perfect ring of brown crust. The skin inside the circle was as white as a plate. But the Italian's face would be worse than that. He was glad they had it bandaged, but it made the eyes so strange. They were still looking at the ceiling. He wondered how many times they had looked at him since his father had shouted last night. He heard him moan again, this time louder still, almost a cry. Mamamia! Even the cop looked up.

Manny turned suddenly to the window. What if it was his real mother the Italian was calling for?

He tried to look out the window, but he saw nothing, only that it was light and the sun glared. He remembered what the cop had said about the Italian's mother, how she lay on the bed screaming. Old Italian women wore black and had grey hair and were short and fat. This was one like that, but sick in bed. He was calling for her.

53

He could see the old woman, but could not imagine the Italian belonging to her. He had only eyes and had killed a cop. If the mother was very old, then he could be almost forty. But Manny could not imagine his own father ever calling to his grandmother like that. He decided the Italian was young, only ten years older than himself maybe. He saw what must have been the black, oily hair, the dark skin. Then the Italian groaned the name loudly. Manny had to turn and look. The eyes—the pupils in the corners and the watery large whites against the white of the bandage— stared back at him. Manny made a little movement with his head, then opened his mouth to say something like—hello. But thinking of the cop, he reddened and, closing his eyes, turned his head away. He bit his lip hard and winced, as though the Italian should know what was sick in him pained too. He raised the sheet and looked down at the thick bandage of his leg. It did pain very much. He even moaned.

During the afternoon the Italian began to move his arm. Once Manny saw it raise to the bandage, the splinted finger rubbing lightly for a second against the gauze where the ear might be. Then the arm fell to the bed again. Manny tried not to think of it and to read the newspaper he had bought from the man who came through the ward after lunch. But there was nothing to interest him. Even in the sports section there was nothing because it was the middle of the week and the colleges only practiced.

The moaning continued, and even now, having heard it for so long, Manny still could not bear it. He wanted very much to go home. He stared out the window. It was only a few feet above the street. He watched the cars pass, watched along the bike path on the other side of the Parkway, watched for the gangs of kids that sauntered by, watched the women sitting on the benches, some with their hands on the silver bars of the carriages. He wondered how the cops, when they didn't really have to, could sit on the old wooden chair reading from the magazines in the middle of all that smell. The Italian couldn't go anywhere.

That evening, during visiting hour, again none of the fellows came, and his father did not either. His mother said he had to work late. She cried a little, but did not say anything about his playing ball. Once, her hand resting on his blanket groped for his, and he let her take it and press it tightly. It was damp, but it made him feel good. The Italian had no visitors again. Manny could see him lying very still with his eyes open to the ceiling. He moaned the one word softly.

The next morning the Italian moved his arm more freely. He brought it up often to rub against the bandage. But he still moaned. He moaned the single word many times, and Manny, having to turn once for the shot the nurse brought, could almost not bear to look or listen. He felt at once a whelming of pity for the Mamamia the Italian called to. It made his eyes feel moist and he wanted again to pick the peeling flakes of skin on his bandaged leg. When he heard the nurse at the side of the Italian's bed, he had to look. She brought something yellowish in a glass with a tube in it and tried to make him drink. She held the glass below the bandaged head and put the tube through the little opening where some of the lip showed. But no liquid left the glass, and the nurse had to take it away. She had not spoken a word. She had not even tried to look at him. But the Italian had never looked at her either. His eyes, blinking slowly, stared at the cop, and the cop, who had heard the nurse come, stared back. He kept the collar of his shirt open, and the redness of his face was on his neck too.

When the moaning stopped during the afternoon, Manny believed the eyes of the Italian had left the cop and were staring at him. He turned his head halfway. He would look at the cop and tell from him. But the cop's chin was on his chest and his eyes were closed. Manny turned his head all the way. The eyes were on him. They met his. The whole bandaged head seemed to have moved for the first time, turned toward Manny. He had to lower his eyes, but he was afraid to move his head. He felt the Italian was waiting for him to say something, wanted him to, and he did not dare try not to.

He groped suddenly for the paper. Leaning as far as he could and with his arm out and his eyes almost closed, he tossed the sheets to the Italian's bed, mumbling, "Here." He tried to smile. He looked toward the cop, but his eyes were still closed, his head still on his chest. He turned back toward the Italian, his mouth still pulled by the smile. The newspaper was on the Italian's chest. He had not touched it. His eyes, white and watery, were on Manny.

"I thought maybe you wanted the sports."

He said the words feebly. He did not know why he said them, or why he had thrown the paper. One of its sheets slipped away, slid nearly to the Italian's hand near the edge of the bed. He raised his arm slightly, then let it drop. He raised it again, letting it fall once more. He kept the finger next to the splint pointed, poking with it into the mattress each time the arm came down. Manny turned his head away and was going to stare out the window, but he heard the Italian make a small squawking noise in his throat, and he turned back. He was doing the same thing with his hand, poking the finger against the white sheet. Manny looked at the bandaged head. The eyes, the pupils in the corners under the fringes of gauze, were still on him. They were blinking slowly, then hard, staying closed for seconds. The hand came up, the elbow resting on the mattress. The Italian pointed a finger at him, then let the arm fall. He poked several times rapidly into the mattress. Manny could not understand. He wanted to speak again, but the words stopped in his throat. He turned his head away and looked out the window. He saw the afternoon light and the cars, and bikes, the women and the carriages. He turned his head back again to the Italian. He stared at the place where the bandage lumped against the nose. He was moaning again the single word, softly, drawn out. The same finger—the nail white and bloodless—pressed itself, extended, against the mattress, raising the hand above it by the length of the fingers. Trembling, Manny turned away, trying not to see the cop. He bit into his lip hard. He needed to go home.

The Italian wanted to change beds with him.

THE BANDAGED MAN

He knew it all at once. The Italian wanted to go home to where the old fat woman with the grey hair was sick in her black dress on the bed. He wanted to die there. He would get into Manny's bed and wait until the cop napped and then get out the window to the street and make his way down the Parkway. He wanted Manny to make up a story for the nurse so she would wheel the beds around. She had done it once before for the man with the moustache who was always getting tests for the pains they could not find and who did not want to be near a window. They had put the old man with the scissors in his bed. Manny would have to tell the nurse he was cold near the window, or he couldn't sleep at night because of the car lights, or the sun in the morning got into his eyes and woke him too soon. That's why the Italian had been watching him, testing him. He wanted his help.

He raised the blanket and looked at his leg. He hooked his good foot beneath the ankle of his bandaged leg and moved it. But it did not change the position of the hip and he was sad for the pain there. He wondered when he would get home and how he would walk on the crutches and if the leg would get better by the time basketball started. He imagined what he would do at home before he went back to school, but his mother always came into his wondering. He looked out the window again, but he could not remember with each new moment what he had seen. Then, as though from far away, at his side, faintly, he heard the clicking of the glass and metal. He lay perfectly still, his hands tightened about the blanket. The nurse had come to fix the bottle at the Italian's bed. He could call to her now and make up his story. He knew the Italian was watching him.

The blanket was wet under his fingers. He turned his head slowly. The cop, the magazine in his hand, his fingers on the corner of a page, was staring at him too. Manny lowered his eyes and rubbed tenderly with his hand on the blanket across the width of bandage beneath. The old man with the scissors called loudly to the nurse for the pan. Manny heard her walk away, but she would be back, and then once more to take away the pan. He could not look toward the window anymore. He closed his eyes, hoping the Italian would think he was asleep. He imagined the Italian, who had killed a cop, pretending sleep near the window during the night and then sitting up painfully crawling to it, rolling over the sill and then out. He would stay close to the building under the wide stone ledge so that the cop, if he heard, could not shoot. He would be strong enough to get all the way home, walking through the dark streets with his eyes peering out from his bandaged head, walking with his hands pressed against his stomach, leaking the trail of blood from one block to the next, the white bandage getting red and wet with it, walking in the cold night in the grey pajamas of the hospital, walking all the way to where the old Mamamia waited. When the cops came for him he would be in the bed with her, holding her hand, and dead. There would be blood on the white sheet.

He heard the nurse at the old man's bed and opened his eyes. She was holding him by the back and getting the pan under without looking at him. Manny turned his head slowly toward the cop and saw him reading the magazine. Quickly, without thinking, he looked toward the Italian. The eyes looked back at him and he thought he saw the bit of lip move. He heard the nurse begin to walk, and he looked away from the Italian toward her. She looked back at him and smiled and his mouth opened. But she kept on walking and no words came.

He'd almost said it. He would when she came back for the pan. He would not look at the cop. He did not turn back to the Italian, but he nodded his head slowly, knowing the other was watching and would understand. He closed his eyes and waited.

He tried to count, but he lost track. He thought of what the fellows would say when he told them what he had done and they read of it in the papers. But then he knew he would not tell them. He saw himself going to school on the crutches and everyone stopping him to see the scar. He saw himself after school practicing running on the bike path to build up the leg again. He would walk with a limp for a long time, and the girls Dox had started to go with would ask about him. His mother would try to keep him from playing ball, and there would be arguments and he would be angry with her for a long time. He thought of many things and they started to get mixed and he felt himself very tired. He saw his father many times reading his paper in the living room after supper, the page stretched between his thick fingers.

He heard the nurse take the pan away and he heard himself telling her, but he could not open his eyes, he was that tired, and faintly, as from far away, he heard the Italian moaning, but he could not hear the word, it was that far away.

When his parents came during visiting hour they laughed and said foolish things and told him he could go home tomorrow morning. He knew he was not well enough and he did not believe them. He told them he wanted to go home that night. His mother said the hospital did not like anyone to leave at night and it would only be a few more hours. He took his mother's hand and said again he wanted to go that night, and his father said what would be the difference? and his mother said there must be a reason, and they stood looking at each other and Manny said he did not want to be next to the Wop anymore. His father said see! see! and left to find the doctor. He came back smiling, the bundle of Manny's clothes in his arms.

He had to stay in bed the first three days. All the fellows kept coming up after school, and Styrass came finally and said he was sorry and Manny laughed. He was glad Matty was there when the family doctor came to take out the stitches because Matty talked always about his boils and how painful it was when the doctor lanced them. They counted the stitches together and there were twenty-four. The doctor, smiling, holding the scissors up, said it would be another day in bed for each stitch and they laughed and went on counting. Afterwards he was on the crutches, doing tricks, pushing down with his arms to keep the rubber caps in the carpet and swinging through, laughing when his mother yelled.

The day before he had to go back to the hospital, terror seized him.

His leg hurt again all day and he knew the doctor, when he touched it, would feel something they had left in the knee, and he would have to stay in the hospital again, in the same bed. His mother annoyed him, hurrying in and out of the room all day. But she put her handkerchief to her eyes when she saw him take the crutches to go to the bathroom. It infuriated him to have her cry over him, and he found reasons to shout at her. Matty came up after supper and Manny kept him there a long time talking of the football season.

He had an argument with his mother the next day because he did not want her to go to the hospital with him. She yelled, but he said he would not go if she came. He let her walk beside him down the stairs, but he insisted he could manage and would not let her touch him. She gave him the two dollars and watched with him in the street until he got into the taxi. He laid the crutches on the floor and sat in the corner with his leg straight out, the heel on the folded chair in front. He could not easily turn his head that way, and he saw only dimly the things they passed on the Parkway.

In the hospital he felt sick with the smell of the carbolic and ether. The nurse put her hand on his shoulder and said how fine he looked and asked him how he felt, and he said he guessed he was O.K. He sat on the bed and she said he would have to get ready for the doctor, and she turned and moved her hands on the table among the jars. She came back and began to cut at the bandage, a small one where the wound had not closed. She kept a hand on his thigh, and he felt ashamed. He thought he should say something.

"How is the Italian?"

"Which one?"

"The bandaged man. The one who . . ."

"Oh, we lost him."

"Lost him? He got a . . ."

The nurse went to the jars again, dipping a gauze pad in one of them. He was not even thinking of whether it would sting. When she came back she did not say anything else.

The doctor told him the knee was fine and that he did not need the bandage anymore and should begin to exercise right away. But Manny could scarcely hear and he did not once look at the leg when the doctor rubbed his fingers on the knee. He did not want to take a taxi home and decided he would use the McDonald Avenue car. He would pass Matty's house before his own and they could talk. He would stay in the candystore until Matty got home from school. His mother would worry and there would be an argument when he got home, but he did not care. The crutches, as he walked, coming down against the dry and fallen leaves, made them rattle. Here and there a woman turned to watch him. He grew tired as he made his way across the five blocks to the streetcar. He had to breathe deeply, but the smell of the hospital still lingered. He would begin to exercise tomorrow. He would run on the Parkway, and each day for a whole year, as though it were a ceremony, he would run a little longer.

ALMOST BROTHERS

The mother of the boy called Dox had died unexpectedly a week ago. His birthday fell one week earlier to the day and year than that of the boy he sat with on the wooden bench on Ocean Parkway whose name was Manny, but who was called Priest by his friends. It was July in 1946, and the war had been over for a year. The boys sat quietly in the hot and humid Brooklyn morning under the motionless leaves of the maple trees. They were exactly the same height, but the one called Priest was thicker than his friend. Dox was broader, but narrower in the waist. He was full of sharp angles and a tough flatness. There was a feline meanness to his body which gave the air of immediate and swift useability. In a boy not yet seventeen, it seemed violent.

Each of the boys ordinarily regarded the other with awe and resentment. Perhaps it was because of the nearness of their births and the essential differences of their natures. Priest looked upon the mysteries of the world with immense feeling, but among his friends and with adults especially, he aspired to decent, explainable behavior. Dox gave all the appearance of an inner life that was emotionless, but he often behaved mysteriously. His many fights might have been attributed to his inability to contain for even a moment the first sign of an emotional stress. He had fought with all his friends, but never with Priest.

Priest had already suffered his own family loss. His older brother had broken down on the landings at Tarawa. He was in the psychiatric ward of the Naval Hospital in Oakland and would never be released. Priest imagined that he shared now with his friend in an experience of family grief; he wanted to make this feeling known to Dox. But Dox rarely spoke of the things which Priest thought of as mysterious.

Priest knew all the boys in the club by a sympathy rare for one so young, and by means of it he held sway over them. But he didn't yet know on this day that he shared no griefs with Dox. It wasn't really grief that Dox felt at the death of his mother, whom he had loved. It was an unnameable humiliation. The proudest of all the boys, if ever he imagined insult he would lash out at once, not one blow but many, his arms flailing so swiftly you could never remember the beginning of the motion. His pride was fearless, but it could also be without honor. He would as soon and as unexplainably turn on a friend a half head shorter than himself as he would on a man a full head taller. Surprisingly, it was Dox who spoke first now.

"I wish the war didn't end," he said.

"What are you talking about?"

"I'd enlist if the war didn't end. I'd do it today. I look old enough."

"What for? What would that change?"

"The war's over. It don't matter."

"You could enlist without a war."

"Why would I?" Dox didn't look at his friend. He hadn't once looked at him. "The war's over."

Priest pondered it for a minute. "You mean there's no one to kill now?"

Dox made no reply, and Priest felt the urge to reveal what had truly happened to his brother. He had never told any of them. He had made all his friends believe his brother's wound had been of the heroic kind, with blood and crippled bone.

"I wanted to enlist when my brother got wounded," he said. Dox didn't answer, and Priest backed off from complicated admissions. "It doesn't work out," he said. "There's no way to get even. I thought about it. I thought a lot. I said to myself if everyone who killed had to be killed . . ."

"What are you talking about?"

Priest, in truth, no longer knew. "There's no one to blame," he blurted out.

"I wish the war hadn't ended," Dox said.

"Ah, Dox," Priest pleaded. "What good would it do? I know what you mean, but what good would it do?" He looked urgently at his friend.

Dox sat with his upper arms on the top slat of the back of the bench. His hands dangled, but not a finger moved. His head was tilted back, and he stared blankly at the leaves of the trees. But he never moved. Even his eyes didn't blink. The few words he had spoken were forced through the ridges of his teeth, a front one chipped at the corner from a reckless dive in the schoolyard. His capacity to remain still was alarming. It always reminded his friends of how fast he could unleash himself.

"Damn it!" Priest cried suddenly. "Why's it have to happen? God, I just saw her the week before. She was coming out of the A & P with bundles and . . ."

Dox moved a finger to scratch at the wheal on his cheek, which always bled in football games. The motion was enough to make Priest stop. Then Dox turned to him, his eyes full of confusion and defeat. It frightened Priest to see debasement in the eyes of the most fearless boy he knew. He said no more. There was nothing he could think of to say.

They sat silent for a while through the slow growth of the morning's heat and humidity. People walked by them, sometimes girls, occasionally riders on the bike path on the other side of the railing from them. Girls and women on the bicycles wore shorts, and the flashes of their pumping thighs, tanned and muscled,

aroused spurts of desire in Priest, for which he felt shame. He
would glance then at Dox, who was already the easy master of
the kinds of girls he would always win. But Dox gave no sign.

They were joined after a while by two of their friends, the one
they called Whistle, whose speech was mutilated by a cleft palate, and Matty, the smallest and youngest of them. They called
him Soupbone, but he was already, of all of them, the richest
in self-esteem. He carried a bat and ball. The two newcomers
were not at ease in the presence of their friends who gave the
appearance of having sat for a long time on the bench. They
didn't sit down. They might have thought that before they came
Dox had talked intimately to Priest about his mother's death.

"Wanna go to the schoolyard?" Matty finally asked Priest. He
didn't look at Dox.

"They're locking it Saturdays," Priest said.

"Bust it open," Whistle said.

"I don't feel like playing," Priest said.

"Let's go to Kelley," Dox said and rose. It was the name of a
park a mile away. They sometimes played games there on Sun-
days; otherwise they seldom used it.

The field was empty when they arrived. They played with a
pitcher, a batter, and two outfielders who wore the gloves Whistle and Matty had brought. They were young enough to want
much from ballplaying, and how they played was a showing forth
of their needs. Thus Priest, who believed in heroes, used his
shoulders and thick wrists to swing for homers. Matty, who
could draw beautifully and already felt his future made secure
by it, believed in style. He trotted with the self-conscious prance
of a trained pony. Whistle, in angry assertions against the crippled roof of his mouth, would be dripping sweat two minutes
after the start of any game of ball. Dox played with a cruel economy, as though he saved himself for the hidden violence which
resides in all physical play. At bat he would lash at the ball with a
sudden twisting of his wrists, hitting wicked line drives flatly
over the infield. Sometimes, in one of their Sunday games, racing

66

to first, he could, without breaking stride, deftly lower his left shoulder and hook it into the first baseman's side to dislodge the caught ball. He had done that once to a grown man and had sent him whirling, head over heels, as though he'd been hit on a highway by a car. He played centerfield with his arms folded over his chest, ankles crossed. Except for the movement by which he occasionally turned his head to spit, he looked as though he slept. But he could spring like a cat from that posture to take balls on the fly which should have been caught by the fielders on either side of him.

On this morning, in the almost empty park, a week after the death of Dox's mother, none of them, except for Whistle, played out the habits of his nature. Priest refused to hit the ball over the fence. Dox pursued the balls listlessly, dropping easy ones. When his turn came to bat, he missed ball after ball which Matty, embarrassed, lobbed ever more softly to him. None of them knew the decent way to call it quits. Until at last Priest, out of his sympathy for what he imagined Dox endured, cried out when he was at bat and Whistle was already releasing the ball to him: "Let's quit and go!" And he drove the ball with all his might, high and far, out toward Dox and left field, out and out, over Dox's head, over the fence, high up on the wall of the house beyond. It banged hard, dropped back to hit the fence and fall into the garden, to be lost from sight among the flowers at the side of the house.

They walked in a group after the ball and would go home from there. The gate to the waist-high iron picket fence was latched from the inside, so Priest worked his hand through to spring it free. There was a small sign on a post driven into the lawn which read SOLD, and below the word was the name of the realtor. Whenever on their Sunday games a ball had gone over the fence, a woman always emerged from the side entrance of the house and found the ball and then walked with it to the front gate and waited there for some boy or man to come for it. In that way she saved her flowers from being trampled on. But neither she nor

67

anyone else had come out this time, and Priest and Whistle, who went in to search for the ball and noticed the drawn shades as well as the sign, were not mindful of the flowers.

After some minutes of looking, they still had no luck. The flowers had not been cared for in a long while. The weeds were high and thick, and the ball had come so hard off the wall it might now be buried deep among them. Dox came to join the search. Only Matty remained in the street before the fence, though it was his ball.

"It's your ball!" Whistle roared at him after more futile minutes of looking, of whacking at the flowers and the weeds. His raised voice was like a seal's.

"Priest hit it," Matty said.

Priest continued to look for the ball, and to observe Dox. Whistle roared back curses at Matty, and Dox raised his head. Priest, looking at his face, imagined he saw in it an emblem of grief.

Then Priest heard the sharp rattling at the side door. He looked up and saw through the panes for the barest moment a face he couldn't distinguish, though he knew it was a man's. The door swung quickly open. The man stood on its threshold glaring at the two boys he could see, Whistle and Priest. He was tall and fat and dressed in G.I. pants and a T-shirt which was sweated through on his shoulders and his belly. His hair was cut short and he wore eyeglasses in round steel rims. His large flabby arms were pale, and his hands, to the wrists, were covered with a grey film of soot, as if he had been sifting ashes. Priest kept staring at the hands.

"Who sent you here?" the man said from his perch on the sill.

His strange hands were on each panel of the doorjamb. He filled the doorway. His voice was strangely high for a man so big, and Priest was immediately afraid.

"Our ball came over the fence," he said.

"There's no ball here," the man said.

Priest glanced down the side of the house toward Dox, who

ignored the man. He was still poking with his toes among the flowers. The man had not yet seen him. Priest began again.

"The woman who lives here always..."

Something passing across the man's face made Priest stop. The man brought his hands away from the doorjamb and stepped down from the sill onto the walk before the flowers. Priest lowered his eyes from the face and stared again at the ashen hands. The man put his hands behind him and glared at Priest, and then at Whistle, who moved now a step closer to his friend. The man still failed to see Dox.

"She doesn't live here," the man said. "You come here to spy on us?" He took a step toward them.

He's crazy, Priest thought at once. Then he thought he would say or do something to let the man know Dox was behind him. No man in that small space between the house and the fence would start up with three of them. He could not explain to himself the air of depravity the man gave off, like the odor of his sweating. When he remembered the man had said "us," he heard Matty call out from the street: "Hey!"

Priest and Whistle turned at once. There, leaning against the corner of the house where the walk turned, was another man. His arms were folded across his chest. It took Priest's breath away. Whistle murmured "Jesus." The man was almost identical to the other one in size, and he wore the same T-shirt and olive-drab pants. His shirt was also sweated through, but his hands were hidden under his crossed arms. He leered at the boys. He, of course, could see down the side of the house to where Dox was. Of the three of them, Priest thought, it was Dox who was free. He could sprint the backyard and find a way out over the fence. But Dox had never run away. Priest felt his knees begin to shake at the inevitable prospect. He appealed once more to the possibilities of good sense. What was wrong in looking for a ball?

"Mister, we just came to find the ball. If you don't want us to, we'll leave. We were in the park, the ball went over the fence. That's all."

The man looked toward the other man at the front of the house. That one was still leering. He uncrossed his arms and pointed toward the rear of the house at Dox. The man with the ashen hands wheeled clumsily, saw Dox, and retreated a step from the walk. Dox merely stood his ground, his feet in a flower-bed. His eyes looked vacantly toward Priest. The man at the front of the house took two steps toward them, and stopped. The other man came off the wall and took a step toward Dox and said, "What are you doing here?"

Dox didn't even look at him. He looked down at the flowers near his legs. It was Whistle who spoke. His voice came loud and fast and was unintelligible to anyone who hadn't lived with him. He knew this was so, and it gave him courage to say what he pleased to adults.

"He told you three times we came for the ball. Are you deaf? Or what?"

The man swung at him. The fat arm whipped out with surprising speed, but his feet were clumsy and the grey fist was a foot away when it lashed past Whistle's face. The man, cursing, then squealing, stepped forward to swing again. He whirled his head for a second to see where Dox was. Whistle wheeled toward the street and raced up the walk. It appeared to Priest that Whistle would go headlong into the other man, who was almost squatting on the walk, his arms spread, his tongue out. But Whistle side-stepped him without breaking stride or turning his head to look. He trampled flowers and leaped to the lawn as the man scooped his arms at the air and then turned. He saw Whistle jump the waist-high hedgerow and the iron picket fence and get out on the street beside Matty.

"Come on, Dox!" Priest shouted.

He banged past the arm of the man who now had to turn again toward him. The man clutched at Priest's sleeve, and the sleeve ripped when Priest tore free. He sailed the fence, stumbling when he hit the pavement. He felt blood on his knee. He turned to look for Dox. Dox had not come after him. He was still toward the back of the house. Over and over Priest asked himself what they had done wrong, what did the men want.

The man nearer to the boys on the street gave them up and moved swiftly toward the other man and Dox. Go now, Priest said to himself for Dox, and then cried out to him, "Come on! Come on, Dox! What are you waiting for?" Dox could dodge them. If anyone could, he could.

"Your stupid ball, " he said to Matty at the fence.

"Don't blame me. Don't blame *them* on me."

"Come on!" Whistle roared at Dox. "Get out of there!"

The three boys stood shoulder to shoulder with their hands gripping the spikes of the fence. Dox had not moved, but he was looking from one to another of the two men who were now at each other's side, whispering. They took up almost all the width between the house and two or three feet from the park fence. The boys all knew that none of them now would get clean away. Dox would suddenly lash out before the man could even see him move or begin to imagine how fast he could. But the man he didn't hit would grab him. There'd be a fight, Dox's fists would swing like stones on a whirling rope in the midst of the big fat men who would eventually weigh him down, and then they would all have to go in.

"Damn Dox," Priest said. "What's he staying there for?"

Then he stared. They all stared. The man with the eyeglasses seized Dox by his shirt at the nape of his neck, and by the belt of his pants in the back. He lifted Dox from the ground. Dox allowed it. Now, holding Dox at his side that way, twisting and knotting his shirt, the man hauled him toward the front of the house. The other man stood where Dox had been, watching, his arms crossed again, his chest heaving slightly from his small exertions with the other boys. The knees of the man who carried Dox thumped against Dox's ribs as he lurched with his burden. He carried Dox like a heavy parcel, like the day's trash. The boys at the fence stared and stared.

Dox was as mild as a puppy hauled by the scruff of its neck.

71

His toes dragged the gravel of the walk; his hands dangled limply. At the hedge the man strained with Dox's weight. He was going to lift him over the fence. Priest stared at them, stared at the man's ashen hands, at Dox's eyes. They gazed back at him from the raised head, large and fearfully wondering. The man swung his arms and grunted. He dumped Dox over the fence, and Dox landed on his behind at the feet of the boys. The other man at the back of the house laughed. His thumbs were in his belt under the roll of sweated through belly fat. He squealed with a laughter that was as obscene and frightening as anything Priest had ever heard or could have imagined.

He was stricken with shame as soon as he started to run, but there was nothing that could stop him from running down the block as fast as he could. He ran with a knowledge and fear which were useless to him, and he sobbed his brother's name with a pity he had never felt before. He didn't stop running until he got to the corner. The others came hard after him, running too, Matty with the baseball bat banging behind him, unaware that he even held it. Dox, without a stop to his running, crossed the street and kept on going away from the three boys who had gathered breathlessly on the corner. They called to him. He didn't heed them. He ran with one hand to his forehead, or over his eyes—they couldn't tell—and he turned the next corner from them and went out of sight.

"Jesus," Whistle said.

"He went off his nut," Matty said. "The thing with his mother made him. I never saw . . ."

"Two bastards," Whistle said. "Just about a ball."

"Four," Matty said. He told them of two more men he had seen peering from behind the drawn window shades.

"His hands were grey," Priest said. "What were his hands grey from?"

"Furnace ashes," Whistle said.

"In July?" Matty said.

They looked at each other in awe. They had all read of dismembered bodies burned in cellar furnaces.

"What were they doing there?" Priest insisted. "Why did they think we were spying?"

On the long walk home they began to talk of Dox. Whistle maintained it was Dox's shame for the way the men had frightened him that made him run off. Matty said no man or men could scare Dox. "If your mother died, would you get in a fight the next week? He ran because he was starting to cry about his mother. He didn't want us to see." Priest, strangely, had the least to contribute. He shifted the talk from Dox and Dox's mother to the idea itself of dying. He provoked them to speculate about diseases they could name, and he intimidated them into silence with his hints of mortality and chance. When they were drawing near to the Parkway and would go separate ways to their homes, they talked again of the men. They had much to tell their other friends, but they pledged themselves not to mention what had happened to Dox.

From his house Priest phoned Dox. He was told by Dox's older brother that Dox was not at home. He didn't call again after supper. He imagined relatives would be there in formal mourning. When he went to sleep, he thought for a long time of the encounter with the strange men. Their images blurred—he couldn't accurately remember their faces—and this intensified his sense of a hidden meaning for their inexplicable behavior. He was up a long time reviewing the string of circumstances, as though they contained a clue or a lesson. He remembered then, or thought he did, the name of the realtor on the sign in front of the house. He knew realtors did business on Sunday, and he went at last to sleep inventing the story which would elicit the information he wanted.

In the morning, however, he could find no such name in the phone book. Dox did not show up for the game scheduled in the neighborhood park, but no one had expected him. Priest took Whistle and Matty aside and tried to talk with them of the men and to check if they had seen and remembered the name on the sign. Neither of them had. They no longer looked upon the incident with his own fervor. Matty lamented the loss of his ball and

73

hinted at compensation. He reminded Priest that he had deliberately hit it over the fence.

By Tuesday Priest had still not seen or heard from Dox. Three times he had called Dox's house: twice he learned Dox was out, and once there was no one at home to answer. His inability to see or talk to Dox fastened him all the more to his speculations about the men. Alone on Tuesday afternoon he went back to get the realtor's name. The sign had been removed. He stood opposite the house on the other side of the street and stared at it in confusion. The shades were no longer drawn, but there was no one and nothing to be seen. It was all ordinary. Even the ballfield in the park, unlike the day on which they had come, was crowded now with kids. He thought of waiting there long enough for a ball to come over the fence. He thought even of crossing the street, knocking on the door, and addressing whichever of the men answered in such a civilized way as would immediately elicit the simple explanations. But as he stood there he experienced so vivid a recollection of Dox's humiliating posture when he was carried to the fence that he left at once and hurried home.

He learned that evening from a friend that Dox had gone once to the cemetery where his mother was buried, far out by subway and buses into Queens. The news stunned him. He imagined that what had happened to Dox at the house was connected with his visit to the cemetery. More than ever he felt himself mysteriously close to Dox, and his heart opened freely, without the old resentment for Dox's unfeeling ways. Dox, too, could give himself to mystery, to wanting and needing to understand it. Priest knew how often he had himself been moved to fight, to lash out—as Dox always did—and had restrained himself by the force of reason, the obligation to understand, which preceded the obligation to do. They were almost brothers, he and Dox, celebrating their birthdays but a week apart. Priest knew it now. In awe of each other's opposite way of working out the same nature—that's why they had never fought.

When Priest got home that night from his walk with his

friend who had told him about the cemetery, it was too late to call
Dox. It was Dox who called him on the next morning, Wednesday.

"You wanna go back with me?" he said.

Priest knew at once what he meant, but he said, "Back where?
Where've you been? I kept trying to get you. Are you all
right?"

"To Kelley Park. The house there."

"What are you gonna do?"

"You wanna come with me?"

"But what for?"

"I'm leaving now. I'll walk with the Highway. You wanna
come, be in front of your house." He hung up.

Priest prepared the arguments by which he would dissuade his
friend. His own idea of going back to the house had never included Dox, which struck him now with a premonition of disaster. He feared not only what could take place out there, but with
it the new sense he had made of his friend. He waited in front of
his house for the ten minutes it would take Dox to walk there.
Images of the two men bloomed in his mind, the ashen hands of
one and the leering smile of the other—both of them shapeless,
fat, sweating. And the two invisible ones, the two Matty had
seen.

Dox came on the other side of the street, walking fast, turning
his head occasionally to spit. His arms were motionless; only his
legs moved, rapidly. He glanced toward Priest's door, saw him,
but did not even slow down. He stared at Priest across the width
of the street and kept on walking. Priest, when he crossed to him,
trotting to catch up, felt as if he were being drawn across the
narrowing distance by some power of Dox's will. But when he
caught up he saw there was nothing in Dox's face, nothing in his
eyes, not the confusion of the week before, and no resolve either.
He merely walked fast. Priest addressed him at once.

"You can't go there. What for? There's no reason for it anymore."

Dox said nothing. He kept on walking, and Priest had to keep walking too. He reminded Dox there were four men, not two. He suggested there might be no one there anyway. He admitted he'd gone back himself and the shades were up and he had seen nothing. He pleaded finally that they might at least go back and get some friends. At last Dox answered him.

"Go home if you want."

They fell silent, but they kept on walking—fast. It was again hot and humid, and behind Dox's ear, running down the tough muscle of his flat neck, there was a single line of sweat. They had accomplished half their walk and Priest still did not ask Dox why he had phoned, why he had not chosen Whistle or Matty to accompany him.

"You're mixing it all up," he said instead. He was picturing Dox at his mother's grave, which could not yet have a stone, standing there above the mound of dirt and the designation of her name on a small card on a piece of wood stuck into the dirt, standing at that one spot for long hours alone, the feline body, vicious in its power to respond, made unendurable in Priest's mind by the stillness of it. Against it the walking was a kind of relief, but they were drawing ever nearer to the house. When they turned the corner to the block itself, he tried one last time.

"All right, then. We're going. But you let me do the talking. Whoever comes to the door, let me tell him. We just came for the ball. Then if . . ."

"What ball?"

Dox slowed his pace. He almost halted as he regarded his friend. Priest felt his face flush, and he could not answer Dox, and they resumed their walking. Again he conjured the picture of the two men, and the two invisible ones.

"Let me talk to them first," he pleaded again, his hand firmly on his friend's shoulder.

"Talk if you want," Dox said, tearing loose of the hand with a wrench of his shoulder, walking, not breaking stride.

Dox worked the latch of the gate when they came before the

house. It creaked loudly when he swung it open. Priest caught it from behind and held it for a moment to keep it from swinging closed. Holding the gate had cost him a stride and he came up the two steps to the front door behind Dox. He wanted to shoulder his way past Dox so that he would be the first to be seen when someone answered the door, but Dox blocked his way. Dox pressed his finger to the bell. He pressed and pressed and the noise inside screamed.

"They heard you. Let go of it!" Priest urged. Dox kept his finger stabbing on the button.

A shade in the front window peeled back, but Priest couldn't see. His heart thumped. The door swung back. The man who had leered at them four days ago stood there. His face fell in surprise. He was wearing a suit and a bow tie. He looked, for the moment, stupefied and harmless. Then the leer began to form in his face and Priest could not collect his wits to begin the reasonable sentence he had rehearsed.

"Look who's here," the man said. "Look who's back." His voice, unlike the other man's, and unlike the recollection Priest had of his squealing laughter, was deep.

"Get the other guy," Dox said. His voice was flat.

The man stared incredulously at Dox, and Priest felt himself beginning to speak. But he had to stop, for he was shamefully about to tell the man that his friend's mother had died. The man was still staring at him when Dox repeated, "Get the other guy."

Then the man moved. He raised his arm and brought his open hand down hard on the side of Dox's face. It made a sound like the popping of a bag, and Priest saw the blood ooze from the wheal on Dox's cheek. He clenched his fists, took a deep breath, and watched Dox. He wanted to swing at the man, he wanted to speak, but he felt himself at the mercy of Dox's will. Dox merely stood there. He did not even look at the man who had struck him. It was as if he'd not been hit, though he wiped with his tongue at the flow of blood. His hands were at his side, unclenched. "Get the other guy," he said again, his voice still hard, flat. Then Priest saw the other man bulging behind the one who had answered the door. The two men, looking at each other, filled the doorway. Dox was in Priest's way and Priest could not see if the man's hands were still grey.

"Listen, we . . ." Priest started to say, his voice thick. "What kind of men are you?" he blurted out. "We only . . ."

"Bastard!" Dox cried, loud, passionately. Then he sprang the step to the sill, his arms flailing even before he had launched himself, like stones whipping on a rope. He banged the man who answered the door out of the way, and now he was at the man who had dumped him over the fence. Again and again he drove his fists into the man's soft belly, his chest. The man, trying to catch at the fists, got his face forward and low. His mouth fell open. His tiny eyes behind the glasses were amazed. Dox hit him there, in the face, again and again, hard, brutally. The man's glasses flew off. Blood streamed from his eye, his nose, his lip. Priest could not see Dox's fists, but he could hear the drumming on flesh and the whack of bone, and he could see the blood staining the man's white shirt in streaks and splotches.

In a moment it was all over. Dox stopped. The man who had opened the door had not the time or the wits or maybe even the courage to respond. He looked in amazement at the beaten man who backed off into the house and wiped at the flow of blood in his face and sobbed.

"Bastard!" Dox shouted again.

Then he leaped off the porch past Priest, nearly knocking him over on his way. He ran swiftly down the walk and through the open gate and was turning up the street before Priest could begin to respond to the tingling in his legs signaling him to run also. The thought crossed his mind that he should swing first. He should lash out and strike the amazed man, the leer all gone now, who was looking up the block to where Dox raced like a cat. If he didn't hit him, it ran through Priest's mind, he would regret it all his life. But his betraying good sense took over, and his legs responded, and he fled the house and raced up the street after Dox, who, still going fast, was halfway to the corner.

At the corner around the street from the house, Dox leaned against a car and caught his breath. He waited for Priest. When Priest got there he leaned against the car also. He wanted to speak, but he couldn't catch his breath. And even as his breath came back he couldn't sort out from all that ran through his mind—from all that he knew now and all that he felt—a single thing to say. He took the handkerchief from his pocket and raised it to Dox's cheek to wipe the blood. Dox raised his hand to move Priest's hand away, but then he dropped his hand. He permitted his friend to wipe the blood.

Priest knew he would have to find Matty or Whistle to tell it to, what Dox had done and he had witnessed. He knew as well that Dox would never tell it. He could see it in his friend's eyes, the absence of the need to tell, or understand. His eyes now were as they always were, as if nothing had happened. Not the man, not even his mother. They were walking, and he was merely Dox again, walking with that threatful conservation of his energy. The world was merely what it always was. Priest had to use all his restraint to keep from turning with his own fists on his friend as they walked. At least he imagined it was restraint. In truth, he too profoundly admired and feared Dox to be able to do it, admired him even as he guessed ahead to the incurable life of violence Dox would always lead. Side by side, in silence, they walked home, both of them turning their heads occasionally to spit.

WHISTLE AND THE HEROES

It is only basketball, yet twice a week, in the early night, Marvin Wessel lives the life of a man. He doesn't play before the Garden crowds, and even the time of club ball is far behind, yet Wednesdays and Fridays are the best days of his week. The community center is open on Monday evenings too, but on that night he drives his mother for her injection. It's a sacrifice for Marvin, and they both know it. She might change the day of her appointment, but he never presses her to. Next to the nights that he plays basketball, giving it up on Monday is the other big thing in his week.

His mother alludes often to a devil, and when the doctor first explained her child's cleft palate, she always spoke of it as more of Satan in her life. As a boy, he knew what she said had something to do with him, and understood no more of it than that. But now he no longer thinks of it. He tries to think of little that is in the past: basketball on the two nights and his job satisfy his idea of time.

Whistle—as his friends have always called him—works as a packer in one of the city's largest department stores. Before that, four years ago, he worked for a button company, but his present job is better. The building is huge and he is shifted among departments often enough to overcome the monotony of his work. The frequent changes make it unnecessary to get too friendly

with anyone, and this, also, satisfies Whistle. He feels no need
for new friends, and his speech makes it difficult to talk to people
he doesn't already know. When the work gets too dull, he thinks
ahead to his two big nights.

On a Wednesday or Friday, Whistle is always nervous. This
happens as early as breakfast. He fries an extra egg and has milk
instead of the usual coffee. He is grateful at these times that his
mother always sleeps late and he can manage the mornings for
himself. On the subway, he pushes back against the jostling
with a little more force, although he is careful to avoid argument.
If he is close to a window, he peers at his face, which is trapped
in the window against the darkness of the tunnel. He thinks he
hardly looks the part he will play that night, and the deception
gives him some kind of advantage over the others in the car. At
work, when he walks from the packing table for empty cartons,
he pushes hard against the balls of his feet. He can feel his calves
tighten, and he has to fight the impulse to run a few steps. Even
when he packs, the work is not enough to wear away the energy
that builds inside him. He is almost pained by the sense of his
body, and he is able to isolate parts of it: the weight of an arm,
the tension in a leg, the bunching behind a shoulder. This impatience for violent movement compels his mind to wander as he
packs, and he lapses into a familiar image of himself. They are
jumping under the backboard for a loose ball, and he suddenly
angles in from the corner of the court and finds an opening. He
cuts in cleanly and leaps with the power of his run to snatch the
ball out of the air and come down without contact some fifteen
feet away toward the other corner, already dribbling quickly
downcourt. The picture excites him, and he works with more
conviction at the carton on his packing table.

At lunch, he runs the short distance to the cafeteria, finding
little spaces in the hurrying noon crowds. He runs with his feet
wide apart and his legs bent slightly at the knees so that he might
veer sharply through any sudden opening. Though he can tell
himself he runs to get a window seat, he doesn't care to under-

stand why this seat isn't so important on other days. He eats quickly, again having milk instead of coffee, and spends the rest of the hour smoking cigarettes and staring out the window. He can usually guess which of the girls that pass are models, and he can even decide between those who work in the high-price houses and the cheaper ones. He has heard enough stories to know they are all tramps, and he has seen it himself when he worked in a dress house. But when one walks by who is beautiful, yet clean—like the fragile girl in a perfume ad—he finds the stories and what he knows hard to believe.

In the afternoon his mind wanders again, and the time passes quickly. If he grows too conscious of his straying thoughts, he works at the packing with a renewed vigor. When it gets toward quitting time, he is pleased by the energy that is still in him. At five o'clock he turns in his slips, knowing that he has packed more than he does on the ordinary days. Men in the same department mutter goodbye to him, and he nods his head and smiles in return. Three middle-aged women work there, but they say nothing to him, though they joke with the other men. In the crowded street he runs again to the subway—the feet wide apart, the knees slightly bent.

When he gets home on Wednesdays or Fridays, he takes the stairs to their first floor Bay Ridge flat two at a time. His mother knows the community center opens at seven, and supper is always ready for him. She finds it a nuisance to have her time fixed this way twice a week, and she complains bitterly about it. She often tells him he must stop playing ball, that he is no longer a boy, that were his father alive he would have to toe the line. But she never forces an argument because she has come herself to depend on these two nights. When he hurries out the door with his gym clothes in a traveling bag, she begins to mutter about her devil as she rubs a hand across her chest.

On the gym floor, Whistle moves with a bird's grace. He uses the game as a gull does the wind, tacking toward the basket in what is almost flight. He is slender and not more than five-ten, and though all the fellows he plays with are much younger than he, many of them are taller and stronger. Some of them, swelling in their late teens, strip to their shorts so that the sweat will shadow the contours of their bodies. But Whistle wears a grey fleece-lined sweater and track pants.

They play on only one basket, yet Whistle rarely stops moving. If there is a loose ball—no matter how far away—he chases for it. If someone is about to shoot, he is already moving toward the backboard for the rebound. Even when he crouches to jump for a ball that has not yet begun to drop, there is so much tension in his poise that there is no apparent halting of motion between the wait and the leap. Yet with all his running, there is a great economy to Whistle's movement. He possesses a flawless instinct for knowing where to be. Despite the smallness of the court, he never collides with the other five who play. There are many such collisions in this unrefereed game, but Whistle is seldom involved in the tangle. The kids, often desperate with his near perfection, claim that his one shortcoming is a fear of the rough stuff, and they try to provoke him. But Whistle knows this is not a part of his game, and he is able, by the certainty of his movements, to avoid it.

It does not matter to him that he is twenty-eight and most of the boys he plays with are still in their teens. Nor does it matter that there is no great audience and the game is only a pick-up affair. It is enough that he performs well and the sweat is on his body. But more than other things, there is that fine chemical change as he plays. Sometimes he will put a hand to his abdomen, as though to feel it. Things inside of him—hard things he is unaware of during the day, but feels now he should be able to touch—loosen as though parts of his body had begun to dissolve. After a few minutes on the gym floor, he can almost hear himself unwinding, as though there were some connection between running and health. When he leaps in from the corner of the court to steal a ball from the taller fellows under the backboard, he may—as he begins to dribble away—raise his head slightly and look back toward the players with a curiously defiant stare in his eyes, a thinning of the lines in his already taut face. Aside from this one lapse, he is all but oblivous to place and time. He does not think once while he plays how much better it all is than his work as a packer, or his life at home. He runs with pursed lips and never speaks, but neither is he aware that he has not spoken.

Yet in his mind there are the impressions of a long time ago. There are many people and various days, but if he were to remember well there would be only one night, there would be the girl and Bernstein. It was eight years ago and a good time in Whistle's life.

It was a winter evening that came with a heavy snow. He would remember that because the girl sat on his lap and he wouldn't help when the car settled on the ice and the fellows got out to push. It was winter, too, because the last he'd ever seen of Bernstein was after the game when the kid had thrown a snowball at the lamppost outside the school, threw it so well that he hit not the post but the lamp fixture, and when it came down it made a splattering thud in the soft snow. Then Bernstein and his gang ran off around the corner, shouting, and Whistle stood there. He looked into the darkness where the lamp had been, looked up at the falling snow, and listened to the echoes of Bernstein's laughter.

It was the winter of the year. Even with the car as crowded as it was, they made vapor funnels with their breathing, and they passed the bottle around often. She swallowed from it along with the other girls, and when she finished and gave the bottle to Whistle, he saw her shoulders shudder and felt her squirm on his lap. She was broad and thin, and her name was Alice. When she turned her face to hand him the bottle, the edge of her profile was rimmed in a soft light. Whistle thought she was very pretty.

It had been Dox's idea that they take the girls to the game. Whistle worked with Dox in the dress house, and Alice worked there too. Dox's date was a model in the place, but Alice worked in the office. Dox insisted she was too thin to be a model, but Whistle thought she was clean and would not be one. He had never spoken to her, and it was Dox who had arranged the date. That made Whistle angry, but he could not understand why. For weeks he had wanted her to see him play. At nights, the desire had made him restless with a new excitement.

After work they went to the New Yorker for dinner. Flip and Artie met them there with their girls, and it was almost a party. They had drinks before dinner, but Artie kept insisting about the game, and so none of the fellows had more than two. Whistle wanted to drink more, but he felt himself tighten when Artie mentioned the game, and he held back.

But in the car when the bottle Dox had bought went around and she would swallow from it and then turn to hand it to him, Whistle was afraid she would hear the beating in his chest. There was the soft light on her face, and she said, "Here, Whistle," without even a smile. But there was an edge to her voice that startled him. He did not think from seeing her at work that she would drink the way she did, and he believed she was doing it because the other girls were. But she didn't say anything or even change the expression on her face when Dox's girl started to curse, and Whistle felt the blood inside him to the ends of his fingers. He wanted to take a long swallow when she said, "Here, Whistle," but Artie still kept on about the game, so he ran a little of it over his lip and passed it on. She sat well back in his lap, and he had a hand on her shoulder. He thought ahead to when he would be running on the gym floor and she would be watching him. Thinking of that relieved the sense of his awkwardness. It would be much easier for him after the game. He could look forward to the party in Dox's basement. He was almost not afraid to think of taking her home by himself afterwards.

But suddenly, even the thought of the game was strangely frightening. She might not know anything about basketball. She might not care at all about how he played. He remembered he had not spoken a full sentence to her since the evening started. That terrified him now. The others were all making noise in the car. When he listened, he could hear Dox's girl laugh loudly. But Alice was quiet. Maybe Dox had spoken to her before the date. Quickly, without thinking, his fingers—as though they were apart from the anguish inside him—tightened about her shoulder. He waited for her to protest, wanting now to be out of the car, not caring anymore about the game. But she didn't speak. She didn't even move. She just sat there on his lap looking out through the opposite window, the light shading the edge of her fine profile. He felt his fingers loosen on her shoulder.

Then Flip, sitting in front with his girl on his lap, twisted his head toward the corner where Whistle sat in the back. Looking past Alice, Whistle could see Flip's thick neck wrinkle in two ugly folds.

"It's awful quiet back there," Flip said. "They must be having fun. Whistle didn't even get out to push." Dox's girl laughed. Whistle thought hard for something to say, but Alice was quiet too. Then Artie's girl, sitting next to Whistle, spoke.

"Nothing's going on. You take care of your own troubles."

"What did I say?" Flip called back. "I thought I was being nice. I was looking out for Alice."

"I'm fine, thank you," Alice said without moving. Her voice, clear, brittle, sounded in Whistle's ear like the tapping of metal. It came upon him quietly—as though the thought had been in his mind for years—that he was going to love her. They were on the bridge now, and the water below them was dark in the twilight. Looking out between the massive, bolted girders at the river, at the boats, at the snow, and at the lights that beamed their narrow yellow tracks across the water, Whistle lost himself for a moment in a surprising calm. It was as though he had done all this—Alice on his lap and his hand on her shoulder—many times before. He thought he would ask her, after the party, when they stood before her door, to go on a boat ride with him when the warmer weather came. When he turned away from the window, he saw that she had raised a hand to her face to touch precisely with a finger near the corner of her eye. The nail was long and polished lightly, in pink.

"There won't be much for us to do at the game, just watching you guys run around," Dox's girl suddenly said.

"Anxious to get to the party?" Dox asked. Whistle knew Dox had smiled.

"It'll be better than the game," she said.

"I suppose it will," Dox said.

"You girls can bet on that," Flip said.

"There he goes again," Artie's girl said.

"For Christ's sake, what the hell's eating you?" Flip answered.

"Oh, can it all already, will you," Dox said. It grew quiet and Whistle wondered why Alice hadn't said anything when they spoke about the game. Then Dox looked quickly at his girl.

"You watch Whistle during the game. That'll give you enough to do."

"Why? Is he something special?" She turned a little to look toward Whistle. He bit his lip to stop the childish grin.

"The best basketball player you ever saw," Flip said.

"So what?" she laughed.

"This one's got the giggles," Flip said. "Listen kid, if girls were basketballs Whistle would have you all screwed by tomorrow." Flip laughed, and Dox's girl laughed. A small knot of breath caught in Whistle's throat. Then Alice laughed, louder than the others, filling the car with the sound of it, tilting her head back so that her hair fell against his face. She jerked on his lap as she laughed, and then began to cough and laugh at the same time. Whistle heard himself mumble, "Take it easy. Take it easy." When she stopped at last, they were all quiet again. Whistle listened to the continuous grinding of the snow beneath the tires.

"It's going to be a rough game," Artie said, breaking the silence.

"Quit worrying," Dox said.

"Is this a very special game?" Alice asked. Whistle shrugged,

then nodded toward Artie. "He thinks so," he heard himself say.
"They're only kids," Artie said, "but they play high school ball
together. They got this guy Bernstein on the team. He's got
offers from colleges already."

"Oh, is that the kid who plays for Madison?" Alice asked.
Whistle looked up eagerly at her. Her mouth was half-parted in
surprise. It was small, pretty. He turned his head away.

"How did you know?" Flip asked.

"He lives on my block. I used to date his brother."

"No shit?" Flip said.

"Bernstein's a nice kid," Alice said. "I've seen him play."

"You watch Whistle tonight," Dox said.

"Are you really that good, Whistle?" she asked, turning her
face down to him. He could not see her face for the shadows,
but he thought surely she must hear the beating of his heart. He
wanted to be out of the car and on the gym floor. He wanted
that very much. He opened his mouth to say something. not
knowing what he would say. But then Dox began.

"He ought to be that good. Hell, even I might be if I worked
at it like him. Hey Artie, you remember when we were kids and
it was ass-cold outside. Below zero, remember? We were going
to a movie—*Captain Blood,* wasn't it? You nearly lost an ear
on the way. And when we passed the schoolyard, there was
Whistle running around in a sweater and steaming like the fourth
of July. He even shoveled the snow away from the backboard,
remember?"

"I ought to," Artie said. "I had to go to the doctor account
of my frozen ear. Whistle, you were a crazy kid."

Whistle smiled.

Flip began to sing a song, and his girl joined in. Then Dox and
Artie sang, and Alice hummed. Whistle thought confidently of
the game. He had hardly spoken to her, had not really touched
her. It would be different afterwards. He would sing with them
on the way to Dox's place. The words were almost in his mouth
now. He liked the light weight of her on his lap, but he wanted to

be in the game already. He thought of it longingly, saw himself angling in from the corner for that free ball. But it was hard for him to think only of the game. He got it mixed with the metallic ring of her voice: "Here, Whistle. Here, Whistle."

When the car pulled up before the community center, Whistle thought he should help Alice out, but she was on his lap and had to leave first. Inside the building, they all lingered for a while at the steps to the locker room.

"You girls keep together," Flip said. "We'll see you after the game." Then, looking at Alice as the fellows started down the stairs, Flip added, "Having fun?"

"Terrific," she said flatly. Whistle, already hurrying down the steps, did not look back. The word, the sound of it, terrified him. He'd been a fool with her. He should've said more in the car. He should've maybe touched her arm now before leaving her. He should've held her hand when they were going through the snow. The steps had been icy too.

"You got a big mouth, Flip," Dox said, as he pushed open the door to the locker room.

"Say, what the hell is all this?" Flip complained. "I ain't said one word tonight when everybody didn't come jumping on me."

"Then shut up!" Dox said.

"Cut it, will you guys. Think about the game a little," Artie said. "It ain't going to be a breeze with that Bernstein kid."

They met the rest of the team in the locker room, and as they dressed Whistle outlined the way they'd play. But even as he spoke, he heard the single sound of her sweet voice. He urged them all to hurry.

When they were finally on the gym floor for the pre-game practice, Whistle moved like a diving gull, as though an idea of his body had become dependent upon it. His teammates sensed the urgency of Whistle's motion, and believing he was being driven only by the thought of Bernstein, their own movements became gracelessly self-conscious. The kids and girls and men of the neighborhood who had come to watch talked in low voices, looking from one end of the court to the other, from Bernstein to Whistle. But Whistle, even up to the moment when the ball was about to go into the air between the two centers, and Bernstein crouched beside him, thought only that she was watching, that her eyes—with the brows arched curiously—were on him. And a second later, when he moved quickly and the ball was in his hands, he thought of nothing when the ball went through the basket. He indistinctly heard the clamor that rose up from the shot he had made, feeling now only the tremendous uncoiling inside him, as though a wall of air had finally burst from his throat. A moment later when he was under and then past the basket and had scored again, his temples beat with the image of his body that had twisted itself between two men, had gone beneath an outstretched hand and angled the ball against the backboard, all in the motion of an instant. He had no thought that he had twice within a minute's time outmaneuvered Bernstein.

So lost was he in the sensation of his running that he could not say when Bernstein first moved in on him, to be no more than six inches away, no matter where Whistle turned or how fast he ran, to stay there continuously as long as Whistle or his team had the ball, hawking him that way with his adolescent face, his eyes bulging, his mouth open, but with no sweat on his body. He did not even know at first that it was Bernstein who had begun to cling to him, and did not know until he had spent the deliberate effort of minutes in trying to shake him off—who would not be shaken—that the stalking figure always inches away was the Bernstein who'd been spoken of so much, who was the high school star, who had the pop-eyes and open mouth and no sweat and who was to be the way of measuring him. It was against this recognition that Whistle made—when he next got his hands on the ball—his first desperate effort to overcome the kid who was taking him. With a violent wrench of his body that feigned movement in a direction he did not go, Whistle got a foot ahead of Bernstein and drove toward the basket. He left his feet, raising the ball for the shot, and then saw, too late, the blur of the hand that came over his shoulder without touching him to hit the ball cleanly from his grasp. Whistle knew without turning it had been Bernstein's hand. He ran wildly to retrieve the ball he had lost, his body colliding against others. When the foul was called against him, and Bernstein, unperturbed, went to the line and quickly made his throw, Whistle began, for the first time, to think not in the images he always made, but of himself against Bernstein; began to think in advance even of what movements he might make with the other hounding him so. With his mind working feverishly as he ran, Whistle lost possession of his game. When he began himself to sense the loss, his thoughts went past Bernstein, went to Alice who was watching him from somewhere in the crowd. Then Bernstein, almost from the center of the court, soon after the foul, lofted a long set-shot that he turned his back on even before he could see it drop cleanly through the basket. Whistle felt an unfamiliar panic as he ran. He even looked for a second toward the crowd, trying to find Alice where he could not see one face in the blur that was before his eyes.

During the time-out that Artie called, Whistle could hear the words, but he did not listen to what the others said to him. He stared across the floor to where Bernstein stood among his teammates, nonchalant, unsweating, listening and talking. Whistle could see now that Bernstein was not even tall, that he was comically thin, with a sunken chest and no spread at all to his shoulders. Bernstein put a finger to his side and scratched slowly, and Whistle—his eyes hot with anger—thought he would like to drive his fist through the ribs where Bernstein's fingers picked indifferently. When they began to play again, Bernstein started to move as he had not before. Something close to fright tore at Whistle as he tried to keep up with him, to try sometimes even to find him. And always, when Whistle had the ball himself, Bernstein was on him, never touching him, but never more than six inches away, his face thrust out to Whistle's so that Whistle saw, whenever he turned, the popped eyes, the open mouth, the dry skin. Whenever he could get close enough to raise his hands for the shot, there was the other hand raised to the same height, blocking or worrying the ball. Whistle swore at himself for his clumsiness, angry with the body that would not move as he wanted it.

At half-time, on the way to the lockers, moving through the crowd, he passed next to Alice, suddenly, unexpectedly. He lowered his head. He was grateful she had not seen him, that she was talking with Sonny who kept score for them and did not play. But when he moved on and heard the brittle pitch of her laughter come after him, he felt anew the weight that had fallen on his heart since the first moment after work.

In the locker room, Whistle sulked and the others left him to himself. He ran his hands nervously over his knees, and the legs felt insensitive to the touch. He began to think then that he was ill, or having a bad night, and then began to believe that, and believed too—as he remembered the two quick baskets he'd made at the beginning of the game—that it might be only a bad stretch. The name Bernstein came to him from all parts of the room, the words "great" and "what a ballplayer" and "what can you do with him," so that Whistle blurted out, "I'm on to the sonofabitch now. I'll get him this half." He spoke so hurriedly and with so little expectation from the others, that they could not understand the words. But they took from the tone what he had meant, and when they ran from the locker room to the gym, they called encouragements to each other.

A minute after play had started again, Whistle was in the corner of the court, and there was a ball loose in the air under the backboard. He angled in quickly toward the ball, feeling the oppressive weight fall out of him as his feet came off the ground with his leap, his hand outstretched under the ball he was about to seize. And then it was not there and his fingers clutched against the empty space. When he turned his head the thin, no-shouldered, unsweating Bernstein was dribbling quickly downcourt. Whistle felt the air go out of him—as though from a blow— then ran wildly after Bernstein, finally leaving his feet in a des-

93

perate lunge for the ball. He came down with a thud against the hard floor. He could feel his fingers claw against the smooth, hot wood. Even in the sudden darkness before his eyes, he knew that he was rolling, felt the joints of his knee and elbow grate against the hardness. Then he knew he was on his feet again and trying to run, but Dox had him by the arms, shouting, "Take it easy, Whistle. Take it easy." They called a foul and Whistle watched Bernstein calmly make it good, watched him while he felt his legs trembling and the blood running from his knee. But he would not leave the game and he was glad about the blood. He began looking once more to the sidelines. He ran wildly after that, not even knowing that Bernstein had begun to ease off, and he fouled freely. He could not hear Dox telling him during the time-outs that it was only a game, that he would be in no shape for the party afterwards, that Alice would get sore.

When they were undressing after the game, Whistle did not know by what score they had lost, nor did he try to think of how many points Bernstein scored and how many he made himself. He started to complain about his knee, and Dox said he would drive him home. But Whistle said no and Dox assumed he would go to the party and went with Flip to find the girls. But Whistle got out of the room later and left the building. He stood for a moment on the corner in the snow that was still falling and saw Bernstein throw the snowball and heard the laughter as they ran away. He started to walk home, not knowing now why he had left. He knew he must have played better than any of the others. Certainly better than Flip. The crowd had clapped when he stayed in the game with the bloody knee. It hurt him now. It hurt a lot. He should get home and clean it out. He wondered if the blood might be staining the snow, but he did not look to see.

He did not go to work the next day, or the day after, then finally quit, telling Dox to say he'd torn the ligament in his knee and the doctor had said to lay off. He learned that Sonny had taken Alice to the party. He could not believe and tried not to care when they told him Sonny had made out.

It was hard to be with the fellows afterwards. No one spoke of

Alice to him. He did not want them to talk of her, though it made him uncomfortable to have them say nothing. But they all talked to him of Bernstein. He'd gone on to college and was the leading scorer on the freshman team. He had scored less against Whistle than he did against some college players. They told Whistle this often, but they could not make him care. He tried never to think again of Bernstein. He tried not to think at all about that night. And sometimes, most often at night, late and in bed, he'd shut his eyes tight when he heard the brittle, metallic, "Here, Whistle. Here, Whistle." He continued to play at the community center, but the club team had broken up and none of the fellows was there. Flip had bought a car and Artie had married. They had parties almost every Saturday night in Dox's basement.

When Whistle's mother some months later insisted they move closer to her relatives, she had—against Whistle's indifference— to abandon unused the many arguments she had prepared.

The three hours are over quickly for Whistle, and only while he takes off the sweated suit in the locker room does he begin to feel the punishment of his body. But under the needling spray of the shower, the fatigue leaves him, and he knows only the pleasant splash of the cool water. He thinks of nothing as the shower breaks against the nape of his neck and, clinging, wets the length of his back. He takes no part in the horseplay, but the others are not angry at his aloofness. They think of Whistle as older and funny, but they never accuse him of playing hero.

Always, after the shower, the close night air of the city lingers on his face with a fragrance it does not really own. When a high breeze slants occasionally from the bay through the rows of houses, Whistle is glad he does not bring the car on the nights he plays. He walks the half mile to home in a measured, predictable stride, and there is an inexpressible assertion for him in the small weight of the traveling bag he carries. He has a choice of streets, but he walks along the busiest one, though he pays no heed to the night-noises. The exhaust from a bus, the shouting from a window, a distant, muffled knock are provoking sounds, but

Whistle is not trapped in their loneliness. He is conscious only of a fine freedom released inside him, of a restored balance in his body. Occasionally a group gathered idly on a corner will begin to suggest things, but only vaguely, and the impressions are already abandoned by the time he crosses the street. Even on other days, it is hard for Whistle to think back in any specific way. The few fellows that haven't married go their ways, and months pass before Whistle will bother to look up any of them. Even on the Mondays that he drives his mother to the doctor, he prefers to sit in the car and wait for her, looking absently out the window, stirred only by the annoyance of having the night at the gym taken away from him.

When Whistle gets home his mother is already asleep. He takes one of the picture magazines that always lie about the kitchen and goes into his room. Undressed, in bed, by the dim light that hangs from the ceiling, he scans the pages, unmindful really of what he sees. When he puts the magazine away and flicks the light switch, he smokes a cigarette. The taste of it sharpens his ease. In the bright glow of the cigarette's end, there is a hypnotic focus for his sleep. Whistle's mind begins to make pictures. He thinks ahead to the weekend and the possibility of driving to Scranton once more, or maybe this time to Fall River. Since he has bought the car, he toys frequently with these trips, but he does not often go. For he always, afterwards, hates the clumsy, unuseable violence he feels toward the women.

When he feels the heat of the cigarette on his fingers, he drops it, still lit, into the ash-tray on the night table. His mind lingers on the impressions of shots he has made that night, of rebounds he has grabbed by angling in that way from the corner of the court. He thinks of Scranton again, and then of the next night that he will play. The poise—so fine before in his enervated body—begins now to crack. Whistle feels once more the dangerous soaring of his anticipations as he waits for sleep.

THE PASSION FOR SILVER'S ARM

There was a white ferocity to the heat of the schoolyard. It was impossible to ignore the August light on the concrete. Frank Weiss sat on the yellow wooden chair against the brick wall of the school and tried to read. The little shade there was no relief from the heat, but the light was darker.

When he looked up from his book to see if the blond fellow was still squatting near the fence, he saw something he was to remember for a long time.

It was a simple thing. It was Silver, the blond fellow with the pink flesh, with the deep torso and the curled and golden hair. He had been squatting on his haunches for over an hour watching the few grimy boys at their little game. Now he had suddenly risen to chase the ball that had gone astray. Loping after it, the muscles of his back slid under the spotless white T-shirt. As he moved in the heat, moved beside the ten-foot-high mesh iron fence topped by four lines of barbed wire, his brilliant hair darted like a flame.

The fellow picked up the ball and still trotting in that heat carried it back to where the boy who pitched waited. The boy was small and dirty. He waited indifferently for the ball the blond fellow did not throw but insisted on carrying back, holding it delicately before him, holding it like an egg, or a chalice. Gently he placed the ball into the soiled hand of the boy who was already turning to pitch it. For a moment the blond fellow lingered there beside him. He did not smile, but he lowered his head. In his hard white-into-pink face, toughened by the prominent bones, the flesh almost luminous in the sunlight, there was for a moment—Frank saw it—a look of care, of hurt, of knowing. Then he backed away a step or two. He turned and strolled to the fence and turned again and then resumed the casual squatting posture which bulged his thighs beneath the khakis. Patient, interested, he watched again as the boys began to play. That was all that Frank Weiss saw.

He tried to go back to his book, but he couldn't. It was more now than the heat and the light.

He had worried that the blond fellow might stir trouble in a schoolyard for children under sixteen. It was an angry neighborhood. But he didn't worry about that now. What kept him from his book was the deepening sense of what he had actually seen. It was the body's act of homage. It was the strong blond fellow's recognition of the small and dirty boy. It was something like that, anyway, he was later to tell his friend Webb when he tried to explain what he had really seen.

This picture would return to vex Frank Weiss. For a long time it would. It would even beyond the few days that followed, days on which Silver—as the dark Italian boys of the schoolyard called the alien man—returned regularly to squat, to watch, and then, at last to talk. On the fourth day, for example, easier now and friendlier, Silver had said to Frank, closing the anecdote with it as he turned his lyric blond head wondrously toward Frank, said in the casual manner of his narratives,

"Yes, he got down on his knees to beg. A thirteen-year-old kid, he got down in the dirt to, to beg! When I shot, from that close, you know, it about blew the sonofabitch's head all over the path."

Frank Weiss was not often the victim of demoralizing poetic insights. Young, having graduated the previous June from one of the city colleges where he had majored with excellence in physics, he was already rigid, dogmatic, assertive. If he heard, not even in an argument but simply whispered somewhere, in a subway, on the street, the words Communist, money, Mississippi, his mind clicked with the whole machinery of a fixed view. You could as well have said to him gravity, the refraction of light. Only twenty-two, he was already committed to a set of deliberate renunciations. For almost a year he had been going with a girl from the college. She was intelligent but uncommitted. In her small and deceptively frail body, however, she concealed an enormous physical energy. They had gotten quite involved. Suddenly Frank decided he had to weigh their relationship carefully. He avoided her for two weeks. Then he met with her in the college cafeteria.

"We can't," he said to her, imagining honesty was always kindness. "Webb, for example. That's a part of it too. It embarrasses you that he's Negro, doesn't it? That we all go out together?"

It was hardly fair to her. She had, after all, in her energy, her thoughtlessness, taught him all that he was perhaps ever to know about making love. But he had deliberated, and he had decided.

It was so with his family too. In his senior year he had taken an afternoon job to support himself and had left home for a small room near the college. There was nothing complicated about his motives. He was suddenly in his twenties, and he wanted to be away. The clutching family routine was uncongenial to his work. There was no rancor he could admit in what he wanted to do, and he attended regularly the ritual of their Friday night suppers. To his parents the abrupt departure of their younger son was the culminating bewilderment of their lives. They were immigrants from Germany, poor, overworked, bitter, and Frank had done to them what they had to fear from the moment he had entered college. It pained him that his parents did not understand, as it had pained him afterwards about the girl. It was trying on Friday nights when his father was so transparently

99

attentive to his older son Joseph. He had not gone to college. He was a postal clerk and had often been accused by his father for his unambitious ways. Nevertheless, Frank fought the occasional temptation to return home. He examined it and knew that this sort of grief was a part of parentage.

So the kind of thing that happened to Frank Weiss during the moment he had watched Silver retrieve the ball was actually a lapse. Now, no matter how he pondered the blond fellow's monstrous tales, all of Frank's proper responses were thwarted. He had to blame it on that foolish image of the first day.

It was troublesome. Occasionally in the last two evenings as he tried to read, he might feel Silver's presence in the room, as though a shade of the blond fellow's roseate flesh had passed through the closed door. Frank would have to visualize again the golden hair, the steel-chip eyes that the shy smile could soften to a gentle blue, the high armored ridges of his cheeks, the sharp nose perfectly centered between eyes and cheeks and above the line of the upper lip, the deep scoop of the lower mouth, the square jut of the jaw. He might even begin to hear Silver speak, hear the echo of the afternoon's stories. The voice had all the infectious quality for a New Yorker of Southern speech: drawling, casual, intrenched. Frank would hear, as though he had never heard it spoken before, that single word Silver uttered with all his native casualness, tossed off, if Frank could admit it, charmingly, that one word of almost all the stories, "Nigger. Nigger."

"So he went mad, this here nigger. He's runnin' all aroun' the deck and runnin' over to the railin' in the middle of the night way out where we was in the middle of the ocean, the middle of nowhere. It was cold too. And there's this nigger, funny as all hell the way they are, tearin' all aroun' and then gettin' over to the rail and yellin' 'I gotta get me home. Ruby's waitin' up all night for me.' So I couldn't help this fit o' laughin' at him and that's where he really went right out of his mind. That's when this

100

happened to my arm, you know, when the crazy nigger come runnin' over like that he ..."

"Your arm?"

"This left one here. Ain't no muscle to the top of it. When I hit him like that it went all red of a sudden and the muscle ..."

"Hit him?"

"The nigger. He come runnin' over to me and made this grab at my throat screamin' somethin' about I was takin' his Ruby away from him and that's why I was laughin' at him for it. Hell, I couldn't help from laughin', him runnin' around like that ravin' he was gonna swim to Newark right out there in the middle of the ocean on a night so cold it would freeze a nigger's heart. So that's when I hit him, when his hand touched my throat. I caught him here under the jaw, and he went about two feet up in the air and his eyeballs sort of popped like a couple of eggs before he come down on the other side of that railin'. That was the last we ever saw of him."

"You left him there?"

"Left him where? He went in the ocean. He wasn't doin' any swimmin' the way I hit him. I caught him right here, you know. What could I do? But that's when it happened to my arm. I couldn't move the arm I hit him with. It just ..."

They were, as they had been for the past four afternoons, against the iron fence of the schoolyard. Frank Weiss sat on the yellow chair and Silver squatted. The sun shimmered on the asphalt and it stunned the air. It was even difficult in that light to look across the yard to where the four boys played one o'cat. They played grudgingly, trying to bear the heat, but the ball was coming apart and with only two fielders the batter stayed up too long and the others cursed and scratched their bare, darkened backs. But Silver was immaculate. His white T-shirt was spotless, his khakis sharply creased. There was no perspiration on his face. The curled blond hair was impeccably in place. Beside him Frank, so conscious of the heat, felt dirty and unresourceful. He watched the middle finger of Silver's pale hand as it

101

traced a pattern on the concrete between his feet. His left arm, of which he still talked, he rested on his left thigh. Occasionally he brought the right hand up from the concrete and touched his left elbow in a gentle caress.

They had discharged him, he was saying, after that happened to his arm. He was in a hospital for two weeks, and then they let him go. His voice cracked a little when he spoke of how the maimed arm had destroyed his hope of becoming a fighter. He spoke of the encouragement he had gotten during his service bouts, and of all the delight: "To get in a ring with one of 'em with him sweatin' and smellin' all over you and just put your head down and keep poundin' away at the nigger, poundin' away." Again Frank wanted to turn on Silver, but he did not. He scarcely glanced at him during the telling of tales, though he felt the need to confront him, to declare himself finally.

"Look, you're lying! Even if you lived in Kentucky, in Harlan County even, still you couldn't live this way. You're making it up. I saw you give that boy the ball, what you looked like then. You know anybody will listen to this kind of story, that's why you're telling them."

The stories were all the same to Frank. They were all tinged with a cunning need to lie. Silver had calculated the obvious method by which a Southerner could be anything at all here in Brooklyn. He must have already found at least a hundred Frank Weisses to tell the stories to, to alarm them with on Brooklyn streets, in Brooklyn bars, in Booklyn schoolyards. But why he himself should be so victimized by Silver, by a Southerner, that puzzled Frank Weiss. It would puzzle him even after that moment in which he was to bring Webb into Silver's life. He must have already on that afternoon when Silver first spoke of his hurt arm been thinking of Webb. He must have been thinking of him as this story of the arm merged with all the others he had already listened to.

Even the first one had been corrupted by that taint of cunning. After a date, homesick, lonely in the North, Silver had gone into the tavern near the Navy Yard for a drink. Badgered by the sailors, the fight broke out quickly. Hollywood could not have done it better, the story of that fight. Silver had told of flying bottles, of shattered glass, splintered chairs, and the one sailor he had flung over his head, over the bar and into the mirror. Frank had to think of how a man would scream when he saw the dagger of glass waiting to puncture his cheek as he dived toward it. And Silver, the one soldier, the one blond perhaps in this Brooklyn tavern, with his back to the bar and standing up for all of them, waiting to be killed, but savage, swinging, feeling damned mean and good, as he said. Then the other soldier was suddenly beside him, swinging also, but hauling Silver at the same time toward the door. The sirens somewhere in the streets grew louder, nearer. Around the corner, under the light of a lamppost on a black street, Silver turned to grasp the hand of the soldier who had befriended him. In the dim light he saw the ripe mulatto flesh.

"I hit the sonofabitch! I had to. Up here, you know, ain't a thing you can be sure of no more."

On the second day after that first visit to the schoolyard, Silver had told him of the Negro who had stopped him on the street to ask the time. Without looking at the man, Silver had raised the watch to his eyes. In the same motion, as though it had been some feint of boxing, lashing out from the level of his eye he dropped the astonished man on the seat of his pants to the sidewalk. The few people who had been near simply gaped.

"They don't even sound like niggers, the niggers up here. You can't tell till you look."

"But the police, don't they ..."

Silver smiled and shrugged. He peeled away the neck of the T-shirt and revealed the purple welt on his shoulder.

"Yes, I do. I get into a mess of trouble up here."

He began on the neighborhood police. They would pick him up after one of his sieges just as regularly and nonchalantly now as they might write out the ticket for the car beside the hydrant.

They would take him down to the station, poke him with the clubs, shout at him the same phrases. That too, by now, was already regular and nonchalant. "You lay off those damned niggers! Where do you think you are? You're gonna get yourself killed up here. Someone's gonna kill you!"

But on the third day Silver told another kind of story. This was the family affair, the courtly heritage unfolded with the same splendid naiveté, with the same myth-making necessity, it would be the story longest to intimidate Frank. The more he turned the story in his mind, the more he adorned it with an imagination of his own that was itself ingenuously cunning.

It was back home in Harlan County. Frank had formed already, from Silver's other stories, an image of the place. This was no blue-grass Kentucky. There was no grass at all. There were hills and mountains and woods and black craters in the very middle of the lands where the coal pits were, and over everything the swirling drifts of dust, from the pits, from the land, somehow from the sky. The men rushed home in the evenings. Weary from the pits, they rushed anyway to plunge into the water of some huge bucket and wash from their skin, from their hair, the black chalk of the coal. Then they were very blond and very pink. At night they must have paraded what they called streets, searching for the black men. And the women stayed home and waited and somehow must have understood.

The story began with Silver's father. He had argued on and off for a year with a fellow miner about money. The quarrel was settled one afternoon by the persuasion of friends. Reluctantly the two men went off to the tavern for a drink. Silver's father was the first up the steps. When his hand touched the door, the other shot him. He shot him twice through the neck and once in the buttock. It was then that Silver's mother took him to the woods. She found him the bush to hide behind beside the path the man would have to use on his way to the pits. She left him there with his father's shotgun and the sack of food for the day. She told the thirteen-year-old blond boy who must have already been the size of a strong man but whose eyes could only have been gentle then, "You wait now. He'll come." She brought him another sack of food on the following morning, and on the succeeding mornings. When the end of August passed into September, she brought him, along with the soiled brown sack, his jacket, his father's muffler and hat, and a blanket. "You wait now. He'll come," she said on every day of those three weeks. And for all that while the boy stayed bound to that bush, except for the short walks he took at night behind the bushes alongside the path and with the shotgun raised. And that was worse than the darkness, the cold, the hunger, the fear. Chained to that one place, his mind spun with what he had never been old enough before even to dream. He came to hate the man for whom he waited with particular feeling. It had little to do with his father.

It was a cold morning when the man did finally come. He was obviously drunk. Out on the path, before the man, his shotgun raised, the knees of the boy trembled, but not with fear. The man's arms jerked from his sides, and the lunchbox he carried clattered to the path in the quiet, cold morning. In his drunken memory as he looked at the gun, the face of the boy must have begun to make a sort of awful sense. It was then the blubbering began. The boy, expressionless, watched him. When the man began to back away, the boy raised the gun. The man stopped. The man had a heavy stubble of beard that had begun to stain with the tobacco that leaked from his mouth. The man fell to the path and cried.

"Yes, he got down on his knees, to beg. A thirteen-year-old kid, he got down in the dirt to beg! When I shot, from that close, you know, it about blew the sonofabitch's head all over the path."

That had happened eight years ago. It was a tale for which Frank Weiss never had the experience and ordinarily lacked the attitude of belief. Yet he lingered on its details now whenever he blinked in fascination at that eight-years' history of casual violence that was Silver's life. And all of it was muddled by that first vision of a strong and gentle blond man and a dirty little boy.

And now Silver lived here in this dark Italian neighborhood of Brooklyn. Perhaps that was the hardest thing for Frank to accept, this end of Silver's life.

Silver worked nights as a mechanic. The pay was better at night, but more important, he would not have to, then, in the subways, stand belly to belly with any nigger who had a token to drop in the turnstiles. He worked here now, and he lived here now because he was married. He met the girl at an Army dance at Fort Hamilton. Her name was Therese. She had been dancing with him, and she rescued him from a fight. In her brother's car in which she had come, she slipped him past the guards and took him home to her house. She led him past the old deaf father who sat on a rocking chair with his face a foot from the television screen, and led him upstairs to her room. He was drunk then, and she had a difficult time at first trying to quiet him. He left in the early morning before the brothers came home. Overseas, he kept a vivid memory of her. He remembered the coal-black hair, the ivory-into-olive flesh. He thought of her often in the hospital. When he was discharged, he found her house after a full week's search on foot. He accomplished it as a woodsman might. Recalling the general Brooklyn neighborhood, and recalling, too, the year and make of the brother's car, he narrowed day by day the circumference of his five in the morning walks when he was sure the car would be before the house. After the week, he found the car and the house. He waited until the brothers left. She met him at the door. She must have dreamed often of that blond man, but she would never have expected his return. They were married six days later. Silver moved into the room with her.

Two days ago Frank had seen her. She had come to the school-yard fence to summon Silver home. Her hair was black and long. Her nose was bent. Her mouth was full and made carmine by the depth of lipstick against the olive shading of the face. Her teeth were very white and perfect. Her eyes were almost black. She wore the black dress of Italians, even young ones, who mourned. She was big, but compact. She seemed capable of an agile sort of ferocity. When she walked away with Silver, she chained his waist with her encircling arm. Against his white T-shirt and below the flaming gold of his head, the arm looked black. She seemed to need, as they walked that way on the Brooklyn street, to claim for anyone who cared to see, how entirely she possessed him, that fair, waxen blond. Frank was certain Silver hated her.

Later Frank was to notice her when she walked the street in the morning. Silver would be home asleep. Often she would be dressed in only shorts and a halter. Her dark flesh glanced with every step. She held her abdomen taut so that her great breasts would rise and thrust. But still there was about her a sense of Silver's presence. It surrounded her. She was showing the neighborhood that stood in awe of Silver how she had done it. It is this black hair and all this dark flesh and this savage walk that brings the blond man here to live and keeps him sleeping now in my room and waiting for me to come back. For the neighborhood must have pondered them. Truly, they feared Silver. It was not only his size, nor that and his quick anger. It must have been, Frank imagined, also the pinkness, the blondness, the ancient fierceness of it.

So the Brooklyn schoolyard was a strange place in which to find him. It was a strange place in which to listen to the drawling, alien, and finally somnolent voice of a blond man from the Kentucky hills who could squat all afternoon, immaculate under the city sun. And Frank Weiss listened. The four dark, half-naked boys suffered their intolerable game with the tearing ball. And Silver casually, contemplatively, pursued his atrocities.

He was still speaking of the veteran's hospital, what they had done to him there, what he had done to them. And still, ruefully, he caressed occasionally with the fingers of his right hand, the elbow of his lame arm. It wasn't even a shock to Frank, what Silver had come to say now. All these past days Frank must have been waiting for this too.

"Here's this Jew doctor then's askin' me all this kinda stuff. I heard about it a little from the other guys, but here this Jew was at the side of my bed askin' me these things like we'd just done a drunk together. I racked him clear to the wall. I just raised out of that bed and hung it on him with the good arm. And let me tell you that Jew made himself a wide circle anytime he had call to come past my bed again. Even the guy in the next bed, he ends up a Jew too. But a nice sort of little guy, this one. But I guess there ain't much Jew comin' out of a feller with a hole in his belly you could hide a grapefruit in."

He paused now to look at the boy who came toward them, shouting all the while he walked, "Hey, Mr. Frank! Mr. Frank!" He held the beaten ball with the soft yellow kapok oozing out of it. He held it away from his body as a boy would naturally hold some little thing that was dead or dying.

"But the arm's comin' aroun' now a little. I do exercises for it. Some of the strength's comin' back. It don't look none too pretty, though."

He raised the arm toward the sky, turning it, staring at it. The muscles of the forearm slipped under the blond hairs, under the pink skin. The upper arm, what could be seen under the sleeve of the T-shirt, was somewhat less thick than the forearm.

"Too bad about the fightin'," he concluded mournfully. "I could've made me some dough, and then she'd come back home to live with me, all right."

The boy dropped the ball at Frank's feet. The others had already left the schoolyard. "It's too hot," the boy complained. He glanced at Silver.

"Hi."

Silver nodded to the boy. He got up without a groan from his squatting. He nodded to Frank, and then, before he turned, suddenly, gently, he smiled. It seemed to Frank more than a smile of parting. It wanted to ask for something, to need something to ask for. Then he strode out of the schoolyard. Along the iron fence on the street side, he moved quickly toward home, toward Therese. The sun found out his golden hair and flamed it like a torch.

And then Frank Weiss, who had lived so long so much without

impulse, submitted to an instinctive need. He did not know that then. He thought he was going to ponder it over the weekend, and he did. But the decision that could not be made out of the thinking had been formed before the thought. Perhaps it had formed on that first day when Silver retrieved the ball. Something gentle and equally irrelevant had to be done for Silver. The story of the doctor in the hospital only tested the motive of that need. So Frank Weiss would send Silver to the doctor he knew of. He would restore the blond man's lame arm.

But of this, Frank Weiss was not that innocent. He must have known there was no doctor who could do anything for the arm. It was not the arm at all.

"A maniac!" his father said.

"A shame!" his mother said.

"Down at the post office the niggers on the trucks would fix him fast," his brother said.

It was the Friday night supper. The flames of the four candles flickered above the table and the tallow sputtered and dripped, congealing on the brass candlesticks, on the flowered tablecloth. Early in the meal, Frank had broken the reticence he maintained with the family. He had begun to talk with them of Silver. He had not wanted to tell any of the stories, but no sooner had he described the blond fellow than he heard himself going the round of tales. He couldn't stop. "So he killed him . . . He was going to tell him the time and then he hit him . . . The fellow went over the railing of the ship . . . He was only thirteen and . . ." There was a charm in the violence itself which he could not escape. Twice, when he saw their faces as they listened he prepared to tell of Silver chasing the ball for the boy, handing it to him, lowering his head, bowing almost. But he could not. He launched immediately into another of the horrors and felt the scratching on the cord of his back. He left after the dessert. He had expected them to react in the way they did. It was his own resentment of their words that perplexed him.

Webb phoned later that evening. The landlady called Frank to the phone, then she sat down in the chair beside it and peered over her glasses and clacked with her needles at the knitting in her lap. But for the landlady, he might have spoken then to Webb of Silver. They arranged to go to the beach the next day. But it rained. The heat at last broke, and it rained on Sunday too. Frank went alone to the movies on Saturday night. Otherwise he remained in his room and read. Occasionally he snatched at the University catalogue and perused the description of courses: critical potentials, molecular beams, methods of particle detection and acceleration, nuclear reactors. The names satisfied him. He glanced at the photos of University dormitories. He had to be pleased too that he and Webb would share a room, the celebrated Calvin Henry Webb. Occasionally, interrupting his visions, Frank would see Silver with the pink and blond arm raised to the sky, hear him drawl again, "It don't look none too pretty, though."

On Monday afternoon the morning rain ceased and the sun began to penetrate again. Silver came to the schoolyard. He walked slowly toward where Frank sat against the school wall, the book on his lap. Already on Silver's face there was the shy, abashed smile, the imperceptible lowering of his head. The last time Frank had thought of Silver—which was only moments ago—he had reasoned out finally what he would do.

"You and I have nothing to talk about anymore," he would say. "I have to read now."

But when Silver without a word squatted beside him, preparing, Frank knew, to unlock again the hoard of stories, Frank closed the book and slipped his finger out of the place. He felt the little shock when he began to speak.

"Listen, Silver, I know a doctor. I mean about the arm. There was a friend of mine could hardly walk once. They said he'd always limp. This doctor did the operation. My friend played football again next year. Maybe he could help you with the arm."

"My arm?"

"Yes."

"He could fix my arm?"

"Maybe he could. You can see him anyway."

"He's your friend?"

"No. I said a friend of mine—I mean he fixed the knee of a friend of mine. His office is right here in Brooklyn."

"How's he gonna fix my arm? They told me I . . ."

"I don't know about how. Don't you want . . ."

"Yes. Sure I do. God!"

"Then come in the office with me. We'll look him up in the phone book."

"Now? In the school?"

"Yes. What's the matter with you?"

"I ain't dressed."

"What difference does that make? I'm not dressed either."

"Your shirt's got a collar."

"I don't have a tie."

"It's got a collar."

Silver fingered the neck of his T-shirt. Frank rose from the chair. Silver got up from his haunches. Squinting against the sunlight, Frank looked up for a moment at the blond fellow. Silver was trying not to, but a smile was breaking the hardness of his face. There was the joy in it now a little boy would try to control but could not when the candy he had long cried for was finally handed to him. Frank turned quickly away and brushed past him.

They walked together into the deepening shade of the schoolyard well enclosed by the two dark wings of the old building. Before the iron door at the head of the few steps, Silver hesitated again. Frank looked irritably at him, and Silver moved. Through the dark, school-smelling corridor, Silver walked with his head slightly lowered, his eyes staring. The doors, opened like flaps down the shadowed corridor, revealed the empty rooms, the rows of empty seats and desks. When they stood before the office door, Silver's eyes fastened on the flag which hung limply from the pole that was locked in its socket on the floor beside the door. He ran his tongue over his lower lip. He walked behind Frank into the cluttered room of worn desks and faded filing cabinets. Miss Murphy, who every day at three played "London Bridges" on the piano for the smaller children, was at one of the desks. She had just finished the lunch she always brought in a plastic bag tied at the neck with a red string. She was large and had a puffed, slow face. But she almost jumped from the chair. She looked past Frank to Silver. Her eyes blinked and her head moved quickly.

"Miss Murphy, this is . . ."

"Yes," she breath d. "Yes, how do you do?"

"Ma'm."

Miss Murphy said she would go for her stroll now. She heaved toward the door in her ponderous stride and Silver, near the door, flattened himself against one of the filing cabinets.

Frank, already at the telephone book, felt his pulse deepen. He had begun to rehearse what he knew he would soon say to Silver. He could no longer delay it.

"Here's the name. McAdoo. Francis A. McAdoo. I suppose the A's for Aloysius." His voice trailed off with the sound of the foolish name . . .

He scribbled the information on a pad. He tore off the sheet and held it toward Silver. Light from the windows trapped Silver's hair as he moved away from the filing cabinets and toward the small white leaf of paper. He had begun to grin again. He took the paper and stared at it, his eyes blinking, as if the writing itself were the miracle.

"If you just call him . . ."

"If he can fix my arm—I mean, if I can fight again . . ."

He stopped. They didn't look at each other as Silver began neatly to fold, and fold, the paper. The sun pierced the windows of the office. It fell on the two of them there in the light middle of the darker room. Frank turned his face away from the brightness.

"Silver," he said, quickly, impulsively, though he had rehearsed it. "Silver, I'm a Jew."

Silver stepped out of the light, moved back against the filing cabinets. When the handle of it touched his back, he jumped away. His hands fumbled at the paper, unfolding it now. His eyes searched for the door, for the windows, but they did not look at Frank. Frank could scarcely hear him when he began to speak.

"But I thought—I mean . . ."

"I know. The kids call me Mr. Frank. My name's Frank Weiss. I look Italian."

The words echoed in his ears with their stupidity, their blunder. He could have been saying Aloysius again. He did not look toward Silver, though he heard the muttering from which all the drawl had seemed to disappear.

"They put me in the coal pits when I was ten. He had that hole in him and he never bitched. Maybe you want to come home and meet Therese."

Frank could hear him leave the office, hear his feet down the corridor. He had deluded himself with the fear that Silver would hit him. It was not to end that easily. Frank Weiss would have to ponder for a while the awful advantage from which he had declared his famous words—that slip of paper with the doctor's name, his gesture for the arm.

"That's what he does now," Frank said on a final note, trying to get Webb to raise his head. "He's been my protector for three days. Today he nearly scared the life out of one of the kids who answered me back. He grabbed the boy by the collar and—well, aren't you going to say anything? How much more do I have to tell you?"

"Say what?" Webb mumbled without looking up.

"Say anything. I've been talking to you for over an hour about him."

"He's talked to you for over a week. What have you said to him? What can you say to anyone who talks like that?"

"You're talking to me, not him."

113

"It's hot here. You want a beer?"

At last Webb moved. He got up from the bed on which he had all the while been lying crosswise, his head against the wall, the tremendous flats of his feet over the edge. He filled the frame of the doorway as he left the room. Frank turned his face to the open window he sat beside on a wooden chair and looked down through the hot evening darkness at the darker Harlem street.

On every wall of every room in the Webb's four room apartment there was at least one photograph of Calvin Webb. His father had put them there. The larger ones were framed, the others simply pasted to the walls like some kind of wallpaper meant to last the life of the walls themselves. In half the pictures he wore the white football uniform of the city college. In some of the others he was behind a table of the college library, the books scattered before him. They had been taken from the various city newspapers in which they had appeared, and from the two national magazines that had taken up the story. For that was the public image of the Negro youth who had overcome, who had demonstrated, who had proved again, and so on. He was the Negro football player who had been offered professional contracts, which he had refused, and the Negro student who had graduated from a city college with a straight "A" average, who had majored in Physics, who had been awarded and accepted a scholarship for graduate work.

But to Frank Weiss, Webb had been, for the four years he knew him, a friend of sorts, and a mystery always. It was like the pictures they had taken of him. Because the photographers could not persuade him to smile—"What for?" Frank had heard him say in his laconic arrogance—and because the skin was as definitely black as it was, beneath the white helmet there would appear nothing but the polished blur of the features of that huge black head. And so with Webb himself. It was the perfection of his gifts that finally overcame anyone who got near to him, and Frank had gotten, he imagined, as near as anyone could. Webb had no attitude toward the perfection, no responsibilities for it.

You had at last to wonder what kind of perfections they were, as you wondered from the photographs, even from looking at him, what the face was really like.

He played football, for example, with a ferocity that concealed his actual cunning. Webb was massive. He would never get on a scale, so they could only guess at his weight. The programs listed it as two hundred and ten, but it may have been more. His legs were thick and his chest was rolled like an old iron stove. The shoulders sloped deeply and from them the ape-like arms swung to his knees. He could move like a cat. On the field, when the ball was in play, he was terrifying to watch. But when he took his position on the line, while he waited through the other team's huddle, while his teammates went through all the rituals of the varied encouragements, the shouts, the ass-slapping, the scraping of the turf with their cleats, Webb simply rested on one knee and waited, conservative, detached. He could have been merely watching the game. He stayed that way until he could see the different colored helmet lowering opposite him. Then slowly his knee came off the ground, his hand went forward and down to the grass, his legs slid back, the line of his back stiffened, and the machinery of his terrible strength coiled, and coiled, and then unwound.

"Getting hit by Cal," one of his teammates told Frank, "it's not like getting hit by a truck must be. It's like something clean, all at once. Like a whack somewhere from a pipe. A heavy pipe."

"But I don't think you even enjoy playing," Frank had said to him once. "I've spent a whole game in those stands watching only you. You almost look bored."

Webb shrugged. "It's a silly game in some ways."

"Then why do you play?"

"I'm too good at it not to. Some of the game's good enough."

His nonchalance, his sullen unreachable indifference, that was the mystery of Calvin Henry Webb. As they sat together in the college cafeteria, someone would approach with the inevitable petition. Frank would read carefully the declaration at the head of

115

the page. Then he might sign; or he might say, "I would if it weren't for the last sentence"; or, "No. I don't feel that way at all." But Webb, whose signature was a prize, would turn his head away. When the paper was shoved under his face he would turn again his great, gleaming head. Slowly his tiny ebony eyes would move up from the hand of the boy or the girl, move up to the arm, to the shoulder, to the face. Then he would mumble in that bass voice of frightening boredom, "Go away." And they did. They would snatch up their paper and run. Or when Frank and he were double-dating, Frank with the girl he had finally to break with, and Webb with any one of the attractive white girls who clinged to him, who wanted, Frank knew, only to touch his dark, unfeatured, unresponsive face. Then too Frank would be unsettled by Webb's indifference, his incapacity to care, to realize everyone stared. At times like these, the words would come that stopped in Frank's throat: how can you ignore all that? Perfect or not, you are black. You are, you know!

And so Frank Weiss had come now and finally to the home of Calvin Henry Webb in Harlem to tell him of the very blond Silver. He did that because he had to see Webb's response, but he knew as he made the subway trip that Webb would only shrug. But he came also because he had in the last three days carefully thought out an arrangement by which Webb and Silver could be brought together. It had become apparent to him this should happen, though he did not know yet for whose benefit it was to be done. There was, after all, nothing Frank Weiss could do for Webb. There was nothing Webb needed done for him. But in Webb's room in the middle of Harlem, staring out the window down to the dark street, Frank knew he would arrange nothing. He would not admit it was treachery, but there was anyway something wrong. It was, at least, unsafe.

But above all Frank Weiss had come here tonight to Webb to talk of Silver because he was baffled. For the last three days he had gone over in his mind what he had wanted to do for Silver. He had given him the doctor's address and it disturbed him now, and sometimes in the image of Webb. He had betrayed his own reason, and he had betrayed Webb. So what he really must have wanted from Webb, perhaps simply from being in his home, was to learn some safe way of betraying Silver.

"Well, what do you think at least of that dark girl he had to marry?" Frank said to him when Webb towered beside him, the black hand hiding the beer it held out. "He's trapped up here by the same—I mean . . ."

Webb was already stretched again crosswise on the bed. Above his head was the large framed photograph of himself: white helmet, white jersey, white pants, the black gleaming indiscernable face.

"Don't you think," Frank began again.

"You mean," Webb said, lowering the can of beer, the teeth flashing for a second in what was almost a smile, "you mean the poor blond man?"

Damn him, Frank swore. He got up from the chair. "I'll call you."

"You didn't finish the beer."

"Forget it."

"Did I disappoint you again, Frank?"

Frank started toward the door. Webb sat up on the edge of the bed. Again on his dark polished face there was the faintest line, the beginning of a smile. His hand almost hid the can of beer it held.

"You want it all both ways, don't you?"

Frank turned at the door. "What do you mean?"

"Like what you did with Evelyn, then with your folks. You want it to be the right thing on paper, you want it to be right the other way. You came here for the paper work, didn't you? You wanted to find some way of getting back to where you could hate this guy again."

"Hate him?"

Frank took a step back into the room. He wanted to stare at Webb, but his friend's face had unlipped now into a bone-white band as he grinned. Frank glanced above his head to the picture of him on the wall.

"Damn you, Cal. You didn't listen to a word I said. You lie there on your fat ass pretending insights and grinning—stop grinning, will you! But you didn't hear me. Hate him? I told you I want to fix his arm. I gave him your doctor's address, didn't I? I told you about that first day, how he . . ."

"Prayed to a dark boy?"

"Cut it out! I didn't say that! And you know as well as I do part of the reason I had it out with Evelyn."

"Paper. It was you she'd live with, Weissy, not me."

Frank stared hard at the photograph. From the distance of the doorway, there was no face in it at all. There was only the white helmet, the white jersey, the white pants, the arrested spring of the form about to dive for the ball, or for another player. So Frank had that inevitable vision of Silver armored also in a football uniform, a black helmet, a black jersey and black pants. The two of them would be racing toward each other from opposite ends of the field. The crowd would see it at once, would be on its feet, hushed, waiting, interested, alarmed. They would collide in the exact middle of the field, in the center of all that watching. The noise of it would boom into the stadium, would rise above its air, would roar out, and out, and beyond.

Frank dove back into the room, into the seat beside the open window.

"Look, Cal, I'll show you how I hate him. This is why I came. What I had in mind. I want you to meet him. I want us to have lunch together. I want you to tell him about the doctor. I want it to come from you too. That you want to help him. He's never known—I mean, he only has to meet you to see . . . He's all set up for it now, Cal. We can save him. We can take this Southerner and . . ."

"You're crazy."

"We could do it. It's just like one and one, Cal. Where he was, that's what made him what he is. Now he's here and we can make it something else. He wants it. He's just waiting for someone to

do it for him. All afternoon he follows me around the yard
and . . ."

"Where he was? You think they're all like that? They'd pop
themselves out of this world so fast . . ."

"Cal, will you come to lunch with him?"

"What for?"

"I just told you. For him."

"No."

"For me."

"No. Look, Frank, you are trying to hate this guy again. And
you're a bloody little bastard too. That's what happens to the
paper boys. You ought to be a little bigger. You could play football. You'd like the game."

Frank rose again from the chair. He looked this time into the
small, unrevealing eyes of Webb.

"Isn't there anything, a single damn little thing in this world
you care about, feel responsible to?"

Webb rose from the bed. He towered over Frank. He was grinning again. His fingernails turned rose as his hand tightened
around the empty beer can. The sides of it collapsed easily. He
turned the can idly as he answered, and it nestled securely in his
huge hands.

"But you know I do, Frank. What I care about keeps me all
here. Good ol' Calvin Henry Webb, the All-American colored
boy. You remember that when we come to room together. Then
we'll get along fine. And look," he called after Frank, stopping
him once more at the door. "I'll be in Brooklyn Wednesday. I'm
modeling again at the Museum. I'll come out for lunch, but with
you. Same place we met last month. I'll get there about one. But
don't bring your golden boy. Don't have him there, Weissy."

"They sure make somethin' pretty out of these places up
here," Silver said.

Frank shrugged and looked vaguely around the cafeteria. The
air was dead and cold as the invisible machinery whirred against
the heat outside. Before them on their table, untouched, were

the cold salad plates they had gotten at the counter. Frank sipped at his coffee, but Silver kept his hands in his lap. Frank imagined it would have been less difficult if Silver had not worn the newly pressed slacks, the dress shirt, the flowered silk tie.

"That's kind of you. That's sure kindly," Silver had stammered when Frank on Monday afternoon had prepared the Wednesday luncheon.

"He's the fellow who had the knee operation," Frank had said. "He'll be able to tell you more about the doctor." That was all Frank had said.

For the rest of that afternoon and for all of Tuesday afternoon, Silver either squatted beside Frank or followed on his heels through the schoolyard as Frank performed his small duties.

"You heard him, boy. No cards in here!" Silver had glared at the offender, and the stunned boy, without even the gesture at saving face, fled the schoolyard, escaped the blond fellow who distressed a neighborhood.

But now Frank feared it was all pointless. He was beginning to believe he and Silver had both faked what they were doing. It was absurd to sit there and suppose they were doing something for a crippled arm, were going to restore in Silver what had been destroyed long before he had ever used the arm to pile a Negro soldier over the railing of a ship to drown on a cold night. Surely Silver too knew the foolishness of it. It was a kind of ritual then, a sort of courtship that involved them both as they waited now for Webb. Silver wanted only to savor what it was for someone to care, to contemplate the servitude of it. He had not, for example, once in the three days of this week uttered the word nigger. So perhaps the luncheon itself would come off. Webb might be finally too indifferent to care. If only Silver had not dressed for the occasion, had at least left off the tie. With his pink, strong fingers Silver kept probing the knot as if it were a noose.

"Maybe we got here too soon," Silver said, his eyes roving the cafeteria.

"He'll be here. He's just bad about time. We might as well eat."

"I reckon we ought to wait."

"We can have the dessert with him."

"I reckon I ought to wait. You say he was able to play football after the operation?"

"Yes. He played at college."

"He went to college?"

"Of course. That's where I know him from."

"Did you learn to be a teacher there? I mean, you gonna do this all the time, teach in the schoolyard?"

Frank had begun to eat hurriedly. He hoped Silver would eat.

"I studied Physics. So did Webb. We're going on to a university together."

Silver stared.

Frank had directed him to a corner table in the rear of the cafeteria. They sat opposite each other against the wall, an empty seat beside each of them. It was Silver who faced the entrance and the street. Frank, when he wanted to glance somewhere, looked at the glaring mosaic tiles that composed the back wall of the cafeteria.

"I walloped Vito last night," Silver declared suddenly, nervously. "Therese's brother, you know. I was tellin' her last night about us havin' lunch together and this here friend of yours comin' to tell me about the operation, how it would go and all. We got on talkin' about my fightin' again, so then Vito sticks in the way those Wops talk, you know."

Silver made a cone of his fingers. Shaking them under his chin, he mimicked the accent.

"'When a muscle's outa de arm, she's a goo'bye. You're a farmer,' the sonofabitch says to me, 'You're a farmer. You ever seen 'em put de head back on a chicken?' I told him times before to keep his mouth shut. He was tryin' to tell me someone's takin' me for a ride. You know, gettin' money back from the doctor or somethin' like that. So I walloped him. Maybe I will have a sip of the coffee, it gets so ass-bitten cold in here. You got to get back to the schoolyard soon?"

"I can come late. There's no one to . . ."

Silver lowered the cup to the table before it had touched his lips. He stared at the salad plate for a second, then turned his face toward the wall.

Frank looked only at Silver, kept watching for him to turn his head again. But he knew that Webb was there, was standing at the table, was getting ready to sit down beside Silver.

Silver's hands tightened around the edge of the table. His head whirled suddenly toward Webb. He seemed ready to lunge. But he collapsed slowly back onto the chair when Frank blurted:

"Silver, this is Webb! He'll help you with your arm!"

Frank turned to look at Webb. He was sitting now beside Silver, but he was staring at Frank. He did not glance at Silver even as he spoke to him.

"Relax, Silver. I can eat fast. I'll be out of here in a minute."

He began to unload the food from his tray. A black hand went hugely around a glass of milk and all the whiteness disappeared. He began to eat, tearing at the small roll that vanished in a minute. Still the eyes, the small jet eyes set deeply into the great iron skull, stared at Frank. He wore a white crew shirt.

The two of them beside each other were huge. Opposite them Frank felt shriveled. He tried to look back at Webb, but he had finally to look away. Webb was not indifferent, detached. The anger burned in his polished face, flared the spread of his nostrils. That's what he must always have looked like down on the field, Frank thought, that anger you couldn't see from anywhere in the stands.

Frank turned his eyes to glance at Silver. Silver was staring back at him, but he could not have been seeing. His eyes didn't look, but they didn't blink either. His blond hair flamed beside Webb's head. His right hand, fisted now, pressed the edge of the table. Little beads of sweat gleamed on it, began to run between the knuckles. Frank looked up and the sweat was on Silver's temples too. And still Silver kept his eyes on Frank. They blinked once, then closed for a second. When he opened the lids again, the eyes were vaguer, moister. The blue seemed dull now, grey. He began to hear Silver's breathing, the sounds in his nose a gagged man would make. The sweat was on his cheeks now, and the sweat was above the locked mouth too. At last Webb spoke. The sound of his voice cracked around the table like a whip.

"Well, it's been done now. Just don't go on sitting there like that. I'd like to get up and leave you in peace, Silver. But I can't do that. No more than you can hit me now because of him."

And still Webb had not looked at Silver. And still Silver sat there, said nothing, stared at Frank, pressed his fist, but did not move. Only a corner of the locked mouth had begun to twitch. But his eyes were clearer, seemed to burn more now and were darker under the blond hair. Frank picked up his fork and plunged it into the salad. But he didn't eat. He began to speak instead.

"Yes, it was me, Silver. I fixed it this way. It's because I want to help you. More than the arm. That's nothing here. I mean, it's what's behind the arm. It's . . ."

"Why don't you stop?" Webb said in that same frighteningly bored voice he would tell a petitioner to go away.

"Yes, and you too, Cal. Help you too. You knew we'd be here, both of us. You had to see him for yourself, this blond. It was you had to learn how to hate him. Because this is what you are inside, what you want to be. This is what you really care about. So the two of you ought to tell each other. You . . ."

It was not Webb getting to his feet that made Frank sputter and finally quit. It was Silver. Frank had been watching him all the time he had spoken to Webb.

The sweat was coming magically out of every pore of Silver's face. It stained his white dress shirt. There was a circle of it showing on the chest beneath the flowered tie. His mouth had fallen open. He was trying to speak, to smile perhaps. He had put his left hand over the cup of coffee. His fingers tightened like a claw around the rim of the cup. He closed his eyes. His hand raised and the cup came off the table. Then there was the shattering noise, and Frank, expecting it, waiting, could not even

jump. The cup and the saucer scattered. Bits of them were over
the table, over the floor. Some of the coffee was on Silver's shirt,
and on Webb's, who whirled now toward Silver. Silver jumped to
his feet and the chair fell away from him. Still he looked only at
Frank. The noises he made in his nose were louder now. His face
was bathed. Even the blond hair, the curled and golden hair,
seemed darker now, and wet. His eyes were clouded again. He
stepped past Webb. He did not look at him. He hurried down
the aisle of the cafeteria. The large busboy who had shouted
something about the broken cup, Silver flung with an arm across
a table.

Frank turned slowly toward Webb. He could not understand
why for Webb and Silver there had not been a fight. It would seem
they should have fought. They could not, both of them, have
been that much surer, wiser than he. Webb sat down again, and
Frank did too, slowly.

"After all those stories," he mumbled, trying to fake what
could not for long bewilder him, "After all those bloody stories,
he couldn't—I mean, he just ran away from you. As soon as you
turned on him he . . ."

Webb was already eating again. "It was you he ran from,
Weissy. I guess he could do for me in a fight well enough. I
don't ever need to get that mad."

"Oh."

Frank continued to stare at Webb's polished, featureless, chew-
ing face. He wanted to keep from thinking of the golden hair,
the dirty boy, the lame arm. But as Frank stared at Webb, in the
wildness now of his imagination, he began to see Silver hurrying
to some violence somewhere, perhaps with Vito, perhaps even
with Therese. Then Frank had to turn from Webb, so strongly
did the black face convince him that Silver was going to beat
Therese, might even kill her.

A GIFT EVERY MORNING

The old man from Warsaw and the old woman from Budapest, having met by chance a week ago, sit on the bench in Brooklyn late in March, each hoping that the sun will last a little longer. It takes the bite out of the wind giving them the prospect of a longer talk. In truth, the old man is contemptuous of her work as a hired housekeeper, while the old woman suspects him of being unskilled in even the most ordinary graces of conversation. But they are in their seventies, and they live alone and go too long without a word to anyone but the storekeepers.

He is a short man in good health, but in his widower's life of the past nine years he has produced the symptoms of fatal illnesses, and from them he suffers every day as though he were truly sick. His fingers are short and thick, and the skin of his face is rough and deeply lined. The woman, however, gives the appearance of the greater age, for her bones are brittle, and her legs, when she is standing, angle outward toward the knees. But her face is full of puckers and pouches, the skin so powdery soft to the touch that grandchildren would remember the texture into their own old age. But she has no grandchildren, nor children either, her husband having died in his early thirties. She came to America only after the uprising in her country, and she still talks often of Europe. She is talking of it now to the old man, who never speaks of Europe anymore. He used to anger his sons with petty old-country chauvinisms, but that was many years ago.

"Here they have not so many nice churches," she says. "At home the church is higher than anything near, and when the bells ring you always look to the sky. You see where the bells are. Everywhere in Europe it is so. Is it not so, sir, in Warsaw too?"

"Warsaw?" He looks toward a cloud gaining on the sun, and shrugs. "Warsaw was clean," he says.

She nods. "It was the same everywhere. In Budapest, in Vienna, in Rome, of course. Even St. Paul's in London. And Warsaw, too, must be so. Do they not have beautiful churches in Warsaw?" She is smiling when he looks at her, and he once more notices the dentures. He turns away. The old woman, quite alert, notices. She is distressed by this trait of contentious coarseness in the man; it stands in the way of any gracious passing of the time of day. At last he answers her, his voice gruff.

"I don't remember such things from so far back."

She apologizes for never having been to Warsaw. "When I was a young girl we went always to Italy and Switzerland, or France. England too. But never to the East." She reflects for a moment. She folds her hands in her lap, then opens them and removes a handkerchief from her coat pocket and folds her hands again, around the handkerchief now. She speaks in a sudden rush of heart. "What excitement I always felt to be on a train that takes you so soon to a different country."

"America is better," he says flatly. It is the first time in his life he has ever said so.

"Oh, the museums here! There is nothing like it in all the world. In London, perhaps. Nowhere else. The Indian Museum. Even an Indian Museum. Have you ever been to the Indian Museum?"

He looks at her blankly.

"Yes," she says, "in Budapest who could have imagined such a country. How big, how busy everyone, and everyone so friendly. In Zurich once . . ."

She recounts the story of an American she met years ago, but the old man ceases to listen. He needs to speak, to tell someone, to tell even her what it has been like for him. He looks down the street and sees a boy on the edge of one of the Parkway benches. The boy is bent hard over his hands as he adjusts the roller skates to his feet. The old man struggles with a childhood picture of his first-born son, the one now in an asylum. He shivers against a new gust of wind, and the unfinished memory vanishes. Numbers scatter insanely in his mind—the stems of the sevens crossed as they were in Europe—but he cannot make these numbers assemble the present age of his son.

"Even with all the cars," he hears the woman say. "Twice it has happened. I am from the market with my packages, and he stops his car. He takes me to the door. A young man with so much to attend to going so far out of his way. I call him my Cavalier of the Strasse." Her eyes behind her glasses go merry with the phrase. Her smile is winsome, like a girl's, and this too offends the old man.

He says nothing. He cannot find his own wedge into her foolish prattle. He doesn't deem cars a subject to be talked about, nor churches either. There are churches, he thinks, and there are rabbis too; but where is there to be found for him on this day the rabbi old enough to take him by the hand through the gaining darkness to say, "My son . . ." He thinks of his own father, but he cannot even begin to recall the face. He tries to recall the face of his older son, but even that is hard. How many years now? It happened in the middle of the war when his other son was a boy and his wife was alive, and since that time, in all these years, he has never seen his older son.

"It was better for me when I was able to work," he blurts out. He leans toward her with a defiant look. Perhaps he means to show how he is the one who advances real conversation.

"For a man especially," she says.

He continues to stare at her. "Now if I walk ten blocks, I'm finished."

She nods. The last glow of the merry look has faded from her eyes. "For a man to lose his health in the last years is very difficult," she says.

"And in the bad weather," he says, "then it's out of the question. Then I'm altogether in the house. Then I'm a prisoner."

"We come now to the spring," she says. "April here on this boulevard—oh, so fine! The leaves are yellow and all the children are playing. When there is sun out, then the children of America are like flowers."

He puts his hand inside his coat and rubs to soothe the soreness. He reminds himself that the cramps from which he is temporarily free will inevitably return. He says nothing for a long while. A phrase she used needles in his mind, irritating. *The last years.* He wonders if she spoke it in spite—like the letter from his younger son which he carries in his pocket. Every day of his pain, the cause of which the doctors, conspiring with his son, will not name to him, deliberately withhold from him, tells him more than he wants to know of his last years. The picture looms for him of the grave that waits for him beside his wife where his name is already cut into the other half of the stone. He never visits the cemetery. He tries to ponder his bewilderment with his vengeful mind that all his life could only manage one idea at a time. He asks himself if he believes that work would make the time pass faster. Would he want that? He thinks of the many times he has sat before the television in the early evening waiting for the torturous passage of an entire hour before his good programs should begin. Then he thinks of the later moment when he has looked at his watch in amazement seeing it is already midnight, and there is nothing before him but the dark night, through which in pain and senseless dreams he will pray for daylight. But what is daylight itself if not the used up time of the night?

"Every morning," the old woman is saying, startling him from the abyss, "every morning is a new gift from God."

All her life she must have been soft, to tell the story she tells now in such inconsequential mildness. She recounts how her New York niece brought her here and provided her with a room in her fine apartment, but how she left the niece after a short while to take his job in Brooklyn keeping house for a middle-aged bachelor man of business who is often away. Her niece is displeased.

"She says it is bad for the family, that I have gone to housekeeper's work. But now, you see, I take my tea when I want. It is not good to be much in the way. I have seen very much. Terrible things. There was too much. The Nazis killed so many. I had so many Jewish friends. The best people in Budapest. Oh, so many doctors and musicians. Then the Russians. There was nothing to eat. They took everything. My last friends all disappeared. I was quite alone. They allowed some to leave, but nothing could we take. A comb and a fork and a spoon, they said. I left everything. All my husband's fine things. At the border they made us strip entirely naked. How does it matter, then, that I do housework for pay? I say to my niece, at my age is not every new morning like a gift from God?"

She smiles at the happy phrase, but she sits very still, has sat motionless during all the long while of her speaking. Across the wide street, beyond the ceaseless traffic of the cars, on the bridle path, two older boys begin to lob a baseball back and forth. The old man turns his head to look down the block again. He sees the boy pumping on his skates, skating toward them, unsteadily, the iron wheels grinding. The boy's shirttail is out beneath his sweater, and a new gust of wind sends it flapping. The old man turns away, looking toward the clouding sky. He speaks at last, his voice an assertion of his tired fortitude.

"The pain begins again."

"The doctors must help you," she says. "Here they have all the best doctors. Is it not so?" She almost admits to herself that something in the man frightens her. It is more than the coarseness.

"There's no use to talk of it," he says, dismissing the subject with a wave of his hand.

"Once I had a heart attack," she says. "It was years ago."

"The way my wife went," he says. "A heart attack. Like that, it was over. Finished."

She waits, thinking he wishes to say more, but he already re-

129

grets the mention of his wife. He knows she will now begin again on her husband. Even at their first meeting she introduced stories of her husband. He was this, he was that, did this, did that. The husband collected coins, had a whole library about the old banks of Europe, tipped his hat to women in the streets of Budapest, wore a suede jacket and a silk scarf so the collar would not soil when he worked in his study over his coins where she brought him tea and cakes and a cloth napkin. It was all nonsense. What did it have to do with what had to be said? Could he really think of reading the letter from his son to such a woman? She is like a child in this recollection of a husband who died so long ago.

"My husband," she says, and the old man turns away, "he worked in a bank in Budapest. What was your line of work? May I ask you?"

"I was not a banker," he says.

"Oh, my husband not either," she says quickly. "Only he worked in a bank. He was a bookkeeper."

"And my work was walking," he says. "Ten, fifteen, sometimes twenty miles a day I used to walk. I was a customer peddler."

She smiles. *"Ich verstehe das nicht."*

He stares at her, his heavy-lidded eyes squinting for the recollection of when he last heard that language in that accent.

"I mean that I didn't understand," she says, smiling. "What is it that your work was?"

"You said Budapest. You're German?"

"Nein. No. No. With my Jewish friends, oh years ago. With their parents sometimes. My husband and I would speak German. The old people could understand it better. It is *gleich* with Yiddish, is it not?"

"But you speak it now to me. What for? You think I don't understand English? I have been here fifty years."

"I meant nothing. Only to . . ."

"I taught myself English. They sent me to a night school with grown people doing A and B and C. So I taught myself. At night, every night, for two whole years I sat with translations in English from Tolstoy and Pushkin, from Peretz and Sholom Aleichem."

"My husband the same. With Italian he . . ."

"So you don't have to say anything to me you don't say in English. If I am old now like the people you talked in German to, you are not so many years younger. We are not in Budapest."

She puts the handkerchief into her coat pocket and rises. Her smile, with its edge of regret, is valiant. "I believe the sun now leaves us a little."

He reaches with his hand, taking hold of her arm. He has never been aware of the force of the weight in his hand in the ungentle ways of his use of it. For the barest moment the old woman fears he has meant to strike her.

"I have a letter," he says.

He takes his hand away and reaches inside to the breast pocket of his suit coat. He feels the envelope. He withdraws his hand, empty.

"Sit awhile," he says, his voice strange with pleading.

She cannot know or guess the effort it costs him to keep her there. He commands it with his sudden fury against the letter itself. How it judges and accuses him! He is not unaware of how its spitefulness points into this afternoon itself, this little passage of the disappearing time with this foolish woman. A sentence from the letter drums in his mind: "In your bitterness you have always shut the door on anything that could be good in life, so much did you mix the unimportant with the real failures." Oh, the sentences he can remember. It was but one of so many burning in his brain.

"So your husband worked in a bank," he says.

The labor by which he finds the mild tones of the conversationalist makes his temples throb. All his life in America there have been nails at his temples. That his own son—not the doomed crazy one but the doctor himself—that he should not acknowledge sufferings but make judgments against a father in his last years, it is the last curse of life itself.

"He was a bookkeeper," she says. "It was in a good bank in

131

Budapest, well situated. When I worked in the embassies we could take lunch together in the park in the good weather."

"When I came years ago to America," he says, "and when you had an accent even after you studied English every night, you couldn't get jobs in a bank. How should a foreigner not speak with an accent? So you tried in business. You tried with a little store."

"We had many friends also shopkeepers," she says. "Then the terrible Nazis..."

"And in America if you are not fast to learn all the crooked ways, it's goodbye business. In banks too."

"My husband was not so. He had not ambition. Only his books and his coins and our time together in the house with the lovely things we had from my parents. Also I worked sometimes. It was fine for us."

They sit for a while in the silence of their summoning of the years. The boy on the roller skates, grinding past them a while ago, is nearer to the other corner now. He sits on a bench again, again bent over, adjusting the skates. The traffic in the wide street goes ceaselessly on, and the two older boys beyond it who were on the bridle path have quit their catch and are going now into an apartment house across the street. Both sides of the wide street are lined with apartment houses, five to six stories high, side to side. The rents are not cheap and the old man could not live in his two rooms if his son did not send him a monthly check. He needs to read her the letter, but he agonizes over the ways and the justifications. There is so much that first needs to be said on his own behalf before he can expose himself to the words written by his son.

"May I show you a picture of my husband?" she says.

"Sure!" he says in an explosion of breath, startling her.

"It is only a small picture."

"Any kind of picture. Show me! I'll look at a picture." He thinks he might perhaps have tea with her later. She will ask him. What would be the harm in it?

"I carried it in my hair across the border," she says. "I was not then young either, but my hair was more thick to hide it with pins. To leave all his things behind. The books and the coins and all our pictures from all the trips before there were all the wars. It was almost enough that I would not come. But I could not stay. That was an impossibility. Here is the picture. This is my husband. Here is Ignace."

She holds out the small snapshot she has removed from the billfold in her coat pocket, but she does not let it go. The picture is encased in a plastic jacket, and the old man has to lower his head and squint his eyes to bring the features of the man out of the glare of light on the plastic. He squints and stares, and then begins to make it out. He gazes in wonder at the stranger's features: the bush of hair, the sad, enormous eyes, the vivid mouth. Above all, the old man is taken by the slow, unfolding shock of the face's arrested youthfulness. The man the old woman prattles of and calls husband is of an age to be her own son. He is even younger by years than the old man's younger son.

He looks up from the picture to the face of the woman beside him. He hopes for some sign which will release him from his growing fears, but he can see only that she is old, old, as old as he is. She is smiling again in that offensive winsomeness so indiscreet to her age, but she is old and she is alone. The length of her years of being alone stretches from the face of the photograph to her own face. To grow old and bent and sparrow-boned and a prey to all diseases, and still to love a boy and call him husband and chatter through the day, as though life itself were not in the spread and drag of time but in a frozen thought and a perpetual recollection.

Unasked for, unwanted, the memorized accusations leap from the letter buried in his pocket. What does it matter that the word love was never his word? He *needed* his wife. He cannot clearly remember her face, and not at all the face of his son ruined in the war. "He was ruined before he went to war," the accusation screams again. The wind smarts his eyes, and he hates the old

133

woman beside him whom he needs so urgently now and to whom he must plead.

"What did I do?" he says in a whisper.

She is still staring at the picture; she does not hear him.

"So many better pictures I had to leave," she says.

Neither of them has heard the stopping of the grinding skates. The boy stands before them, one skate loosed from his foot and held to his ankle by the strap. He is holding out his skate key.

"Do my skate," he pleads.

His eyes are bright and his cheeks scarlet with the risen blood of his exertions. His shirttails are out and the sole of his shoe is tearing loose where his skate clamp has to bite it.

"Do my skate," he pleads again, shoving the key into the man's hand.

Numbly the old man takes the key and bends over the skate, his eyes blinded with the smarting, his temples pounding, his fingers wooden and without the skill or recollection to do the little task. The boy stares at the top of the man's head, and then, with the rough treatment of his foot, his eyes dart uncertainly toward the woman. The man cannot manage the key and the clamp, and the bending aggravates the soreness in his stomach. His breath is short.

"Find your mother!" he shouts abruptly, straightening, slamming the key into the boy's hand. "It's not a playground here!"

The boy, taking fright, stands there staring. His lip begins to tremble.

"Ah," says the old woman, "it is not so big a thing. It is not a thing to cry for. Perhaps I will know."

She takes the key from the boy, but she cannot bend far enough from the bench to reach his foot. The boy tries to raise his foot, but he cannot balance himself on the one skate. The old woman gets off the bench and lowers herself slowly until she is kneeling on the asphalt, her coat a cushion for her knees. She tries to work with one hand, and then knows she can't do it, but with only one hand she can't replace the snapshot in the billfold.

Or perhaps her coat, twisted, is too rigidly pinned under her knees for her to free the pocket to get the billfold. She extends the snapshot to the old man, and he, surrendered to a revery which pounds the nails into his temples, takes it.

He cannot put up the wall to hold back the flood of Warsaw. There is the cafe where the writers met in the summer underneath the awning, and where once he talked to Sholem Asch. There is the theater where he saw his first Shakespeare, and there the small outlying villages with the animal manure in the streets where he and the other young actors tried to give small performances. And there also is the small, bearded father with the skull cap (who would be how old now?) who tells him sternly: "Don't dream so much, don't read so much. Follow God!" Those his very words.

What, then, he pleads, can a letter-writing son now know who was only a boy in the Depression playing ball in the streets? Who was fed and clothed on relief checks. Who cannot know what it is to be servile in a grocery store in the need of pennies and at the mercy of the ignorant and unfeeling who speak without accents and have no dreams to fail them, who never made a dream that made them cross an ocean in steerage, huddled like sheep, but sick like men in the constant storms. Let his son go to Poland to live, untrained to earn a living, and let him raise his children there to speak flawlessly the language their father will never master. Let him live long enough to receive from one of his sons the letter of accusation. And let him know the sickness that . . .

He stops. He draws back in shame from the peril of what he wishes for. His head clears for the moment, and in the moment he must fly the recognition that he acts out what the letter describes. He retreats at once to his sickness, the malignant wound growing, ever growing in spite of all the letters from his son of reassurance, denial, and finally the one of accusation. And the growing and the fatal outcome is also an accomplishment of the passage of time.

He thinks of the time it takes him to write the occasional letter to his grandchildren in his desire, now that they are well into school, to spell his words correctly. He would sit with the bulky two-volume dictionary that belonged so many years ago to his older son, having to search for the simplest words. It takes hours to compose the eight, nine sentences, for how are you to find in the dictionary the words you need to spell correctly when they are not to be found when you cannot spell them? But he has not wanted his grandchildren to hold him in blame, and the fire of the wish had given him the patience for the letters. That, in the last sense, is what it all is, and the old man knows it. It is not the sickness, it has never truly been sickness that poisons his last years. It is blame. It is the worst of all poisons: the need to blame and to be free of blame. Someone must be made to know it. His son must know, the world must know, he cries to himself, who has no world. So the old woman must know.

He stares once more at the picture of the face so full of messages. He did not live long enough, this coin collector from Budapest, to know of blame. He is tempted to ask her from what cause it was that a man died so young, but he fears the answer will distract his mind, and his mind, pursuing justice, insists that at least she know the difference between himself and her. Alike in age and alike before the waiting grave, her girlish foolishness that makes the difference derives from the picture itself. It was all over for her before the years had the chance to impose failure and spread blame. She can labor now and pant over the boy's skates and kneel at his feet. The old man knows it for what it is, a pointing of the finger at his own refusal. But does she know, he asks, almost ready to ask it aloud, that those who were not altogether alone and were made always in the eyes of the others to see their own failure, when they were finally alone are most alone?

"Foolish woman!" he cries, rising. "Stay there. You belong there."

He flings the snapshot to the bench. It is caught immediately in a gust of wind. It scrapes along the bench, twirls once, twice in the air, rises, spirals, then falls at the roots of a tree. The old woman utters a cry, a sob, and the old man starts instinctively after the picture. But he would have to go around the woman and the boy, and, for a moment, he stops. The woman, clutching the bench, hauls herself up. She hurries toward the tree, her bowed legs feeble for the task. The boy, one skate grinding, the other scraping, gets there first. The picture lifts again with the rising wind, and the boy falls on it, holding it, smothering it. When the old woman gets there she moves in starts and fits around the prone boy to see if he has caught the picture. She looks in terror down the block to where it might have blown away.

At last the boy digs it out with his hand and scrambles up to give it to her. He clutches it tightly that it will not blow away again. She takes it from him in two hands, pinching tightly at the corners of the now crumpled picture. She rubs it on her coat against her chest. The old man, seeing the picture safe, has started to walk away. She comes after him, but he continues walking. He walks faster than she can, and she begins to try to run. She pulls at his sleeve. Roughly he pulls his arm away.

"It's all right," he says. "You have your picture."

She is trying to speak to him, but she cannot catch her breath.

"I would have got your picture," he says. "If not the boy, then me. You have your picture."

She is still trying to catch her breath. Her head bobs, her eyes bulge behind the glasses. Her voice is scarcely audible when she manages, through her gasps, to speak.

"I don't hear you!" he shouts. "You have the picture. What's the matter with you?"

"No, you haven't," she says. "I must say it to you. You haven't suffered enough. You don't know. No, you haven't suffered enough."

She turns from him, shaking her head, holding her chest. The boy, who had been looking at them, has run away from his fright of her emotion. He is down at the corner on a bench again, staring at his skates. The old woman crosses the narrower street

137

behind the benches, walking slowly toward the row of apartment houses. The wind whips at the curl of hair under her hat.

The old man, motionless, staring after her, her words throbbing in his head, the letter he has not read to her in his pocket, shouts after her.

"I don't suffer? I don't suffer?" he shouts into the teeth of the now howling wind. "What do you know?" he screams. He wanted to accuse her, even of being only a maid in someone else's house, but his mind, clouded with the sight of her faltering steps beside the hedgerows, sinks into uncertainties.

ON A TRAIN IN GERMANY

The American was on an expense account, but on this train he boarded in Munich he would travel second class. After two weeks in several German cities, he had to spend a day in Zurich before flying home. What he wanted from his train ride was a slow trip over the Bavarian plain and through the Austrian Alps in the company of ordinary native travelers. Years and years ago he had flown over this country as a bombardier during the great war, and this present journey was to be devoted to the flow of sentiments and the sorting of confusions. Those bombing runs over Munich in his youth had terrified him, and on each flight out of Italy over the jagged and snow-forbidding Alps he had prayed for the luck that would return him alive, and he had prayed for a future of peace when he might someday come back and look up from the ground at these mountains with eyes of wonder and gratitude.

The American understood German, for it had been spoken in his Milwaukee home when he was a boy. But he himself could only haltingly speak the language. It gave him all the advantage now of a natural eavesdropper, for he was identified everywhere and immediately as an American. He worked for a Milwaukee television station that was planning a documentary on the New Germany, and his task for the past two weeks had been to collect German film that would be edited at home. One of his hopes for the present train ride was to experience a more spontaneous sense of things than had so far come his way through arranged interviews in which English was the language, through short plane hops, rented cars, and the predictably gracious, almost servile encounters in expensive hotels and restaurants. After boarding the train he chose a compartment in which three young people were already seated.

Two young women with a young man between them, they occupied the three forward seats. The three seats opposite them were empty when the American entered, and he took the one at the window. The young people greeted him with quick smiles and nods, and then returned to the high spirits of their talking. The American soon decided they were university students and friends. It was December, the holidays had started, and by the skiing gear piled on the luggage rack above them, the American understood the purpose of their traveling.

In a few moments a Tirolean in his native dress entered the compartment and took the seat beside the American. He wore the grey loden jacket with the green striped border, over which the rucksack was still strapped to his back, stained lederhosen, grey loden stockings and mountain shoes. He mumbled *Gruss Gott* and then removed the rucksack and placed it between his feet. Only then did he look at his fellow passengers, staring at them with a dull and arrogant moroseness. The students ignored him. The American nodded, then turned toward his window. The Tirolean's face, coarse in every feature, was raw and red from the cold. He might have been the American's forty-five; he might have been much younger.

The remaining seat was soon taken by a middle-aged woman who wore a dark cloth coat with a cheap fur collar. She arrived in an air of confusion and anxiety accompanied by a man her age who was seeing her off. He raised her suitcase to the rack while she placed a parcel on her seat. He nodded and smiled obsequiously to the others in the compartment, especially to the well-dressed American, then retired into the narrow corridor with the woman. The compartment door closed behind them. No one inside could hear a word of the conversation in which the woman spoke with apparent fervor, and the man tried to calm her with movements of his hands. He played with the buttons of her coat, he caressed her cheek, he held her hands. They were very much in the way of corridor traffic, and the obsequious man soon left. He appeared again on the platform, and the woman lowered the window to talk. When the train started, the American saw the man throw a kiss; but his jaw loosened immediately into an expression of relief. Then the woman had trouble with the compartment door. The Tirolean, staring, ignored her. The American was rising when the young man sprang up and went to her aid. The woman, to his embarrassment, thanked him profusely, as if she were undeserving. She removed the parcel and then kept it on her lap when she sat. She turned her head into the corner and sighed loudly.

The young woman opposite the American was tall and vivid, with dark, alert eyes. Her hair was black and long, falling to the shoulders of her white turtle-neck sweater. She was easily amused, and when she laughed she threw her head far back and whacked her knee in rapid slaps. The girl who sat opposite the nervous woman had turned in her seat to face her friends, perhaps to avoid staring at the woman. She was smaller and plainer than her friend, and she often drew back her upper lip in a way that made her look both rodent-like and wise. Her speech was laconic and probably full of irony, for hers were the remarks which brought paroxysms of laughter from her girl friend.

The young man between them glanced occasionally at the American. He wore a blue sweater under a checked jacket; his arms were often folded over his chest. His face was gentle and open, with thick eyebrows winging a broad nose over a thick mouth. He nodded a great deal without talking, and there was a quality in his eyes, a patient sympathy, which made the American decide the fellow must often be called upon to listen to the troubles of his friends.

The train, after jolting starts and stops in the huge railroad yards which the American had once bombed, had picked up speed and was passing through a district of warehouses and factories. Staring through his window, he saw a sky that was not unlike that of his own Midwest in December: low, grey, and in its flint hardness seeded for soft snow. From out of that sky he had bombed these rails, dropped bombs on these factories and warehouses, and cried his silent prayers when the flak was heavy and the plane bucked in the air like the rocking horse of his boyhood. Everything below him had been unreal—the toy city, the puffs of smoke, the abstract murder—and real only was the blood pumped from his terrified heart, throbbing and clamoring under the roar of the engines of his plane. He had tried in recent years to explain to his two adolescent sons who loved the bravery of football what the mysteries were at the heart of real fear, but he could not wind his moral lessons past their boredom. He resigned himself to the knowledge that it could not be taught, for he remembered how his own father's stories of the earlier great war had bored him too.

The Tirolean beside him was working at his rucksack. He removed food wrapped in newspaper: a thick, greasy sausage and a block of whitish cheese. He held them both in one hand, and with the penknife in the other he cut slices. His fingers were gnarled and clumsy, but he managed to spear the slice on the tip of his knife blade and carry it quickly to the gaping mouth of his lowering head. He then wiped the knife with great care on his filthy lederhosen while he chewed with smacking noises and vacant eyes. Only the American, in sidelong glances, paid attention to him. The woman was still angled into the corner of her seat, her face hidden from the American. The students were talking about a friend, who was apparently an actor meeting them at the ski resort. They were charming the American with their airs of youthful ardor and rich associations.

He returned to his window, smoked a cigarette, and stared through the smoke he blew at the disappearing Munich suburbs and the stretches behind the houses of the December-brown fields of the Bavarian plain. He had stared for a long time in a revery full of pictures and without thought when he was called back to the compartment by the gruff voice of the Tirolean. The man addressed him, but the American could not understand the dialect. Neither could he understand the gestures made at him by the food-laden hands. The American made a gesture of his own to indicate he didn't understand. The Tirolean ignored him and talked in a louder voice. The American shrugged.

"He wants you to change seats with him," said the young woman, smiling ironically, pulling back her upper lip. Her English, though her accent was heavy, was perfectly clear. It surprised the American. "He wants the room to put down his food." She indicated the little shelf at the window ledge on which there was the ash-tray the American had been using.

"You do not have to do it," said the young woman opposite him. Her English was also clear. She shook her head. "I would not do it." She glanced at the Tirolean, her dark eyes narrowing with resentment.

The Tirolean ignored the young women he knew to be German and who had just spoken in a language he could not understand. He continued to stare at the American, pointed with his knife to the table, held up the food in his other hand, nodded, and spoke again. The young man, speaking German, addressed the Tirolean.

"It is not necessary for the stranger to exchange seats with you. Make a table of your rucksack."

The Tirolean stared at the youth, smiled, then returned his eyes to the American. But he didn't speak.

"It is possible he belongs third-class," the dark-eyed girl explained to the American. "They all do that. We will see when the conductor comes." She swept her eyes over the Tirolean and added, "I think he is very much third-class."

The American tried to indicate to the Tirolean that he wanted to look out the window. It was important enough for him to be an issue by itself, and he suppressed the impulsive secondary thought which argued against his being brutishly ordered around in this of all places. The Tirolean remained speechless and expressionless. He cut a slice from the sausage while he stared through heavy-lidded eyes at the small shelf. The American, before returning to his window, caught another glimpse of the woman on the other side of the Tirolean. She had come slightly forward in her seat and was staring at the young man out of reddened eyes. She continued holding tightly to the parcel in her lap.

Settling at the window again, the American stared out at the tawny landscape of the winter farms, the farms of Germany, on one of which his own father, at the beginning of the century, had been raised. It was one half of the American's origins, this ordinary land of this guilty country. It had been his father's, and his father in America, forgetting his old grievances, had praised it with feeling to his growing son. And then the war began, and he never spoke of Germany again. But a country doesn't go away, and when the American himself was old enough to confront it, and then was brought to it, he suffered a confusion of shame and anger for the fact that his father had been German. For the shoring up of his courage against the terror of his bombing runs, he had tried to imagine personal reasons for the impersonal death he released with a finger. Now, with his train ride into that past just commencing, as he stared into the uninforming land, looking at it for what might humanize it into the truly ordinary, he admitted to a kind of childishness that had made him imagine a short train trip so many years later could help sort old confusions. There was nothing to them now. This land he looked at owed him no special explanations, and he surely owed it no generalized tributes.

When the conductor came the young woman opposite the American snorted with satisfaction. She actually slapped her knee. The Tirolean, it turned out, was indeed third-class. There were words the American couldn't altogether follow, for the conductor's accent was similar to the Tirolean's. It ended shortly when the Tirolean produced a battered coin purse and grubbed in it with his heavy fingers for the change that would permit him to remain. The conductor frowned impatiently at the extra clerical work involved for him, then turned to the woman, took her ticket and punched it. She spoke then for the first time, looking past the conductor to the young man.

"I go to Naples."

The conductor nodded.

"My old mother there is very sick. I go to take care of her."

The conductor nodded again, glancing at her this time. Her voice was hoarse and quavered with fear. Even the students now listened to her.

"Last month she was also sick. And I went and came back. Now I have to go again to Naples."

The conductor nodded, grunted something, and as he went out the door mumbled *Wiedersehen* in the same sing-song way he had said *Gruss Gott* on entering. He shot the Tirolean one more withering look through the compartment glass, but the Tirolean did not see him. He worked at the straps of the rucksack.

"Naples," the woman repeated, to the young man, or to herself. Her lip rouge was smeared, and a band of hair had fallen loose to lie on her cheek. Her eyes, surrounded by reddened flesh, blinked and blinked. The young man nodded awkwardly to her, then returned his attention to his companions. The woman, sighing deeply, went back to her corner.

"*Schnee!*" the girl opposite the American sang out, pointing at the window. And so it was, the snow falling lightly over the farm fields out of the iron sky. The sight of it made the girl ecstatic, and she pinched the cheek of the young man, who patted hers in return. When they settled down some moments later and began again to speak, the American, looking from time to time out the window at the ever-thickening snow, listened.

"I would not call that acting," the young man said. "Prancing and all kinds of carrying on, but not acting."

145

"He is your best friend and you say that of him?" said the lively girl.

"I talk only about his acting. As his friend I am concerned that he should not throw away everything for this bad acting."

"To teach is better? To be with idiots every day?"

"Better that than to be an idiot himself."

"It was not all *his* bad acting," the smaller girl said. "You cannot act alone. They are all amateurs. They pay no attention to each other. They speak lines. Each for himself."

"All the same," the young man said, "to have conviction when you act you must at least . . ." He paused, apparently searching for the right word. He was perhaps about to say it when the lively girl, pouting, interrupted.

"So. Everything is already so grave. Go with Maillinger, and you have to be serious."

He raised his eyebrows. "Who was it who invented, and made, and sold the study sheets to get the money for all of us to go now?"

"Precisely," the smaller girl said, and pulled back her upper lip.

They began to talk of the skiing. They were gay in a moment, and the American marveled at their ability to slide through moods and subjects. He turned to the window and confronted the snow. The train's advance toward the mountains was carrying them into heavier snow. The flakes, battered by the chute of blown air made by the onrushing train, whirled away from the window in a dizzying white spiral. It was not a bomber's sky, nor was it going to be a tourist's sky either. There would be little to see out the window if the storm came full, and the tops of the mountains he had wanted to wonder at would be hidden from him.

The train stopped at a town named Rosenheim, and he watched the snowflaked, waiting people on the platform craning necks to search for those they had come to meet, or for the cars with empty seats. A child flung herself into a man's encircling arms, and a railroad man with an oil can walked alongside the train. Except for the German spoken through the station's loudspeaker, it was all common enough for the American to be a scene from home. When the train started again and they were, in a few minutes, at the outskirts of town, he saw a huge factory with a towering, grimy smokestack. It was surely old enough to have survived the war. Thus was everything only, and more and more persistently, ordinary life, even to the new ripple of laughter from the girl opposite him which turned him back to the compartment again.

She whacked on her thigh again and again, and with her other hand she rubbed at her tearing eyes. Again she must have been responding to something her girl friend had said, for the ironic face was puckered with satisfaction. The Tirolean, who had been dozing, opened his eyes, but the heavy lids dropped over them again in a moment. The American glanced up at the gear on the rack above them, the high-polished metal of the red and blue skis, the poles strapped to them by their strong leather thongs, and all of it laid neatly over the suitcases. He was giving up his mind to pictures of holidays and war, when the woman suddenly stood up. She put the parcel on her seat, but she gave no sign of leaving the compartment. The American and the students looked at her, waiting.

She looked nervously at all of them, but her longest glances were for the young man. She pulled at a button of the cloth coat she still wore. The skin on her face was loose, and with her watered eyes and smeared rouge she looked blurred, like a snapshot out of focus. Wearily, she raised her hands before her chest, the palms up, then she dropped her arms. She began to speak to the young man, but so rapidly and in so hoarse a voice that the American could not understand her. Repeatedly she used the phrase *nicht gut*. She raised an arm again, extending it toward the young man. *"Bitte, bitte,"* she pleaded. She held a hand on the latch of the compartment door and asked him again. "Please. Come with me outside. For a moment only. Please!"

The young man, blushing, exchanged a look with the smaller girl, then rose. He got to the door in time to hold it for the

147

woman, and when he stepped into the corridor beside her he glanced through the window at his friends and raised his heavy eyebrows. The woman turned her back on the compartment, and the American could hear nothing. The woman gestured with her arms. Once she pointed toward the corridor windows, and once she clutched her hair. The young man looked bewildered. His eyes roved the corridor, but he lowered them from time to time to look at the woman.

"Always Maillinger," the young woman opposite him whispered to her friend. "His face is too serious. You will never have him to yourself."

"She has been crying to herself in the corner," the friend said. She turned toward the corridor.

The Tirolean again opened his eyes, turned his head toward the corridor, swung it slowly back to take in the young women for a moment before his chin fell to his chest and his eyes closed again. The ironic girl observed to her friend that she now thought it all had something to do with the woman's passport. The American looked toward the corridor and saw the woman holding the stiff booklet in her hand. The young man shook his head, nodded, then shook it again. He had taken on the posture of a burdened kindness and embarrassment.

They came back into the compartment. The young man's companions tried not to stare at him, for he could not now tell them what had been said. He made a light comment on the snow. The woman, having taken up her parcel, was in her corner again. Her occasional sighs and sobs were even louder now. The young man sat on the edge of his seat, his legs apart and his hands clasped in the gap between them. He occasionally glanced at the woman with an air of sympathy and resentment. His friends made efforts to bring him back to them, but for a while he only gave short answers. Gradually the lively girl picked him up with chatter about the snow and skiing conditions. The American could not believe the woman's passport problems were serious. He even looked forward to the situation becoming public at

the border, supplying him with more second-class local color to
report on to his family, to colleagues.

Shortly, in the increasing snowfall, they arrived at Kufstein,
the border town. When the train stopped, the Tirolean roused. The
woman stood up, holding tightly to her parcel. She smiled weakly at
the young man, and then she wailed. It was so loud and sudden a
noise that the Tirolean's mouth gaped. He turned to stare at her.
They all stared at her. The young man spoke to her. His voice was
reassuring, yet he shook his head with the impatience of a parent.

"It is a small thing. You have to be calm. There is no war now.
I have promised you. If you have difficulties, I will come after
you."

It was almost public now, and the girl opposite the American
asked, "What is it?"

"A small thing," he shrugged. "Last month when she came back
from Italy she forgot to have her re-entry stamped."

The girl waved her hand. "Nothing," she said to the woman. "It
is nothing."

The woman sobbed and shook her head; she sat down again and
cried openly. Wiping at her eyes, she made a wider smear of her
rouge. The Tirolean, fishing in his rucksack, removed his own
passport. He mumbled a word which the American thought meant
"crazy," and the young man shot him a fierce look. The American
heard a near compartment door open and close and assumed it was
the border guard. He turned to his window. The incident was now
perhaps more excitement than he wanted; the woman's anxiety
tyrannized the compartment. Even if it came to nothing, she could
continue to cheat him of the private experience he had longed for in
the journey through the mountains. When the guard opened their
door, the American thought of changing his compartment once the
train got underway again.

The guard wore a long heavy coat on which the melting snow
gave off a slight wool odor. He began with the students, glanced
quickly at their passports, inquired perfunctorily of what they

carried in their suitcases, and said something to the lively girl which the American missed. It made the girl smile. The American offered his passport, but the guard waved it back with his hand. The identifying blue was apparently enough : American. He asked no questions about the American's suitcase. He took the Tirolean's passport, opened it, returned it, asked of the things in the rucksack but paid no attention to the grunted answer. They all turned with him toward the woman in the corner. She immediately burst into tears. She put her hands over her face and wailed. The astonished guard fell back toward the door.

The young man looked at the smaller girl and winced. He rose, took a step toward the guard and began whispering to him. He kept his back to the woman. The American couldn't hear, but the smaller girl who was nearest to them did. At least her eyes widened and her upper lip pulled back. She looked around the two men to glance at the woman. Then she looked at her girl friend and made the face the American took to mean of now knowing the secret but not being able to tell. The woman continued sobbing. The Tirolean turned to the American and grinned. He repeated the word the American had taken for "crazy." The young man reached behind the guard and opened the door. They both stepped out to the corridor. The guard closed the door, leaning against it as he listened. The woman took her hands from her face, stared through the corridor window at the men, glanced at the staring girls, then moved deeper into her corner away from the Tirolean. Then she came forward in her seat. She addressed the young woman, making a great effort to control her voice.

"A misfortune. Such a misfortune. It was something I forgot. I forget so many things now. My mother is so sick. Otherwise I would never travel. My God. My God."

She stood up. Her eyes wandered to the luggage rack above the girls. She put her parcel on the seat. Then, as though she had been too long paralyzed at the rail of a bridge, she yanked open the door and flung herself against the guard. She was waving her passport. The door fell closed again. The smaller girl turned immediately to her friend. Her voice was lowered, but the American heard her clearly.

"I think she is a Jew. I think that is what Maillinger told the guard."

The other girl took in her breath. Then she nodded and blew the breath out.

The American turned toward the corridor. The guard was looking at the woman's passport. He was shaking his head. The American was confused. He saw nothing momentous in the girl's revelation. He hadn't forgotten where he was and what that one word had meant here. But what the young man had said was true: the war was over. There were no more bombs to drop, no flak to survive, the mountains were no longer graveyards for American planes, and German citizens, Jews or otherwise, could come and go. If her passport was clerically inaccurate, the American was certain it could be adjusted. In any case, there were no barbarians waiting for the woman. No guns were drawn. No rifle butts were raised. The guard's face was as commonplace as the young man's. Both of them could have been walking the streets of Milwaukee. The snow falling outside in a now windless drop of slowly spinning flakes was at least as white as the snow at home. Perhaps the single word of the ox-like Tirolean had been the pathetic summary of it all.

In the corridor the guard was indicating with his arm that the woman should walk before him. She put her hands to her fur collar, and then disappeared from the American's view. The guard followed after. The young man hesitated for a moment, then he too left.

"Ach, your Maillinger now goes all the way to the bureau with them," the girl opposite the American said.

But the young man was back in a moment. He opened the door and took his seat. He scratched behind an ear and shook his head. The smaller girl questioned him at once.

"Is that the reason? Is she a Jew?"

He nodded. The Tirolean stared from one to another of them. He rammed his tongue to the side of his cheek, and his cheek bloomed like a tumor. His hands engulfed the knees of his lederhosen. His eyes had blinked for a moment when *the* word had been spoken, but he was now once more expressionless. The young man sighed.

"She is excitable, foolish. It will all be straightened out."

"Perhaps we should find another compartment," said the girl opposite the American.

"I promised to take care of the parcel. And to go to the bureau if she is not back soon."

He glanced at the American; his friends did too. It was now in the compartment with them, a spoken word, an emphatic presence, a substance without a form, but so full of history that the American himself had to be scrutinized for his reaction to it, as if that one word had betrayed the American to the students, informing them that he did indeed understand German. He resented it.

What the hell! he declared to himself. He got up. This was not his grief. He didn't even know that there was cause for grief. Surely the woman would be back. The guard hadn't even taken her belongings. He stepped around the rucksack, opened the door, and went into the corridor. He would search for a dining car. Halfway down the corridor he stopped. Outside the window he saw the woman walking on the platform beside the guard. Another guard had joined them. In a few steps they were out of the American's sight. He stepped to a corridor window and lowered it. The snow streamed about his face.

The train was long and his own car was well toward the rear. The three people he stared after had a way to go. The woman was between the two guards. They were both much taller than she. Their long coats, belted in the back, ended well down on their calves. They wore black boots, vivid against the snow. The guard who had joined the other one walked with his hands clasped behind his back. He wore black leather gloves. The woman hurried her steps to keep up with the guards. She swayed as she walked, but the guiding presence of the tall man on each side contained her. The path of their footprints in the snow on the unsheltered part of the platform trailed after them. Passengers milling on the platform made way for them, and they veered only once to make room for the cart from which a coatless youth sold food through the corridor windows. They were halfway to the station house, and the American, continuing to watch them through the falling snow, unaware that the snow was falling on his hair and wetting his face, experienced for the moment the traveler's strange loss of the knowledge of where he was, who he was. What he looked at began to bear the odd familiarity of something previously witnessed, but impersonally, as if he himself had not been present. It might have been witnessed in a movie, or suddenly recalled from a forgotten book. Or it might have been the flashing embodiment of a generalized terror, riding always before him and drifting always out of sight, like the glimpse at his own day of dying, and leaving behind only the progress of the footprints in the piling snow, the guards on either side.

They were almost to the station now, and he fixed his eyes on the woman's back. It was bent; one of the shoulders was lowered. He stared and stared at it, his face streaming now with the snow-water running from his hair. He stared at it until the three of them went through a door and disappeared from his view. He raised his gaze beyond the station and thought he saw the mountains hulking in the grey light beyond the snow. He felt himself empty. He believed himself to be standing aside of an illusion he had carried for years, one that had shamed him and that he had nevertheless, he understood now, courted as an aspect of the bravery of a youth's participation in warfare. But the casting away of an illusion left him no lighter. It had come to him now with all the guilt of truth. He had never really known an abiding terror. He had been afraid. He had feared for his life. But out of and against his fear he had been granted the chance and the power to drop his avenging bombs. There had been no one to shove his face into the nameless and abiding terror, commanding him to live with it—live with it forever!

He raised the window and returned to his compartment. The students were once more in that lively conversation he had come upon over an hour ago in Munich, but they fell into an immediate silence when he entered. The Tirolean was now in the American's seat. There was a sausage on the little shelf, and he was cutting a stack of slices from it with his knife. Perhaps he meant only to finish the task, gather the greasy stuff into his hand, and then return to his seat. The American turned to the young man. They all heard his voice in a full sentence for the first time.

"Please ask that ox to get out of my seat."

Immediately he changed his mind. In a faltering German he told the young man not to bother. It didn't matter. With his foot he moved the rucksack across the floor to the Tirolean's feet. He took the middle seat. The students stared at him. He folded his arms across his chest and waited. He waited a long time for the woman's return, but the parcel and the suitcase remained, and he believed she would return. And he was right. The young man, who had begun to get up every few minutes and go to a corridor window, returned on his last trip to announce that she was coming. He said she came alone. There was no guard with her. He blew his breath in relief.

The American, who would be sitting beside her, prepared himself for her return. He knew the familiar foolishness of the new sentiment he aspired to, but he was no longer free to set it aside. In silence through the mountains, seated beside her, he would try to know a little of what she felt, or feel what she knew.

He shook his head at the Tirolean, who, grunting at him, offered wurst.

NO MEDAL FOR SONNY

Nobody looking at me today—a balding, modestly satisfied, middle-aged lawyer—would believe that I played football at college. It was the last thing I would have thought of for myself when I entered college. I didn't weigh much, I was not a great athlete, and though I loved to watch the game, I had no great desire to play it. But football, even in ordinary times, was only a minor affair at our streetcar college, and I was there during the war. The captain, who was quarterback, wrote poetry—that gives you an idea. He was the one who talked me into going out for it. "Look," he said, "Jim Thorpe alone with some kid at center to snap him the ball could beat the eleven of us." Even so, I didn't make the first team. I seldom got into a game.

What I remember of football, then, has nothing to do with my own great old days of glory. So I don't bore friends, and I don't even advise my son through weekends of television football. I can't. It's gotten complicated beyond all bearing for just a game. I mean all those monster technicians running in and out every minute with some small specialty that's supposed to make a major difference—and probably does. But I still assume the heart of the thing is what it always was: ruin the other man who has the ball; prevent that ruin when your own man has it. The rest of the stuff is just a style. No matter how much beef they add to the men who play, no matter what fancy names they give to new formations, the

155

same old primitive quality is the essential one : a rage to hit and an indifference to the harm it does.

I am still fascinated by it because I used to wonder even when I played where they got it from, the rage and the indifference. I never had it, and on the bench I had a lot of time to watch it. I saw it always in Sonny Schaefer, and I have never seen more of it in anyone. He was a marvel to all of us. Whenever I think of football guts, I remember Sonny. I remember him in images of collision up and down the field, and I remember a crippling moment that didn't take place on a field, that had nothing to do with football—apparently.

He had sandy hair, a broad face, and a span of fading kid's freckles across his cheeks and the bridge of his nose. He was of average height, fairly broad, and very deep in the chest. He was mild, a little gullible, quiet, almost sweet. He had fair skin and blushed quickly—his smile was like a gift. Except in the locker room or on the field, I never saw much of him, despite the fact that he was in one of my classes. He sat in the back of the room next to the girl he was in love with. She was tiny and beautiful. The two of them together made you think he was her protecting knight of gentleness, in which case the football field had to be the country where he fought her dragons.

He loved to tackle. He played fullback and backed up the right side of the line on defense. I was tall and skinny, so the coach put me on an end with the scrubs. It was the right end, so I never had to clear Sonny out of the way when the scrubs had the ball in practice. But there were times when I had to cut into his spot for a pass. As soon as my fingers touched the ball, I would almost close my eyes and begin to wait even as I tried to take my first stride away. I was waiting for Sonny to come banging into me. He always did. And it always took my breath away. I would be swept off my feet and sent hurtling through the air, mildly conscious of a vise-like pressure around my thighs and of a weight I was dragging or that was driving me backward. He laid himself out above the grass like a swan diver, his back arched, his toes pointed. He hit you first with the high part of his chest. Then his arms locked your legs. Sometimes he'd begin to turn you before you hit the ground, and you had this momentary airborne sense of the two of you turning like a long driven shaft, and then you'd hit the grass and he might be on the bottom, but the momentum of his turning carried him over you, and you had a glimpse of the top of his helmet. Then it was gone, and your legs were released, and he was gone, off you already, running to his spot for the next play. He could tackle as well as anyone I ever saw play. He had a deadly, almost disinterested instinct for the man who had the ball.

He was adequate as an offensive fullback, but the excitement of watching him tackle diminished all his other accomplishments. He liked, for instance, to block, and you'd imagine he'd be perfect clearing the way before a halfback. In a sense, he was. He brought into that part of the game the same savage grace with which he tackled. But there was judgment, as well as instinct, involved in this, and too often he merely flung himself at the defensive man nearest to him. Sometimes he was cutting down a man who had already lost his chance at the ball carrier. Our coach, Seabury, got sore throats trying to teach him differences, but I think now that the nice skills of the game bored Sonny. He was in it for something else. For him all the rules of football only made possible and permissible something between him and the ball carrier. He didn't really care whether we won or lost.

We didn't know that then. We equated the desire to win with the evidence of the beating you took, and no one on the field, game after game, took the beating Sonny did. As the game progressed and he made more and more of the tackles, the exhaustion would set in. The arch in his back would level out a little when he tackled, the shoulders and chest would drop a bit. Many times it was his face that made first contact with the ball carrier. By half time he was stretched out on a table in the locker room like a beaten prize fighter, his face pulpy, his eyes glassy. So when he swung his legs off the table and dragged himself out for another whole half of the same thing, we had to believe he was doing it for us, that he wanted us to win. But any torturer could have told us that a man so beat up couldn't care less about who literally won. It was for something else he went out there to make his tackles and take his beating.

I saw him once at the movies on a Saturday night after a game. He had his girl with him. We were all just going in. He had his arm around the girl's shoulder, and to anyone looking at them it might have made the picture of a kind of marvelous sweetness—this burly guy with a bruised face and the tiny, beautiful, almost doll-like female to whom he seemed to offer malehood. Actually, he surrendered it. When he left her to pay the cashier, he nearly fell on his face. She'd been holding *him* up. I sat a row behind them. He slept through almost all the picture. When we came out together he had a handkerchief to his nose. The rag was vivid with new blood and brown with old. The girl told me it had been bleeding on and off through the movie.

"Why do you let him play like that?" she cried, turning on me in the theater lobby.

Her eyes were flashing. She looked like a child about to stamp her foot. From the anger in her face you'd think she believed everyone but Sonny was responsible for the ferocity with which he played.

I knew she saw the home games because she was always waiting for him outside the locker room. But she never made the trips when we played away. She never saw the Connecticut game. If she had, she never would have believed that anyone but Sonny himself had anything to do with the way he played.

It was a beautiful October Saturday, and the trees beyond the fences at both end zones were full of leaves of scarlet, rust, gold. It was football weather. I've always thought of it as that teasing snap of bright air which promises the player he can do extraordinary things, and promises anyone watching that he deserves to witness them. It must have gotten to Sonny, for he went on to give all of us something to witness.

By the end of the first period the few thousands in the stands had caught on to the real drama of the game. Whenever Connecticut ran the ball, the loudspeaker comment at the end of the play was always the same: ". . . tackled by Number Thirty-five Schaefer." Everyone began to watch him.

Connecticut ran out of the old single wing that even then was beginning to disappear. They played for four, five yards at a shot, a sustained march the hard way, holding onto the ball, eating up the time. Neither team had a scouting system, so they knew nothing of Sonny other than what they were learning right out there on the field. For a long time they kept on running most of their plays to his side. I suppose they were making enough first downs not to pay too much attention to who was making the tackles. When they did catch on and started going to the other side, it didn't really matter. They picked up a few extra yards for the time it took Sonny to get over there, but three out of four times, right side or left, it was Sonny who made our tackles.

He was groggy well before half time, coming up higher on his tackles, getting more of his face in the way, but never failing. I remember the play in which their fullback came ripping up the guard on Sonny's side through a hole wide enough for a parade. He ran straight up with a couple of men in front of him to cut Sonny down. It was the kind of moment that made you stand up at once, thinking: touchdown. No one could explain afterwards how Sonny had slipped the interference. What we saw was a big man going full steam with the ball, and then being suddenly stopped. Not as if he had run into a wall, but as though he had actually been caught, as though he himself were the ball, picked out of the air to be run back the other way. Because Sonny, perhaps too tired to leave his feet, had his shoulder in the ball carrier's abdomen, his face in his chest, and then drove him back through that same hole he had ripped through, back and back, yard after yard, and long after the whistle had blown the play dead. When they finally got Sonny to let go, it was obvious to us he was beginning not to know where he was. He kept turning around, searching for our bench, for the coach, for the scrimmage line. He had that look on his face of a boy who had won a fight and was trying to remember where and why it had started.

At half time he was stretched out on the concrete floor of the locker room. They had given out oranges, and Sonny was lying there with a wedge of one stuck in his mouth like a teething ring. His eyes were closed. He didn't even open them when the trainer raised Sonny's arm and taped the cleat gash he had on his wrist.

We tried to get him out of the game soon after the second half had begun. The captain himself pleaded with Seabury.

"Sonny's punchy. Get him out of there. It's only a game."

The coach sneered. "Bet a buck he makes the next tackle." And Sonny did.

He almost had to be taken by the hand now to be shown his spot behind the right side of the line. He tottered there as though he would keel over. He staggered around in little loops, pulling at his helmet and throwing his head back. We had those old leather helmets, and Sonny, waiting for the play to begin, would tear open the strap, put his fingers into the earholes and pull the helmet out from the sides of his head. You couldn't tell whether he imagined he was being choked, or he was trying to hold himself up by taking a good grip with his fingers on something he was wearing on his own head. And then Connecticut would break the huddle, and Sonny would clamp the helmet strap and turn toward the sound of signals.

Then the play: the rush of bodies, the collisions, the blur of the colors of the uniforms on that bright day, and then the end of the inevitable announcement: ". . . tackle by Number Thirty-five, Schaefer."

A better team than Connecticut could have made use of Sonny's great day. They could have thrown passes around him; they could have tried to fake him on traps, he was floating and charging so much. But they were small-time, too, and inexpert; and they were, anyway, by the third period, two field goals ahead. So they chose to hold the ball as long as they could, grind out the little yardage, hoping to get their remarkable kicker close enough for another try. What difference did it make to them who made the tackles? Someone had to.

I got into the game myself toward the close. The right end got something in his eye they couldn't remove during the time out. I was in on defense for three plays. Sonny made the tackles on two of them. I could hear him behind me, waiting for the play to begin. He was whimpering. I turned my head for a second to look at him. He was pulling at his helmet, his body weaving around the spot he was trying to stand on. His face was scarlet. You couldn't see the freckles in it. You could hardly see the bruises. The sweat streamed off him as though he had just turned his face into the nozzle of a hose. The whimpering went on—a little puppy noise of hurt. And then the play came, and there was the pile-up at the right side, the indecisive thudding of bodies and pads, and then that one sharp banging blow you could actually hear as though it were a fist smacked into a palm in an empty room, and right after it a voiced sound that was not a grunt of effort, but a kind of snarl. I knew it came from Sonny. I can hear it still—so full of its desperate satisfaction, so full of an immediate pain emptying out a kind of need.

By the time the game ended, I'd learned some things I hadn't known before: that a coach could love the game and not care much for the men who played it; that the men themselves during the game made it more than a game, or we simply would have quit until the coach had gotten Sonny off the field; and that Sonny himself, the way he played, needed the game. It was his needs and not his skills that made him great. In the newspapers, they call it desire, but I wonder. Desire for what?

Sonny was drafted shortly after the season ended. In the spring word came back to us he'd been killed in combat in Bavaria. We heard of the medal awared him posthumously for conspicuous bravery, and shortly after that we heard some of the story of how he died. The medal was sent to his family, and perhaps they tried to give it to the girl he loved. She said nothing of it when she spoke to me of Sonny a few weeks after I heard the news, but I don't think she would have taken any medal for his bravery. It was not only that I heard her speak against the bravery; it was that I had seen Sonny himself demonstrate against it at the party for him before he left for the Army. It was a sweet, crippling moment, as vivid in my memory of him as any image of his violence on the football field.

The party was given by his girl friend at her house, and I went because the poet-quarterback and I were double-dating. He'd been invited and insisted I go along. The party was in the finished basement where there were no rugs and we could dance. We drank beer and ate sandwiches of various meats at a time when the stuff was rationed. We danced, we told football stories, we sang, we gave Sonny presents, and we offered male observations and jokes about soldiers and the war. It must have been December, but with the gang of us there and the heat turned up, it grew very warm. Some of us took off our jackets, though Sonny didn't. He danced with his girl as often as she was willing, and he was very good at it. She was, too. I don't remember what was in fashion then, but in the swinging numbers the skirt of her dress flared like a cheerleader's. Sweat began to trickle down Sonny's face, and he occasionally wiped at it with a handkerchief as he danced. Whenever I looked at him, his eyes were always on the girl. They glowed with that regard he must have had for her tiny, fragile perfection.

I stayed late, long after most of the others had left. Our poet-quarterback was having too good a time to leave, and I was stuck waiting for him because I'd promised him a ride back. He'd had a lot of beer, and, as always when he got a little high, he recited pieces of poems he had memorized. His other little talent was to imitate Al Jolson; he sang song after song. There were only the six of us left. When he began to sing "The Anniversary Waltz," Sonny and his girl danced. That was more than twenty years ago, but I can close my eyes now and see them again, dancing a waltz on that large linoleum floor, see it as if they were dancing now, no older than they were then, but in a true commemoration, nevertheless, of a real anniversary.

The quarterback stood in a corner of the room, transported by his nasal mimicry of the sentimental voice and the mournful tune. And Sonny and the girl danced to it, around and around the room, her head thrown back so she could see into his face. And he moved her as if she truly weighed no more than a doll, and flawlessly she followed him, the one long step and the two short ones; and his face was broken in that boy's smile so entire in its fulfillment of a pleasure that you could not have imagined for him that he ever laid a hand on another man, football or otherwise, and surely not with the savagery with which he did so, against himself as well as the other one.

Finally the singing voice broke down, and then quit. Sonny and the girl danced a moment or two longer in the surprising silence, and then, in the middle of the room, they stopped. Then it happened. The small girl, exhausted, her face flushed, her chest rising and falling, started to move away, perhaps for a chair. Sonny caught her hand and gently pulled her back. He bent at the knees to bring his face close to hers. He put the heels of his hand together and cupped them under the chin of the girl he loved; his palms and his fingers, like leaves, shielded the sides of her face. He said nothing for a moment, only looked at her. He was crying. You could see the tears. His face was covered with sweat, but you could see the tears. He spoke in a low voice, but it wasn't a whisper. We all heard him.

"I love you," he said. "I love you. Oh God, I love you. I don't want to go to the war. They'll kill me. I know they will. I love you so much."

When she spoke to me after Sonny's death—it wasn't more than five months later—she said almost the same thing she had that night at the movie after a game. I was again in a class of hers, and she'd stayed out of school for a few weeks after the news had come. She wanted to make up work, and she called on me for it after the class ended. We kept busy with it for a few minutes in the empty room, while every thought I had of something I might say was blocked by my sense of its inappropriateness. When others started arriving for the next class, I suggested a stroll on the campus. I took her in a direction away from the gym and the football field. We sat on a bench behind the library, where I copied out assignments for her and turned in my mind whether I should tell her I had passed my physical and would soon be going into the Army. Suddenly she stood up and looked away. Then she faced me and asked it.

"Why did they let him fight like that?" she said. "Why did they?"

Again she looked like a little girl who would toss her head and stamp her foot. There was nothing I could say; I walked with her to the streetcar. She began to talk about Sonny. I thought at first she was only recollecting anecdotes, and then I realized she was trying to tell me something by them. I began to put it together only afterward, when I walked back across the campus and went up into the stands to watch the spring practice I wasn't involved in because I would be leaving soon. It was springtime, and I was young, and I was about to go to war, and I suppose it was because I had a mixed sense of mission and fear that I resisted for a while understanding the fragments of stories about Sonny she had told me.

She told me of the look on his face when they were in the subway together and the crowded train had stopped for a long time in a tunnel and he whispered to her that he thought he smelled smoke. And how he had gone white during the elevator ride to the observation floor in the Empire State Building. And once on a class picnic to Bear Mountain they decided to stay overnight in the woods, and she knew in the morning from looking at him that he had not slept at all, had stayed up all night hearing and imagining noises. I sat up there above the football field and with a professional air I watched the players making familiar patterns, and I understood she'd been trying to tell me so that someone besides herself would know that Sonny had had so strong a fear of so many inconsequential things. Maybe she was trying to tell me it was the anxiety itself he feared most, since it must have shamed him so much.

I turned my head to where a quick, snapping thud told me a clean tackle had been made, and when the man got off the ball carrier I watched him trotting away and wondered at the show of satisfaction he gave off in every stride he took. I tried to summon a sense of landscape for a place called Bavaria, and I thought of what we had heard of how Sonny had been killed. Our coach had told us.

He learned it in a letter from one of Sonny's Army buddies to whom Sonny must have talked a lot about football.

He was part of a small scouting party that got lost too far behind enemy lines to try to make it back again. They hid in the woods near a large farmhouse; they wanted to get into it to wait until their own troops caught up. But there was a German military truck parked near the house. They never saw anyone going into or out of the house, but lights went on in the evening, and they had to believe there were soldiers inside. They didn't know how many. They waited and waited. They stayed in the woods all night, and all the next day and the next night. On the following morning they could hear artillery, and then the sound of vehicles on the highway. They guessed the Germans were moving out of the nearby town, and they guessed those in the house would soon come out and get in the truck and join them. As soon as the first one came out the door, and before his buddies could stop him, Sonny broke out from behind his tree and began racing across the open field toward the startled German soldier.

It was not the soldier Sonny ran at who killed him. Apparently that one kept on standing there and staring at Sonny because Sonny gave no sign that he even intended to use the rifle he carried in one hand as he ran. A second German, who'd come through the door, shot at once and killed Sonny before he too was shot by one of the Americans still in the woods. The soldier Sonny had gone after threw down his rifle and raised his arms over his head, but someone from the woods shot again and killed him, too. There were no other Germans in the house.

Up there in the stands above the football field on which Sonny had played, I understood what that waiting out there in the woods must have been like for him. I understood that whimpering noise I heard from him in the Connecticut game, and the snarling sound he'd made when he tackled the man on the next play. And I wondered if he'd had even a moment's consciousness after he'd been shot to wonder himself if anyone among all of those who ever watched him, anyone besides the tiny girl he loved, understood how much of a beating he had really taken on every tackle he ever made, driven as he was by his nature to find a visible enemy, a ball carrier, to undo the humiliating shame he suffered for all the things he feared in every ordinary day.

I AM TAKING MURRAY'S PLACE

I work in this place, Hector's Auto Service. For about six years I been working there. We own the building, the boss, I mean, Mr. Hector, and for two months now I've been manager of the place. The way we do, a guy cracks up his car, and he calls his insurance man and they tell him: bring the car to Hector's. Or it's a bad wreck and they tell him call us; then we send out the truck and bring him in. That's my job sometimes, going out to the wrecks and estimating cost of repairs. I do everything in the place. I take care of the books, I help out on cars, I order parts, I boss the help, and since I became manager I do hiring. Which is how all this started with Marvin Alfedora. He came looking for a job at our place the first time I started this hiring.

It's a big place, the biggest independent auto repair outfit in New York, which means the biggest in the country. And I'm the manager of the place. I think about it when I drive into work from where we live in Kew Gardens. I'm the manager. I'm the manager. How many driving their cars into New York have a better job there than the one I have? My wife says I have a big head about this manager thing, since if you came over New York in an airplane you wouldn't even see our place. Which is one way to look at it, if you're a pilot, or a bird. Most of the people I know still work on the ground, and with them any auto insurance guy in New York knows our place. He knows me too. But what I have to tell is about Marvin Alfe-

167

dora who came to work for us a couple months ago. He only lasted two weeks. Sometimes I still hear him here. Sometimes I see him.

Before I got to be manager, my wife did another kind of needling for about three years. It was all about this Murray who used to be manager before me. A skinny little man with a ratty mustache and rat's eyes who only talked about his ulcers, like they were jewels in his belly, and all he ever thought about was what he was gonna eat next, and all he could eat anyway was the crud in baby jars, which he'd rack up about a dozen of on his desk for lunch. Then he'd hang his head over them and lap through it all like a kid on a malted. He'd finish one jar and slide it with the back of his hand off the desk and into the waste basket. Then he racked up the next one. Right in the office.

He was the one kept me from my raises. The boss couldn't pay out to two people for one man's work. That's what my wife was always needling me about. For the last three years it was like that. Putting up with Murray, with lousy pay, with all the headaches for the kind of work it is, six floors and still not enough space for all the wrecks, the boss yelling, "Space is money! Get the cars out!" and the customers piling up in the office on Fridays yelling they want their cars, and the idiots we got working there yelling about what did I want them to do with this car and that one, and the insurance guys calling up, and the goddamned racket all day from the hammering on the cars. By the time I got home every night my head was split like an apple. Then my wife would start through dinner. Then there was nothing left of the day except a couple of hours in front of the television. I was thirty-six already and closer to dead than to the time I was born. I oughta have something a little better out of the one life I got.

Then about a month ago Murray comes in and quits. Just like that he quits the place he'd been at sixteen years.

"It's damp here. I'm sick of car wrecks. I gotta go to Florida. I'll die in this cold place."

That's all he said. He packed up his baby crud in a crate big enough for an engine, and goodbye Murray.

168

I Am Taking Murray's Place

I was the manager now for one hundred fifty dollars per week and a bonus thrown in the end of the year. I called my wife and she came in, and we had dinner at the Copa. We even danced. It was like it used to be at the beginning.

Marvin Alfedora came after that.

We didn't need anyone for Murray's place since I'd been doing all the work anyway. But the boss fired the girl that worked the switchboard and typed a little cause he thought it would be a good idea to get a guy for that who could later on help in the shop a little. I hadda do the interviewing. I put the ad in the *Times,* and the next morning there was a line of them about twenty long when I got to work. All this talk about good times and my wife yelling before I got to be manager, like you hop out and get another job anywhere just like that. Anyways, even I'd never done any hiring before I knew you didn't take one from the first guys showed up no matter how good. I didn't really want anybody too good, somebody already ambitious to be a manager. So about eleven o'clock I'd gone through everyone answered the ad and there were no more coming in. All I had was the names and phone numbers of about four of them. Then the boss came in to meet the new man. When I told him there wasn't any yet, he said this place wasn't United States Steel. Just take someone who could talk and type a little. That's what I did. Marvin Alfedora.

We shut up at six when we're not going overtime. He came in five minutes before that. Who ever heard of coming on a job interview at supper time? But he breezed in and looked around like it was five in the morning and he was first on line.

He had the biggest head I ever saw. It looked even bigger the way his shoulders were like a couple of clothes hooks sticking off his neck. His nose was big and wide and heavy, sort of his whole face the first look you got. He had bad eyes. Those metal framed glasses no one wears anymore and the lenses in them so thick that when he was working in the office and the sun came in about one o'clock, all you could see on his head were those two blinding things, like headlights.

169

After his nose and eyes, everything else disappeared. He had all right teeth, but with his mouth that far back it gave me chills a little when he smiled. Like a lot of little bones on an X-ray.

His voice was from his nose somewhere. It was deep, but with something droning in it all the time—like a not-so-hot motor. Mainly it was the way he had of saying things. For instance, the first words he spoke to me.

"Are you the people," he said, "that advertised in today's edition of the New York *Times* for a young man to do office work in a position that had a future? I am particularly interested in the part about a future."

I kept staring at him.

"Are you?" he says.

"What?"

"Are you the people?"

I nodded.

So he shoved his hand out to me. "I am Marvin Alfedora. I am twenty-nine. I am Turkish."

What did he have to tell me that for? Who cares about Turks?

"What's your experience?" I says.

"Yes," he says. That's all.

"Yes what?"

"I served for three years with the United States Signal Corps at Fort Monmouth. I am very talented with radios, and now I am beginning to learn about television."

"We have no television here. What do I care about Fort Monmouth? I mean what's your business experience?"

He grins. He would always be grinning.

"I have always worked for the government," he buzzes, and all of a sudden I couldn't help it. I was looking right in his nose for the fan belt. "I have worked two years for the federal government and six months after that for the municipal government."

"Office work?"

"It was not office work."

"So what work was it? Look, I ain't got all night! You come in here six o'clock looking for a job I already seen a hundred applicants for and . . ."

"Yes. I worked for the United States Postal Office, Central Annex, Brooklyn. I also worked for the New York Transit Commission. But that was not in one place. That was all over the subways."

"What all over the subways?"

"I put the bulbs in the sockets."

"Put the what in?"

"Yes. I had a very long pole with a little wire basket at the end of it into which the bulbs were fit. By reaching up the pole I could take the old bulb out of the socket and then lower the pole and unscrew the bulb and then screw in the new one. Then I would . . ."

"All right! All right! We didn't advertise for bulb screwers! Did you do office work for the post office?"

"No. I sorted letters. I stood in front of the little slots we had for different towns. I worked the towns for one state mainly. I was in front of Indiana. The slot for Indianapolis would always fill up first, but there was a town called French Lick and every once in a while there was something to go in the slot for French Lick. I got to make a game of that and I could make the time pass by . . ."

"Look, just answer me what I ask you. Don't tell me about any French Lick. What's the matter with you? You said you worked there two years. Why'd they fire you?"

"Oh, no! I resigned. I wrote a letter to . . ."

"All right! Why'd you quit?"

"My feet hurt."

I looked at him.

"You see, I had to stand all the time. They had some stools, but there were women working and I always gave my stool to a woman. Most of the men . . ."

"Look, Mr. Alfedora, we need someone with office experience. Thanks for coming in, but the way I ran the ad, you remember . . ."

"Yes!"

He begins to grin again. He doesn't make any move to leave, so I turned my back on him for a while. But I don't hear any door slam, and then I hear this coughing. When I turn around he's waving a paper at me. It turns out to be a certificate from a business school he'd gone to he said for six months.

Well, I hired him. That's the mystery of it. Maybe it was the boss had given me the needle in the afternoon about being too particular. Maybe I thought he was just right for the job it was—you know, where he wouldn't think like someone else might that the job wasn't up to his qualifications. Hell, if he could get that worked up about screwing bulbs, he might think working an eight-phone monitor board and doing a little typing in Hector's Auto Service was already one foot in General Motors. Maybe it was the way he looked and talked about all that crap made me ...

Anyways, he started the next morning right on time. The first couple of days he was there I went out a lot on calls, and I couldn't show him the little things made up the routine we had in the office. So what happened these first few days I guess you could expect whenever someone new comes to a place. Little things got all screwed up, and you had to take time out to do it right again or explain it to him. But he'd forget what you said to him and ask again five minutes later. For instance, I had him typing out these Claims of Loss we have to do for the insurance companies. You have to fill in the name of the insured in three different places, and on the second day he was doing this, the particular lady's name was Frances M. Ryan.

"Mr. Luffin," he calls to me when I was on the telephone, "Mr. Luffin, is this Frances M. Ryan or is it Frances N. Ryan?"

"M for Mary," I tell him.

Five minutes later when he has to do the name the second time and I'm in the back of the shop getting the right color seat covers for a Chevy has to go by noon, there's Marvin crept up behind me when I didn't know anyone was there. He scared the ass off me. He says to me again, "Mr. Luffin, did you say Frances

M. Ryan or Frances N. Ryan?" So this time I yelled at him even though he never blinked an eye when you yelled at him, "I already told you! M. like in Mary!" When he asked me the third time I was in the can and reading the paper in the only minute I get to myself in the place. I hear him yelling at me through the door about the M and the N again. I yelled back at him to leave the goddamned thing out, they didn't need no middle initial.

He got the telephones mixed up on the first day. We have this little monitor board is nothing very complicated, but like everything else it's once you learn how. Marvin had me talking to the boss in his office upstairs and all the time the boss thought he was talking to one of the insurance brokers who had stopped sending us work for a couple of months. I thought I was talking to Cavanaugh from Allied Accessories that we stopped getting our radios from and were going direct to Motorola. We were at it maybe two minutes, me and the boss. He was talking to me in that greasy way he had for insurance guys. I was yelling at him the way you always have to with Cavanaugh. Otherwise he yells at you. After two minutes me and the boss caught on finally. He started in about the last insurance smoker, and I was yelling about the price for the six tube sets without pushbuttons. The boss had a fit about it the whole day, and I laughed with my wife about it at night.

But those were little things could maybe happen to anyone on a new job. I couldn't by the first few days even guess what we going to be in for. Marvin just worked out there in the office and no one paid him any particular attention except the shop guys could see he was somebody new and looked at him a little when they heard him talking. He came to work on time every morning. He wore starchy white shirts and a tie pin and cuff links and always kept his jacket on, but I didn't say anything about that. I figured he wanted to look like Herbert Hoover in Hector's Auto Service, it was all right with me.

He brought little things in every day to help him with his work, like a kid with school supplies the beginning of the term. He brought a cushion to sit on the first day. The next day he had another cushion for his back. He got one of them upright boards typists use to keep their copy on. Then he brought a paperweight with the snow inside when you turned it, and he brought five different kinds of lead pencils. He brought a calendar with one of those farms and snow on it and took down the one we had, the kind you'd find in any place like ours. He liked snow. So he'd sit there in the office with his enormous head, and those eyeglasses shining at one o'clock, and his big nose, and those little shoulders in his jacket, and starched shirt and tie, all propped up in his pillows and minding his work. He kept making little mistakes and nagging me with questions, but otherwise it was all right—for a while. Then one day it was near the end of his first week, and I'd been out all afternoon on calls. I came back near quitting time and there was Marvin in the office grinning at me. The office was different. What he did was he cleaned up a lot and moved some of the furniture around. It really looked a little better, maybe. So I told him, "Very good, Marvin." Something like that. I think that's when it all began, right after that.

First thing the next morning he has a few minutes free and tells me he's going around the shop. "I ought to familiarize myself with the work," he says. I tell him to keep out of trouble, but I thought it could be a good idea if he went. Maybe he could do some little things in the shop for me after a while.

It was at lunch time when Collela, he's the one mechanic we got, comes screaming to me about he was laying under the car getting the oil pan back on after he'd traced a leak in the bearings. He had only his feet sticking out under the car when this face comes under the door upside down and yells at him, "What are you doing?" Well, here was Marvin all dressed up, and Collela thought it was some kind of fire inspector caught him smoking under the car. So he tried to put out the cigarette before he crawled out. He hid the butt in his cuff and burned his ankle cause the cigarette wasn't out yet. Then he remembered seeing Marvin from the office. So he chased him all over with a wrench and at lunch he told me to keep the queer out of the shop or he'd call the union. So after lunch I was gonna sound off to Marvin when I hear him answering the phone.

"No, this is Marvin. I am taking Murray's place."

Maybe he answered the phone like that before, but this was the first I heard it. I told him he didn't have to say all that. All he hadda say was: hold on please, I'll get Mr. Luffin. Was it so hard to do? That same afternoon I'm in the office and the phone rings and there he goes again.

"This is Marvin. I am taking Murray's place."

"I just finished telling you not to say that!"

I yanked the phone out of his hand. I'm ready to have it out with him right then when he turns his big head to me and buzzes through his nose.

"You remarked yesterday that I was doing very well, Mr. Luffin."

"Well, you ain't today! When someone asks for Murray, just . . ."

"But the advertisement in the *Times* said the position was one with a future. I told you in our interview I was especially interested in a place that had a future for me."

"Never mind that! We were talking about the phone."

I try to stop yelling and make it plain to him again. After all, it got me a little sore. It was me was taking Murray's place—after six years. It finally comes out he heard the boss talking about opening another place in Westchester, and Marvin has figured out I would go there, and he would stay on to be the manager. He would be taking Murray's place. I told him be a good boy and just do what I said for him to do, and in a way he had a future there cause he could learn about the repair business if he kept his ears open and watched the work sometime. But he had to shut up and never bother the men in the shop. Again I said the wrong thing. Why couldn't I just tell him stick to the office or get the hell out?

It happened the next day. I was out to lunch. So was Collins. He'd been working on this '50 Olds a couple of hours tracing out the wiring on the signal lights. He had it all set up except he needed a new bulb in the right front parking lamp. Collins is a slob. A clock watcher too. Right on the tick of twelve he's out of the place no matter what he leaves in the middle of. Anyone else would take another five minutes and get the bulb in. Especially since the '50 Olds is hard to work on the way they put the wire junction block for the lights under the radiator baffle pans. It takes twenty minutes just getting them out of there before you even begin on the two hours it takes on the wires.

Well, what Marvin did in the morning was go back in the shop like I said he someday could and asked Collins what he was doing. When Collins clocked out just before I went to lunch I heard him tell Marvin, "She's all set." I was actually a little glad somebody in the place was talking to him. But what Marvin must've done was go back to the car and check the signal lights. When he saw they didn't work in the front right, he got at the junction block. He figured he was an electrician cause he plays with a radio at home. So he went to work. He did Collins' wiring all over again. He cut wires and he spliced them into other lines and then he saw he not only can't get the front right on, he can't even get the headlights on. Now it's time for Collins to get back from lunch. Soon's I come back from my lousy twenty minutes sandwich, Marvin says not a word to me and dives out to lunch. When Collins comes back the slob goes and puts the pans back on before he even tries the new bulb. Then after he gets the bulb in I pass by, and he's standing there next to the Olds scratching his head. He starts running back and forth between the dash and the front end scratching his stupid head. So I cursed him for putting the pans back on.

He swears on his mother his wiring was all set up, but there's nothing to do except he has to take off the pans again. I'm in the office when I hear him let out this yell. Like an old lady and a tom-cat might yell stepping on each other in the dark.

I figured right away it was Marvin. I waited for him to come back from lunch to fire him. It worked out I couldn't do it. Soon's he gets back to the office, there's Collins. He must've figured it out too, and he's got Marvin by the throat and shaking him up and down and Marvin's making dying noises. I had to grab hold of Collins and throw him out. So Collins wants to fight with me till I grabbed hold of a tire hammer and got him back into the shop telling him I was still running the place. I was the manager. I couldn't therefore fire Marvin right on the spot and make myself chicken to Collins. So that day close to quitting time I had a call on a wreck out in Brooklyn where we don't usually go. I figured I could tell Marvin in the car he didn't have to come back to work anymore. We'd mail him his check. I offered him a ride home. Just before we left someone calls up and once more he says it after what he'd done with those wires and after what I told him.

"This is Marvin. I am taking Murray's place."

That settled it. I waited till we got out in the street traffic and onto the West Side Highway. I didn't say anything until then, and Marvin didn't say boo neither. When I turned around to tell him, I thought he was dead.

He was scrunched up against the door. His little shoulders were sticking off the front of his neck, and his big head was way over the back of the seat. His mouth was half open. Under those binoculars, his eyeballs were rolled back somewhere inside his head. All you could see was the whites—the way people die. I started saying his name and looking for a place to pull the car over. All of a sudden he begins to snore. Out of that nose it was like the horn went off. I call his name, but he doesn't even move. I figure the hell with it. I'll get him up when I stop the car. "Good morning, Alfedora. You're fired."

The wreck was out in Flatbush. When I got off the Parkway and stopped for the first red light, Marvin's sitting straight up.

"I always fall asleep in a moving car," he says. "It has something to do with my thyroid. Once in the Army this officer— Oh, I live right around the corner from here, Mr. Luffin. Please come up to the house with me. My mother will be very happy to meet you."

"I gotta go to the wreck. Look, Marvin . . ."

"But I want to show you some things. We're right at my house."

Around the corner, and the second house is his—over a store. When he gets ready to open the door, I put my hand on his shoulder to hold him back. I nearly had him around the throat, there

177

was so little to his shoulder. I yanked him back. "Look, Marvin, about the job . . ." Then this old lady turns out to be his mother got her face in the window. She was smiling at me like I was some girl he brought home to marry. She must've been waiting on the street for him.

"She doesn't speak English very well," he says, "but I can talk to her for you."

They started yelling at each other in a language I never in my life heard anything like. It must have been from Turkey. Before I know it the old lady comes around my side of the car, opens the door, takes my hand, and pulls me out. She begins hugging me. Right out there in the street! She was a short old lady, but going around her was three Marvins. What the hell was I gonna do? Next thing you know I'm up in the house. I never in all my life smelled anything like what she had cooking for supper. It was steaming up the whole place. Marvin had to take those glasses off and wipe them down. How could I tell it to him now in his own house with the old lady there? And him smiling at me?

All right—I'd tell him tomorrow he was fired. Now the thing was to get out of there. But the old lady kept jabbering away in Turkey all the while she was blocking the door. I kept telling Marvin I had this wreck to go to before I started for home, but he kept standing there in the living room between me and the old lady and grinning, first at her, then at me.

Then Marvin says to me, "My mother wants you to come for supper with Mrs. Luffin."

Maybe I smiled. Then the old lady says something to Marvin and he right away yells at her. But I mean really screams. He pulls at his hair too. So she turns around and talks to me. I don't know what she's talking about. I really want to get the hell out of there. All over the wall they got these pictures in glass frames that must've been people in the family. But like a zoo. I mean, talk about ugly. One of the men's got a big mustache and those white eyes Marvin scared the hell out of me with in the car. She started screaming back at Marvin, so he takes my hand and leads me out of the room to where the closed door was.

"She thinks I should bring a lunchbox to work. She wants to ask you. Every night we argue about it. I try to explain to her this is not like my previous employment with the government. She doesn't understand about business."

The old lady followed after us to the closed door. So Marvin opened it and pulled me into the room and then slammed the door in her face. She must have been trying to pass me some signal the way she kept making faces when the door closed on her. And wringing her hands. And all the time Marvin is grinning.

This room I was in must've been his. If the language they talked and the food they cooked was nothing I ever heard or smelled before, this room with a bed in it was like nothing I ever saw before for sleeping. In one corner on the floor there was this TV set without a cabinet. In all the other corners on the floor there were radio sets that didn't have cabinets either. In the middle of the floor was this automobile engine! Laying all around it were these brand new socket wrenches. He grins at me. He sings it out.

"I am going to work on it!"

What could I say?

"And look at this!" he says.

He takes me over to the bed and picks up some of the books are on it. He shows them to me. They're all brand new, and all about automobiles. One was on office management.

"Look at this," he says. He walks around the engine and goes to a table's got all kinds of parts and tubes and wires and screws and old tools. He comes back with some sheets of paper with lines all over it. He puts it in my hand.

"How'd you get it up here?"

He looks at me stupid a minute, then he sees where I'm looking.

"Oh, that—the engine. I paid some movers to get it through the window. It was only ten dollars and the engine only cost ten. I had forty dollars left over for the books and tools. With next week's check I can buy a new suit. I notice you have no jacket under your white coat, but I would want to wear one. But how do you like that?" He pops these papers I'm holding and begins to grin at me again, his teeth in that way-back mouth like two racks of bones.

179

I didn't know what the papers were. There were all kinds of lines on them in different colors, the arrows, and numbers with marks for feet and inches. I said, "Looks like some kind of floor plan."

"Yes," he grins again. "Of the office and the first floor of the shop. Tomorrow on my lunch hour I will take the measurements for the second floor."

Right then I should've told him. "The only tomorrow for a nut like you is the booby hatch. You're fired!" I wanted to remind him we do body work, not mechanical stuff. What he needed in his room was a wrecked car he could bang on with a hammer while the old lady yelled at him in Turkey in between cooking that stuff I could still smell through the walls. I held out his floor plans for him to take back. I held them far out and turned my head away, and then he takes my other hand and starts shaking it up and down right over the engine.

"I want to thank you, Mr. Luffin," he says. "I look forward to our working together when Mr. Hector opens the new branch for the business. My mother is very encouraged. She worries since my father died that I won't be able to support her."

He lets go of my hand and takes the papers from me and moves away some of the junk on the table. He puts the papers down exactly in the corner. He smiles at the engine, then he smiles at his new books on the bed. When he started smiling at me I beat it for the door. I said something about the wreck I had to see.

I went where I remembered the stairs were, but they weren't there. I was near this other room where the door was open with a light on. The old lady was there. Before I could beat it she hauled me in. She was pointing at a picture and nodding her head and saying, "Hoozbahnd, Hoozbahnd, Hoozbahnd." It looked just like Marvin. It was the size of a subway poster. It wasn't on any wall but nailed across the whole damned window like a shade. She kept on pointing now to where Marvin was. She held my arm with the other hand and said things she must've thought was English about Marvin. She pointed to her chest and said, "sick, sick." The rest of it, I think, was about if she was gonna die, what was gonna happen to Marvin.

"No place. No bodee."

She kept saying it over and over. I tried to pull away my arm and tried not to look at the picture on the wall. Then Marvin came running in and screaming at her, and she started screaming back the way they did before about the lunchbox. Then she let go of my arm because she was all of a sudden hugging and kissing Marvin. I beat it.

I started right out for home and then hadda go back half the goddamned way when I remembered the wreck I'd forgotten about. I told my wife when I got home. One of the neighbors was over after supper, and we talked about it. I couldn't stop laughing. I really couldn't stop, tears and all. Before I went to sleep, I got sick. I really did. Maybe I remembered the smell of that cooking.

Anyways, it was Tuesday the next day and I was able to keep Marvin to Friday. I figured what the hell, we kept him till pay day it would make the books easier. Only the boss could fire him if I didn't, but the boss only made faces and noises in his throat. But he never told me to fire him. He never even told me after what happened with Jefferson, the colored guy on the second floor does car painting. On Marvin's lunch hour he actually went up there to measure out the second floor. He couldn't see Jeff is under the car getting the spray gun through to the other side, having to do it that way we're so jammed for space. Jeff went right to the boss instead of me even though I was up in the boss's office talking to him.

"He kept pokin' my ass under the car with that there yardstick. I almost busted my head on the muffler. You don't fire him there's a lotta men roun' here are gonna walk out that door on you. Why the hell don't somebody fire him?"

So a lot of the shop men were talking about him by now. When Jeff went out I could hardly look at the boss. I screwed on the first job of hiring I hadda do. But the boss didn't yell. It was like he was apologizing when he asked me why I couldn't get the guy to stay in the office. Why couldn't I get him to stop saying he was taking Murray's place on the telephone? Even one of the insurance guys came to me once and said, "That's a real nut you have in the office now," and said it like it was my fault. Not about how I had hired him, but like it was my fault he was a nut.

I fired him on Friday. I had to. Friday he drove us all crazy, and in the end it was like no one wanted the blame for firing him. He didn't even know all week that he isn't doing anything right and doesn't listen to a word you tell him. All the time he's in the office when he's not wandering around the shop, he keeps sitting propped up on his pillows, wearing his jacket with those little hook shoulders and the starched collars, and rearranging things every day on the desk, and buying more of them goddamned school supplies, and his glasses shining all the time at one o'clock, and his voice droning away on the telephone, still telling everyone he was Marvin taking Murray's place. I couldn't stand to hear him say that anymore. The way he kept saying *place*, like Murray's place was the name of a street. It made me sick. When I got home at night I started in about him until my wife yelled, "Shut up already about this crazy guy! Can't you talk about something else." But on Friday I fired him.

It's our worst day. All the cars we got in the place, the people want them for the weekend no matter what kind of work we got on them or when it was we towed them in. From three oclock on it's a booby hatch. I never get home on Fridays till maybe nine o'clock. I have to do last minute jobs on the cars, take care of the payroll, jockey the cars in and out of the jam we always got. Marvin started right off on this day about two o'clock with some Oriental. It was all I needed. The customers are beginning to pile up in the office and I hear the telephone going all the time and no one's answering it. There's Marvin and this Oriental turned out to be from the U.N. head to head over the counter. They're hollering at each other, and not hearing each other, and smiling all the time. I told Marvin get at the phones. I got the little Oriental aside and told him his car was ready. He kept on smiling and bowing the way they do, and then I went after Marvin and he tells me he was very interested in the Oriental. He asked the fellow how he could plant some Japanese cherry blossoms in front of his house. There wasn't room in front of his house, the way I remember, for planting one radish. There was nothing in front of his house except the pavement. The man didn't know what the hell Marvin was talking about anyway. He was a chauffeur and his boss was a U.N. delegate that had his car with us. Marvin didn't even know the man had a car there. Maybe he thought an Oriental would drop in on Friday afternoon just to talk about Japanese gardens with Marvin Alfedora.

By this time there was so much noise and rush in the office I was sure everything would get screwed up. I reminded Marvin they all had to sign their Proofs of Loss, and he had to get the deductible money from them before they drove the cars out. Then I hadda go back to the shop. Ten minutes later he comes after me on the floor to tell me a guy called up to say the parts were ready.

"What parts?"

"I thought you would know," he says.

So I have to run to the office and call up eight dealers that took twenty minutes before I got the one wants our driver to pick up hub caps on this Cadillac. A half hour later I'm out on the floor helping to get the roof on a convertible. There's Marvin again. He wants to know if we need Proof of Loss signatures on the cars come from out of state.

"Oh," he says, his face falling a little bit when I tell him sure I do.

"What do you mean?" I holler at him. "What car you talking about?"

"The New Mexico one."

"He didn't sign? Where is he?"

"He drove away. He said an out of state . . ."

"He didn't sign!"

"No. He said . . ."

"That was a nine-hundred-dollar job! New Mexico!"

183

I was running to the office, but that was the one thing Marvin had right. New Mexico was gone, and it would take us who knows how long tracking him down through the insurance company. So I wheeled on Marvin. I was ready to fire him right there in the office. But he wasn't in the office. I wanted to go after him, but the phones were going again. And there were all the customers piled up in the office I had to talk to, and then I hear Collins way back in the shop beginning to curse, and in two minutes the boss is next to me whistling under his breath, his face all purple.

"Fire him! Fire him! Right away you have to fire him before he puts me out of business."

Then he ran away. Then Johnny, the idiot errand boy ran in and tells me Marvin was back in the shop trying to get the cars all ready for me to jockey out, and he snapped the hood on these two cars Collins still had to put on the hood cable for. That's only ten minutes work, the cable, but it takes two hours if you have to open the hood there's no cable inside. And the customers are there yelling to Collins to hurry up, and he has to tell them it will be two hours more on each car. So I'm as mad as I can ever get, and I can't even go looking for Marvin I'm so busy. There's no one in the office now, and they're all yelling at me to get their cars out, so I have to go looking for him anyway to get someone on the telephone at least for a minute because the boss comes down to talk to the customers, smiling and singing, "We're short-handed today, gentlemen! We're short-handed!"

I took the elevator up to the second floor 'cause I didn't wanna pass Collins, but Marvin wasn't there. I find him way the hell up on the fourth floor. He's measuring again. With the goddamn yardstick, crawling around on his hands and knees cause it's where we keep all the wrecks we ain't started on and there's no room up there.

"I thought I would get out of the way," he says with this grin on his face. In one hand he's got those papers with the colored lines.

"The boss wants to see you right away in the office," I said.

The way he shot out of there for the staircase he must've thought I was leaving that afternoon for the place in Westchester we were never gonna have, and he was taking over here. I got even madder. I couldn't stand it the way he couldn't understand. I figured I was up on the fourth floor I'd find this Ford some guy downstairs was screaming for we hadda put a bumper on. I find the car all the way over in a corner and I'm trying to think the best way to jockey it to the elevator when Marvin's there again. It turns out the boss didn't tell him. That got me even madder. Who the hell was he we couldn't even fire him?

"Mr. Hector said I should see you. He said you had the information for me. What is it? What is it?"

He had to yell to where I was in the corner. I had to yell back. I told him.

"Your services are no longer necessary to our company, Mr. Alfedora."

I wasn't making fun of him. It just came out like that.

"What? Speak louder, please!"

"You're fired!"

"I am fired?"

"You're fired!"

"I don't understand. I have only tried to help the firm."

"Help? Do you know what the hell's going on downstairs? What you cost us already since you been here?"

"Oh. You mean that New Mexico car. But I have figured . . ."

"I mean everything! What's the matter with you, anyway? Every break I gave you! Why can't you be normal? Why can't you do anything right?"

"But I have done things right. I refused to take the lunchbox. I studied all night. You were there when . . ."

"I gotta move this car!"

"But I have never been fired. On my other two jobs I resigned."

"Then go resign! Quit! Get out of here!"

185

His head and neck were sticking up over the roof of one of the wrecks, and I could see his Adam's apple going up and down on his starched collar.

"All right. I will tell Mr. Hector I resign. I will tell him my place is better with radio and television. Electronics is a new place."

"Get out of here! Jesus, get out of here or I will go out of my head!"

"Goodbye, Mr. Luffin."

"Goodbye! Goodbye!"

He backs off toward the stairs. He waves at me all the time. He bumps into all the cars. That's the way I last saw him, going backwards down the stairs and waving to me.

I went crazy trying to straighten things out the rest of the day. I went home with my head split like an apple. I couldn't even watch TV. My wife says it was all my fault. I was the one hired him. That's the way I keep thinking about it now. I can't get it out of my head. I keep thinking all the mistakes crazy Marvin Alfedora made were my fault.

What for? I gave him every break. What did I ever do to him?

The new guy I hired is all right. He brags about his broads. He smells up his hair, and he whistles. But he does his work. He answers the phone and all he says is like he's supposed to, "Hector's, at your service."

But like I said, I still hear Marvin. Sometimes I even think I hear him creeping up on me when I'm working in the place somewhere, like he's moving around with his stupid yardstick in and out the wrecks.

THE MURAL AT CASTLEREAGH'S

When Ben Lewis was fifteen years old and in high school, he was failing his English course, so he made another of his many drawings of Ferris wheels and called it "Bessarabian Circles," and another drawing of the great crowd on the beach and called it "They Come Naked Near My House." He gave the drawings to his English teacher for her classroom, and the astonished woman rubbed out the titles with a soap eraser and then neatly printed "The Ferris Wheel" and "The Beach" and entered the drawings in a high school contest. Ben won the contest and added to his local fame; the teacher whose name he would forget would remember him forever, and Ben passed the English course with a respectable grade. When Ben was thirty-six and an artist, his talent was still used on occasion for extraordinary purchases, and he had lost none of his fondness for metaphor. Though he had long ago abandoned Ferris wheels and beaches and had turned now to the Bible, the titles he gave to the prints he made were still outlandish.

At this moment of a May evening he was working in his living room on the copper plate that was on his lap. He was cutting the third of the rams into the lower right hand corner and thinking vaguely of how Abraham would get into the title. The chair in which he sat, the one his father had made, was next to the best light in the room, but it was very uncomfortable, and Ben was not distressed when the phone rang. He carried the plate and the cutting tool with him when he went to answer the phone.

He smiled immediately. He put his hand over the mouthpiece and his lips formed for his wife the name Nehemiah. Maggie, who sprawled on the sofa, nodded, smiled, and returned to her book. Ben edged with the telephone toward the hallway, a maneuver which would relieve the self-consciousness he always felt before Maggie for his part in these conversations with Nehemiah. As usual, Nehemiah plunged in without a greeting.

"I have something very good for you, Benny."

"Nem, I listen," Ben said.

Nehemiah switched to the doleful voice he reserved for heavy matters of business. The tone was full of caution and misgivings.

"It's going to be a very high class job, Benny. A very large item."

Ben said what he always did. "Do you have anyone in New Haven who could do it better?" He looked toward the living room, but Maggie was out of his vision.

"I know, Benny, I know. Who was the one in high school went around tellin' everybody it's Benny's the one got it in his fingers?"

Everyone in high school had said something of this sort about Ben, and Ben had not really known Nehemiah in high school. It was simply another of the little legends which had been manufactured between Nehemiah and himself, so Ben responded, "It was you, Nem."

"So now I got something very big and very good for you."

"I listen, Nem."

"It's a deadline and it's a very big item. Two weeks, Benny. Can you deliver for me?"

"For you, Nem, I'll go night and day."

There was a slight pause and then Nehemiah said, "That's equitable."

Ben smiled. He saw Nehemiah's mournful mouth as it calculated the precise word, prepared it, rolled it, and then released it over the phone : equitable.

"The particulars, Nem?"

188

"First, I have to ask, and you should answer me frankly, Benny. How are you on trees?"

"On trees? Wonderful, Nem."

"And castles?"

"Also wonderful."

"And all the other crap—some horses and knights and maybe a few coats of arms?"

"With my eyes closed. What are we doing?"

"So, good! We got a deal. We can go right away. It's a restaurant will be on the Derby Road near the Yale Bowl. He's ready to open in three weeks. He's real crazy for it to look like an English manor house or something. He's got royal blood you'll hear the way he talks. He . . ."

"A mural, Nem?"

"Forty by six. You can do it in two weeks?"

"That's a lot of feet. But I'll go night and day for you. How much, Nem?"

"We'll work it out it should be mutually *equitable* for us."

"It'll be a lot of work."

"Look, Benny, I'll tell you right away there's money here. He's a Castlerech."

Nehemiah hacked against the last syllable as though it were a fishbone he had swallowed.

"He's what?"

"A Castle*rech*!" Nehemiah roared. "A regular Castle, then r-e-a-g-h. Castle*rech*!"

Ben had to take the phone from his ear. "Nem, you'll choke yourself. I never heard of him."

There was a pause, and when Nehemiah resumed, his voice, with all the old regret, unfurled like a banner for his people.

"You never heard the name? Benny, I'm surprised. A cultured fellow like you? In England it's a very big name. One of 'em was a viscount, a Marquis of Londonderry."

He pronounced it Marcus, but Ben frowned at the turn the conversation had taken. Too often in the recent past it lay between

Nehemiah and himself, these little departures, these little dead ends in the middle of the ways they should have maintained for their conversations. Nehemiah sensed the danger.

"You'll come to the shop, Benny? Tomorrow? At your convenience?"

"First thing."

"Fine! As long as it shouldn't interfere with things at your place. How are things at your place?"

"Fine."

Nehemiah, whenever he spoke to Ben of Yale, where Ben taught drawing, referred to it as your place.

"As long as you shouldn't struggle," Nehemiah approved. "Then I'll see you tomorrow, Benny?"

"Tomorrow. But forty by six in two weeks . . ."

"So tomorrow we'll talk everything over. You'll say my greetings to Maggie?"

"Yes."

"A lovely girl, Benny, we talk sometimes on the phone you're not in."

"Yes."

"And the boy is all right? I sometimes can hear him on the phone. What's his name again—Kevin?"

"Yes."

"So tomorrow. You're sure it'll be all right with the trees? You'll make the plain regular English ones?"

"I told you all right."

"So, all right. All right! Tomorrow."

Ben heard the click of Nehemiah's phone. They never said goodbye. It was as though some aspect of their conversations could not risk the farewells. Ben, still holding the copper plate and the cutting tool, returned to the living room, to the absurd lyre-backed Sheraton chair his father had made with the great skill of old country hands and a false, rootless taste. Maggie had already put the book aside and was sitting up on the sofa. She knew the mild irritation that was apt to be Ben's final mood in the recent conversations with Nehemiah, but she imagined it was only a matter of the time he had to give up for the work he disliked to do for the extra money he had to earn. She tried to smile.

"What's the word of the week?"

"Equitable."

"It was beneficial the last time." She raised an eyebrow. "And the job?"

"Three hundred I guess. Maybe three and a half."

Ben shrugged, and then he dug deeply with the tool into the plate at the horn of one of the rams. Maggie had already returned to the novel, but she looked up to blink when Ben, without raising his head from his work, said simply, " 'Abraham Loves Isaac.' I'll call it that."

Neither Ben nor Nehemiah was a native of New Haven, and the high school to which Nehemiah always referred was in Brooklyn. But Brooklyn was long ago for both of them, and Ben himself had come to New Haven almost two years ago from Spain, not from Brooklyn. He was driving on Goffe Street about a year after he arrived and waiting at an intersection of a Negro neighborhood for a change of light. It was then that he saw the name painted on a store window: Nehemiah Carp; and over it, in larger letters: Restaurant Interiors. It was one of those Brooklyn names from long ago he had never forgotten. Tessie Pepe, Marvin Alfedora, Herschel Schreck. He remembered nothing of them but the names, but it pleased him when the names came unexpectedly to his mind. He imagined the recollection was a gesture toward that community spirit he totally lacked. But Ben drove on and quickly recovered from the little shock that someone whose name he remembered from high school was here in New Haven. It occurred to him that he might call up Nehemiah and say hello, but he never did. It was Nehemiah who called, and he called at Yale. It was all rather uncanny, for only a week had passed since Ben had first seen the name.

"Is this Professor Lewis?"

"This is Mr. Lewis."

"This is Nehemiah Carp."

Elaborately formal, Nehemiah proceeded to unravel identifications: the high school, teachers, a stage design they had worked on together. Ben remembered nothing, but Nehemiah asked to meet him in the bar of the Hotel Taft. Ben deferred to a heavy schedule and Nehemiah paused. Then he spoke with even more formality, but ambiguously, about a matter of business.

When they met, Ben still failed to remember him. He was short and boneless and dark, and had a mournful mouth and very black, groomed and wavy hair. Ben ordered a martini and Nehemiah asked for a shot of whiskey which he swallowed in a gulp, throwing back his head and shuddering when it went down. He did not order again, and while Ben sipped at the martini Nehemiah drummed on the table with his hairy, pudgy fingers.

The meeting could have been worse. Nehemiah dragged in nothing about the other years. He knew of Ben's work, had seen his show at the Yale Gallery after reading of it in the *Register*. The other day he had seen a poster on Christian Missions outside the Congregational Church. There was an unsigned drawing on it he had identified immediately as Ben's, and if Ben didn't too much mind that sort of thing—Nehemiah lowered his eyes at the difficulty—then they could perhaps, every once in a while, work together at something that would bring some extra money to Ben. Nehemiah handled it very delicately. The word money slipped from a net of polite expressions, and then, quickly, was hauled back.

Nehemiah had a habit of tilting his head and then winking when he established a certain point, as if he approved of his listener's cunning as well as his own. When he confessed that restaurant interiors were his business and then added, "that kind of crap," he made the gesture. It was then that Ben remembered him. He remembered a melancholy, self-debasing boy in high school who worked stubbornly at his drawings and then tilted his head and winked when he was told they were no good. Suddenly Ben knew that Nehemiah was rich. All the little Michelangelos he had ever known who had turned to something artsy-craftsy were now rich.

Nehemiah pledged that when something good turned up he would call Ben. For a month nothing turned up but he called Ben anyway, about twice a week and always at Yale. The conversations were brief and Nehemiah was still very formal. Apparently he only wanted to inform Ben that nothing as yet had turned up, but once he talked hesitantly of a party at his house, some old friends from Brooklyn. Ben said nothing inquisitive and the matter was quickly dropped. At the end of the month Nehemiah finally had a little work for Ben, and Ben, after classes, went out to Nehemiah's shop on Goffe Street.

It was a preposterous junk house and a different Nehemiah Carp. He danced capers like a court jester. He tumbled toward the door to greet Ben and he hauled him in, pumping Ben's arm in the first handshake that passed between them, tugging him by the clasped hand in and out of the spaces that could be found on the junk-strewn floor. There was lumber of all sizes and unmatched pieces of furniture and cartons of tiles and tilting decks of tiles that were not even in cartons and foam rubber and barrels of kapok and feathers and baskets of sheepskins and coils of rope and bundles of masks and overturned statuettes. There were shelves along the walls that sagged with rolls of wallpaper and cans of paint. Tools of all sorts lay on tables, and in a corner that was almost utterly dark and with no bulb near it anywhere that could give it light, there was a power saw, and a power drill, and something else that might have been a sewing machine.

"There's a cellar and an upstairs too!" Nehemiah sang.

Ben detected a slight shift of manner in Nehemiah's voice. When Nehemiah swooped into his monologue, the dialect became so obvious that Ben realized for the first time how Nehemiah's speech, until now, in the hotel and over the phone, had been almost faultless. Now Nehemiah stood in the middle of the junk-strewn floor and his kind of Brooklyn rose into his voice like a call to arms.

"So here it is, my fake shop. For every fake in Connecticut wants a showplace out of his restaurant, for such a fake I have something here. He wants for instance a Singapore room, I got enough bamboo strips in the cellar I could make a curtain would cover the Yale Bowl. Upstairs I got a staple gun is the size of a cannon, so with a bang-bang I can give him a Singapore room. And if he wants instead a Zanzibar den, I got African masks in the cellar from Greenwich Village. I get 'em a dozen for thirty-two fifty. So I make him wait a month and he starts to holler where are the masks and I tell him the natives are knockin' 'em out in Africa, he should have patience it takes a while. I get fifteen dollars a piece for the masks alone. Upstairs and downstairs and on this floor I have for everything. I got Indian feathers and wagon wheels and muskets and scabbards and mermaids' tails and whole fishes, is a very big thing now, fishes. I got cornucopias and I got elephant tusks I make 'em on the lathe out of birch trees. I got Japanese lanterns and Australian boomerangs and pictures of naked women would decorate a whole ceiling, each breast is like a zeppelin. And I can also make a little zeppelin for an airport restaurant, and I got stuffed birds, and for the Yalees I got even stuffed bulldogs. You would be surprised how in New Haven it's so easy to pick up a dead bulldog. And I got also in the cellar . . . So what's the use I should go on? I could tell you only from all this crap I live. I live pretty good. You'll have to see the house someday I got in Woodbridge they had it in the magazines."

He stopped abruptly and turned on Ben. He swallowed once, as though some device in his throat shifted gears, and then his voice slipped into mournful reverence.

"Benny, I saw your show in the Yale Gallery. The prints were something terrific."

Ben was a normally restrained, even inhibited man, but he had roared with laughter. He knew that Nehemiah had cast his accents at last for the high school years, for the Brooklyn boy who was an artist and taught at Yale, but Ben could not stop laughing. He doubled up with it. Unwilling in the past, wherever he had been, to accept such overtures from the Nehemiahs he ran into everywhere, denying that anyone else's sense of loss could resemble his own, he had rejected what he always described to Maggie as the delicatessen mentality. But New Haven had become something different from all the other places, and Nehemiah Carp had made his pitch and Ben had acquiesced. Before he left the junk shop he took with him the little job of hand painted tiles to be set in a bar top that was to take him three hours and for which he would get sixty dollars. His uprooting must have been more calamitous than he suspected. The cadences of Nehemiah's speech, more than his self-abuse, more than his praise, reached out warmly to Ben. And Nehemiah himself must have guessed that Ben's laughter lived around the edges of a rich regret, for he had tilted his head and winked.

When Ben's father came to America he told the immigration officer that his name was Lubovowitz. The officer, without looking up from the form on which he wrote, said. "You think I'll spell some goddamned name like that? Your name is Lewis."

He was already thirty-four, but the man took the new name with a shrug, as he was to take all the hazards of his life with the same historic shrug. Because he had a relative there, he opened his unprofitable furniture repair shop in Coney Island and he shrugged at the bizarreness of the new world around him. Two daughters and the son Ben came to him, and when the man was confronted with the extraordinary talent the boy already showed at ten, he shrugged, guessing the son would have to go his own way. So he shrugged again when Ben took the scholarship to Cooper Union and left Coney Island for the windowless rooms of Greenwich Village. It was the same gesture when the man's wife died, though he did lament that she would have been happier to have been buried in Kishinev. And when Ben, already teaching a course at the Art Students League where he met Maggie, phoned his father to say he was getting married, he really expected that the man would shrug. He was surprised when his father exclaimed into the telephone: "What's her name? Halloran?" Though he did not attend the civil ceremony, he must have finally shrugged, for he was already seventy and he went to work on the Sheraton chair which took him three weeks to make.

There would be times when Ben regretted the fateful resignation of his father. It made things too painless for Ben—unopposed, unrecalled. From his earliest adolescence he knew that he would leave the Coney Island he loved to draw pictures of. Given over to summer amusements, the place had to be temporary, but he was to imagine later that the leave-taking should have been harder than it was. Together with Maggie he was to begin a series of familiar enough journeys: teaching jobs and fellowships took them to Idaho, to Italy, to Kentucky, and then to Italy again and a final year in Spain before Yale. He was worldly enough to dismiss provincial misgivings, but he sometimes thought there should have been more anguish than there actually was. There should have been some calamity in having their only child, a son, born in Amalfi, of all unlikely places. But there never was. Ben simply lacked an austere enough sense of place, of knowledge he had forsworn, of a father he had not even overthrown. When his father died, and they learned of it in Amalfi just before Kevin's birth, it was too easy for Ben himself to shrug, to let the relatives attend to the funeral, to send telegrams of easy consolation to his married sisters, now in Los Angeles. Perhaps that was why Ben kept the old man's chair with them wherever they went, kept a gayly painted crate decorated with steamship stickers—that they otherwise used for an end table—for the very purpose of shipping the chair. Against the classic resignation of his kind of father, Ben needed some tangible evidence of something that had once actually lived for him and was now lost.

Perhaps it had been too easy for him also because—like Coney Island—all the other places had been temporary. When there was no real prospect of staying on, there was no reason to contemplate what had ever been left. With New Haven and Yale there was at last the threat of permanence, and Ben, for the first time, had something to contend with. He was about to build a world for himself, and it had nothing to do with the only other world he had ever really known. The distance between Coney Island and Yale was comic, and Ben, homeless for so long, had gone into the Yale world with a vengeance. It was a strange design for an artist to luxuriate in: the cocktail parties, Ivy league games in the Bowl, bull sessions with colleagues at the Faculty Club, the fake Gothic architecture, the money, the certainties, the very faces of his students. But sometimes, suddenly, in the midst of any one of these pleasures, Ben would draw away in shock at the new thing he confronted, and he would reach out in a blurred pity for the man who had left his Bessarabia at thirty-four to surrender his name on a Hoboken pier and live forever in Coney Island, and he reached out in anger too. Sometimes, but never expressed, he would divert the anger against Yale. And in the prints of peculiar Bible scenes he had taken to making, there was something enormously fugitive, a frivolity of lines that could have suggested the loss of Ferris wheels and carousels and boorish, naked people near his house.

Perhaps what Ben really needed was the better part of two worlds, something of the old place that would not yet force him back there, and just that much of Yale as he could afford, as would tolerate the other thing. He might have guessed that only something fake and itself uprooted could satisfy a need so impossible, even so fake.

Out of this need Ben had laughed on that first day in Nehemiah's shop. In the nine months between then and the mural at Castlereagh's before them now, they had gone the inevitable road. Soon enough it had become Benny and Nem, and their conversations were manufactured like a notorious conspiracy against the Yale Ben never spoke of and Nehemiah always inquired for. It was obvious to Ben that Nehemiah saw in him an entry into Yale, and equally obvious that Nehemiah wanted Yale because he was in New Haven and because he believed he had long ago betrayed, not himself, but the world of art and high seriousness. He had made his own short journey from Brooklyn to New Haven fourteen years ago to be a stagehand at the Schubert Theater with the vague hope of coming back to New York as a stage designer. But he met Sandra Berg, married her, and allowed her father to put him into business. He made a small fortune of his own, but he fanned a great lust for the uncertain thing he imagined he had lost.

197

But Ben, insistent upon the separation of his two worlds, had so far been useless to him. Ben ignored invitations, remained blank to overtures. So Nehemiah had recently devised his own little ways of striking back. He did not give up on what he wanted, but as he began to see its possibilities diminish, he occasionally provoked his Yale friend with a cruelty he believed to be no greater than Ben's. He not only of late properly reminded Ben of another world, but he sometimes tried, obliquely, awkwardly, to suggest that Ben, a Jewish boy from Coney Island, had no right to any other world, especially Yale. If it was cruel it was also too obvious, too simple. He mistook entirely the metaphoric nature of Ben's regrets.

But such lapses had so far been mild and occasional, and they were the only expense the relationship amounted to for Ben. He did the sham work, he pocketed the money that helped pay off the debts accumulated in the years of travel, and enjoyed the vaguer consolations: the laughter and the regret, the unexpressed kind of conspiracy against Yale which he actually needed, and sometimes, on the very rare good times, a precise sense of something renounced that his shrugging father had never been able to supply. And that last stroke—it was the least expensive of all. The mournful, boneless Nehemiah was anything but the image of a father. Above all, Ben knew that between them it was all fake enough to be a momentary bulwark, fake enough to be a temporary amusement.

The three of them at Castlereagh's were like a vaudeville act. Nehemiah, whenever it was necessary to have Ben present before a client, dressed the part of an entrepreneur: a pin-striped blue suit with the jacket open to reveal the too tight, buttoned vest on the highest mound of which he stored the pudgy hands, the hairy fingers interlocked, the thumbs free to twiddle in idle satisfaction and management. But all of that and even the groomed and wavy hair could not relieve the mournful mouth, the little soft man's professional melancholy. Beside him before the bar stood Ben, who was taller, and thin enough to be almost emaciated, and with a slight slipping of his shoulders, a marked depression of chest and a sallow complexion, and a bent nose and stern mouth that made him look almost like an American Indian destroyed by a liver ailment. He had a crew cut and wore a tweed jacket with leather elbow patches. Finally there was Castlereagh. He stood behind the bar with a tumbler full of Scotch in his hand, quite drunk, but like the alcoholic he was, quite coherent. He was a big man, heavy now who must have been only broad once. He had silver hair and a trim silver mustache beneath a great hawk nose that could have been broken in a fight, though his eyes were gentle, blue and constantly watering behind his rimless glasses. His skin was as white as his hair, but there were little petals of scarlet in his cheeks. He blinked dubiously at the twosome before him and then swept the hand that held the Scotch toward the long blank wall where the mural was to be hung. When he spoke the accent was so transparently British that Ben knew him immediately for what he was, and for an alarming moment he suspected it could even be Brooklyn.

"And you're the artist bloke's goin' to do me the battle on that wall's out of Henry the Fifth. Eight times I saw that film, I did. Eight times! I got all the bleedin' photos you'll need to copy it from. I got them right . . ." and his voice disappeared as he swept the hand with the Scotch somewhere else and then raised a finger of the other hand to wipe with it beneath his glasses and peer more steadily at Ben, who had already turned to Nehemiah, who had already tilted his head and winked at Ben.

They had all the props they needed for a vaudeville act too. Above the door where they had entered were two crossed metallic lances, and there were flanking pairs of wooden lances in upright sentry at the waiters' doors to the kitchen. There were herald's trumpets angled out of the corners of the wall, and down the length and across the width of the high ceiling there was a patchwork of dark timbers that should have been hewn oak and that Ben guessed were made of cardboard, creosote, and bang-bang staples. Mounted on the wall opposite to where the mural would be were the torsos of the knights, in coats of mail and helmets. There were four of them and Ben knew they would hang there, faceless, to stare blankly at his mural for as long as Nehemiah's glue lasted. Ben stared at them in disbelief, which Nehemiah thought was awe, so he took his hands from the mound of his vest and with an arm against the small of Ben's back he swept Ben to the wall of the knights where they could look up for a closer view and were out of the hearing of Castlereagh, who had finally dived below the bar to rummage for his bleedin' photos. Nehemiah whispered, looking at Ben and not at the knights.

"Underneath there's a sweatshirt, I stuffed it with old newspapers and sometimes a telephone book should put a little spine in him. The helmet is from sheet metal with silver paint and underneath is one of those heads from a millinery. And the coat of mail? Benny, make a guess."

"Nem, I wouldn't dare."

"Go ahead, guess."

"Staples."

"A sardine net, I let it soak in the glue barrel and painted it silver."

Ben nodded toward the bar. "He knows?"

"Him? What should he know? He knows dead knights is one thing I don't have in the shop, and for real armor who would come to me?"

Castlereagh reappeared behind the bar and said loudly, though to himself, "Here's the goddamned things!" His glass was empty and he was groping for the bottle on the bar as he thumbed the photos, gazed at them as a soldier would at the family snapshot, shuffled them in one huge hand. Ben submitted to a disarming shame, almost sorrow, for the man's ways. He turned to the wall of the knights again and lowered his head to whisper at Nehemiah.

"Where's your Marcus from?"

"Marcus?" Nehemiah repeated blankly and then recovered. "Oh, you mean the Marcus! From Boston yet. Don't let on you know. He talks nice, hah? Come over here with me a minute you can maybe give me an idea."

He led Ben past the bar and Castlereagh, who had found the

Scotch and was drinking and staring suspiciously above the glass at them as they walked to a table near the wall where the mural would be. Nehemiah, grunting, pushed aside the heavy table, which was of oak, and pointed to what had been lying underneath: swords and picks and maces and halberds.

"This crap you'll have an idea maybe what I can do with I hadda put the table over it. You know, a man could fall down in here and whissht!" Nehemiah snapped his soft wrist, "Like that he could lose his manhood. Castrated!"

Ben smiled. "To lose it in here, Nem, he doesn't have to fall down."

Nehemiah grinned, shrugged, made a vague gesture with his hand, and then suddenly whipped his head to search Ben's face. But Castlereagh was there to rescue them. He had lumbered after them with the photos, which he extended now to Ben with an insistent smile. His teeth were dark and decaying, and Ben was unprepared for it; the hair was that silver, the mustache so trim. He regretted the remark he could not have helped but make to Nehemiah, and fearing now that the day might turn on him and leave him a victim to the classes he still had to teach, he tried to retrieve through Castlereagh that original spirit which would carry him through, which alone seemed to justify all of it. He did not even take the proffered photos. He turned instead to the blank wall and he could hear the cadence of his speech even before it became speech.

"You really want all that cowboy and Indian crap up there? Forty feet of it and underneath where people are going to have to sit and eat?"

Castlereagh's eyes opened wide and his jaw sagged. Nehemiah, who always left to Ben the haggling for the details of the work Ben himself was to do, smiled quickly, as though he, too, at the sound of Ben's voice, had been reassured. But slowly the smile slipped away and the lower lip drooped mournfully. He took a sword and a mace from the pile, and the pin-striped figure, as though in war, waddled toward the wall of the knights.

It got increasingly hard for Ben, and the spirit he sought for eluded him. It was not that Castlereagh was for so long adamant, but that he was entirely baffled. He could not understand Ben's point, and he interrupted constantly to flourish the photos, to assert the goddamned bloody film he had seen eight times, and Ben began to feel he struggled with some substantial invention of a man's life, held in his hand in glossy photos of white horses and virile men seen through the mist of watery eyes and the ceaseless Scotch. It was strange how little Castlereagh's accent irritated, and Ben experienced this vague pain for the clumsy man who swung his head in circles to stare from the photos to the blank wall to Ben. There was something austere about the man's unremitting fakery, and Ben slipped imperceptibly out of the ritualized speech that the spirit of his relations with Nehemiah demanded. Finally they were able to settle for a pastoral scene of castles for the wall, and heraldic shields to be hung from the beams. It was then, after they had agreed, that Castlereagh swept his arm toward the restaurant in a gesture that could have included all of them, as well as everything.

"I ain't the one to say it ain't all a bit of a fake. But you'll do a dandy job on these castles for me, won't you now? If it's all right then maybe you can do Agincourt for me from these here photos. For my house or something, you know."

Nehemiah came back to them toting the weapons. He tossed them on the pile and Ben and Castlereagh leaped at the ringing clatter. Nehemiah was smiling when he turned toward them and declaimed into the echo of the crashing armory.

"He'll do you a mural, Castlerech, will put England right here for you in your New Haven restaurant you wouldn't have to ever go home again it's such a trip across the ocean. Wait, you'll see how equitable it'll be for all of us. Only the best in the business make walls for Nehemiah Carp's Restaurant Interiors."

When they were outside and Nehemiah had closed the door behind him he said at once, "Benny, I'll give you four hundred for the job."

Ben said nothing. He was trying to shake off the distress which had started with the imagination he should not have allowed himself in Castlereagh's. He knew Nehemiah would talk inside his new Buick station wagon, for he drove in a constant panic and worked it off in the nervousness of his own voice.

"I apologize it had to take so long with him, Benny. From all that about his Hen-ery and his pictures you could get a little sick. You remember last night on the telephone I asked you about the castles and the trees. I knew already it would end like this, didn't I?"

"Last night you were convinced he was an English Duke."

"A Marcus. But on the telephone. You know us on the telephone, Benny." Nehemiah had no trust in mirrors, and when he changed lanes he twisted his head like a bird and bulged his eyes to see the traffic behind him, and then he went on. "In Boston, you know, he was a buyer for one of those shops. What do they call 'em around your place? Men's furnishers? So sometimes they used to send him to England the American clothes aren't good enough for the fakers. Also he's got a son met a Limey girl in the war and stayed over there. Also I got it on good advice he's an orphan so the name he must've made up when he was a kid already. And the little extra money he made in the stock market he couldn't lose with such a name, and so he wants to make an English restaurant, but in America, not in England."

Ben was looking straight ahead, but he knew that Nehemiah had tilted his head and winked. Ben should have maintained his part, but the day had gone completely sour.

"Do you enjoy it?" he challenged pointlessly. "I mean, being a detective."

Nehemiah was innocent. "Ah, Benny. With everybody I do business with I have to find out. I gotta know he can meet the expenses. I mean when we start out he should have it to cover what it's going to cost him."

Ben turned on him, his sallow cheeks flushing with his anger. He said the obvious thing at last, what he could least afford to say.

"What do you want, Nehemiah?"

"What do I want?" Nehemiah blinked. "What do you mean,

Benny, what I want? What do you want? What does anyone want?"

"What do you want from *me*, Nehemiah?"

"From you? What should I want from you? What's the matter, Benny? Between us it's all a joke. Ah, look, look over there, Benny. Look at your place." He pointed with his arm out the window toward the Yale Bowl. He read from what was painted above one of the entryways, and made it sound vaguely like a Yiddish slur. " 'Portal Fourteen.' Anywhere else in America they call it a gate. Benny, tell me—you said something before it was about manhood. And you're not afraid in your place you could lose your manhood, also without falling down?"

If Nehemiah had again tilted his head and winked, Ben would have quit right there. He would not even have done the mural for Castlereagh's. But Nehemiah stared through the windshield and bulged his eyes at the traffic. Ben was no good at this sort of thing. He plunged toward the disaster.

"I wish I could help you. I wish they taught restaurant interiors and you could join the faculty."

Nehemiah shrugged and waved a hand and muttered something incoherent about the taste of martinis. They drove in silence the rest of the short way to Nehemiah's shop, and in silence they got the materials Ben would need for the job, and silently they carried them to Ben's car that had been parked outside the shop. When Ben got behind the wheel, Nehemiah stood for a moment at the door beside him. He said something about Castlereagh opening in two weeks and there wasn't much time. He spoke in an almost proper syntax, and his tone was mournful enough to be rabbinical. Then he shook his head and bit his lip. He stretched his arms out, one toward his shop and the other toward what could have been New Haven or Yale or everything.

"Ah, Benny," he chanted. "Why? Why? It was that Irishman's fault. In the middle of all this, between us there should be—Ah Benny! Two Jewish boys here from the same high school in Brooklyn, there should be love!"

Ben suffered through his class that afternoon. Several times he faltered during the brief lecture before he set them loose on their drawings. It was May, and the students—so bland and unmarked—were already looking forward to home and the pleasures of their summer. He heard himself holding forth on the way in which the drawn line, isolated from the continuity of the form which it helped compose, had to be determined by the way in which it excluded space as well as from the more obvious ways in which it included form. He had said the same thing before other classes, but now the words galled him and he wondered what they meant. He only wanted of them that they draw a decent picture, no more, it seemed to him, than he had ever wanted of himself. More than ever the voice in which he spoke seemed disembodied, lost in borrowed accents of language he had heard in the places he had been. He imagined Nehemiah in the room, nodding his head mournfully, waiting to shout to all the Yalees that the artist to whom they listened, whose work they stood in awe of, that he was Nem's little Benny.

"From high school I know him. On trees and castles he's wonderful. Only the best in the business. He'll go night and day for me."

Before Ben went home he stopped at the library. He took out Boutell's *Manual of Heraldry*, two illustrated Waverley novels, and a volume on the lake country. It was a short way home to the block of decaying brownstones where they had rented cheaply from the University in the dimming shadow of the great Whitney Gymnasium, and Ben, oppressed by the work which stretched before him for the next two weeks, sketched the argument he would probably have with Maggie, tolerant, literal Maggie.

It was about rams, finally. It started after Kevin was put to bed and they talked of the debts that were to be paid out of the four hundred dollars. They decided to cheat a little and cheered themselves with how they might spend the fifty dollars they would withhold. Maggie wanted a party—they owed an evening to so many—but Ben said he needed his time for the damned mural and she'd do better to be thinking of how to keep all of them out of the house instead of screaming for them to come on up. He hadn't even time for his own work and had long ago to postpone painting, paying as he still was for all the goddamned wandering they had done, as though it were Maggie who had won the the *Prix de Rome*. He retreated finally, offering as excuse an upsetting day with the patron saint from Brooklyn. He summarized it too vaguely, and Maggie inclined toward Nehemiah, imagining it all had to do with a choice of loyalty between Nehemiah and Castlereagh. They quibbled about Castlereagh until Ben didn't know how Castlereagh had gotten into it all. That's when he went for the copper plates and sat down to work on it at the kitchen table, while Maggie continued with her cup of coffee. When she looked up at him and simply said, "Another Bible one?" she had it in mind that some comment about his work might still retrieve the evening. Ben glared at her.

"So what? If you start that hunting for relatives routine again . . ."

"Now listen, why are you so . . ."

"What made you say it anyway? How do you know it'll have anything to do with the Bible? There's nothing here but some rams."

"They're Biblical rams," she pouted.

"What the hell does that mean, they're Biblical rams? If I make some rams, I make some rams. They still have rams you know."

"And they have rams in the Bible too, and you've been on a Bible kick ever since Kevin was born. So I just said . . ."

"You wouldn't know a ram if it walked through the door."

"Oh, but you saw a lot of them in Coney Island!" Maggie sneered, giving up her hopes for the evening.

"Just as many as you ever saw in Detroit."

"What I was able to see in Detroit you . . ."

"Look, a ram's a ram, dammit!"

Ben, of all people, should have known better. Addicted as he was to metaphor, a ram in one of his pictures was many things more than a ram, though he would never know exactly what else it ever was. His outburst was only a perfunctory way of ending the evening of a day that had already died in the morning, and he carried the copper plate and the cutting tool up to the narrow attic he had made into a studio of sorts. He carried with him also the image of Maggie in her anger, how Irish it was, how remote from him it made her.

They had married a month after meeting at the Art Students League, where she was making innocently exact charcoal figures in the one class Ben taught. But Maggie Halloran did not have to telephone her parents in Detroit to hear them say "What's his name?" When she left for New York she took with her the traditional final slam to the front door, and the three letters she was to write would go unanswered. Ben knew some of the stories of her ways in New York and guessed that she married him as the last in a series of enormous deviations from the Hallorans of Detroit. But she was a beautiful girl of honey-colored hair and pale complexion, high-boned cheeks and the calm, devotional mouth of a nun. Ben was aware of his own cadaverous figure, and he believed sometimes that she had married his work and hoped that she might grow accustomed to him, for she had said "My God!" when she looked for the first time at his drawings. He was never to make up his mind whether it was the one real triumph or the definite failure of his life, for it was always his work that purchased and redeemed everything. But most importantly Maggie had kept Ben sane by her literal ways. She abhorred those very extravagances of religion which alone of all the religious possibilities appealed to him, but she kept the parched flowers of her confirmation pressed in the dictionary. She wanted the name Kevin for their son because it was her father's name and she knew he had been a beautiful boy, but nothing more than the practical clumsiness of their wanderings had ever disturbed her. She enjoyed Italy because the Italians were so Italian, and in Spain the Spaniards were Spanish, and Kentucky had been full of Southerners. Often had wanted to invite Nehemiah and his wife, just to see him, she argued, and to find out some things about Ben in high school. "I never knew him in high school," Ben would explain again, and she would quell him with the final lucidity of her mind: "He would know something anyway."

Ben carried that to the attic with him too, images of Nehemiah and Castlereagh. He worked late into the night and, stubbornly, for the rest of the week on the print. Nehemiah didn't call him once for what should have been the usual rigamarole about the progress of the mural. Once Maggie prodded him about it and he flared. "I'm in the middle of something else! Why don't you take the kid to the Baldwins'?" He was always urging her to take Kevin to Dale Baldwin's, who raised horses and his children on a farm when he wasn't teaching Spanish at Yale. Ben imagined a farm was good for a boy, but it was a vague belief. He was terrified sometimes when he imagined his son might grow up with a fondness for hunting, or fishing, or skiing. Maggie did not take Kevin to the farm, but she cleared out of the house with the boy and left Ben to his work and his mood. He was able to print the etching on the morning that was exactly a week after the meeting at Castlereagh's.

The right side, where the rams flocked in the lower corner, innocently, stupidly, was dense and cluttered, and the wing of the hovering angel was lost in the flesh and horns of the rams. In the center, below the head of the angel, was the head of Abraham, who appeared abject and defenseless despite the swirl of lines obscuring his features. His lank arm was plunging in a clear space at the left of the print over the face of the boy that was drawn in bare lines in the clear space to where the eye went immediately. The face of the boy seemed almost knowledgeable in its astonishment, and because the head of the boy was drawn on a horizontal plane to the other vertical figures, it seemed that the arm of Abraham, even when the angel might arrest it, would somehow, in its own inertia, fall enough to wound the boy. Behind Abraham's arm and above the head of Isaac, drawn vaguely in the upper left hand corner, was the outline of the dwelling, what could have been the ancestral home, but which might have been, for the frivolity of its lines, the beginning of a carousel, a Ferris wheel. But that was

the only frivolity, for Ben's rendering of the Bible was irreproach-
ably austere.

When he rolled the print that morning on University equipment,
a colleague was there to glance at it, and he said also, and only,
"God!" and Ben returned to the attic to begin on the masonite
panels for the mural at Castlereagh's.

There were still no reminding phone calls from Nehemiah, but
Ben did begin to go night and day. It was mechanical work, and
fake, but complicated slightly by an impression he had that he must
strive to do it well. Sometimes he imagined he was in that way getting back at Nehemiah with it, and at other times he thought of it
as a final act of loyalty to Nehemiah. Occasionally he thought it was
all for Castlereagh, but essentially he knew always that it was for
four hundred dollars. He actually finished the mural in five days
and spent the remaining time in leisurely fashion on the heraldic
shields.

Nehemiah was already at Castlereagh's when Ben arrived on the
appointed morning. Some waiters were there and a curious cook
strolled out of the kitchen. They all watched Ben as he unwrapped
the masonite panels from the newspapers in which he had protected
them and began to mount the mural. Nehemiah, in another pin-
striped suit, stood solemnly behind the taller, gawking Castlereagh, who exclaimed, even before the last panel was up, "It's
England I'll be damned! I tell you it's England!" He kept repeating
it to the waiters, to the cook, to Nehemiah.

It was well done. It was dominated in the center by some fifteen
feet of castle, colored in a soft greyish brown of evening. The castle
bristled with chimney clusters, towers, and turrets; there were
archways and windows, nooks and pennants. Two rows of erect and
tidy poplars led to the middle of the castle, and beyond them, over
the bottom of the castle, were the darker greens of the tops of great
spreading trees. On the far right of the mural was another, smaller
castle built upon the moat, and here the yellow orange of the castle
dropped shafts of gold light from the base of the towers into the
solemn blue water beneath it. There were shrubs and meadows and

knolls and lawns and a dozen little surprises of yellow and purple light.

Ben got off the ladder, and Castlereagh, his eyes watering, pounded him on the back, hugged the embarrassed cook, and swore for the English blood that from somewhere in his family line Ben must have had a claim to. Nehemiah remained solemn, and he was solemn when they left, and he had to shout back to the babbling Castlereagh that he would return in the evening to hang the shields, to dispose of the extra weapons, and to pick up his little check. Outside, as they waited the moment before parting for their cars, Nehemiah, solemnly, praised Ben's work.

"I went night and day for you," Ben smiled. "And I said I was wonderful on castles. And also on trees."

"You should have another hundred for it," Nehemiah said, and drew out from his billfold and handed to Ben the check that was already made out for five hundred. Ben stared at the check, and for the first time Nehemiah smiled, but mournfully. "So? I knew you'd go night and day for me, Benny. Two weeks passed and I didn't hear from you, but I knew."

Nehemiah waddled to his car, and for the rest of the day, even as he handed the check to Maggie in the evening, Ben had to ponder what the hundred dollar tribute, or bribe, was for. But Ben discovered little by thinking things through, and later in the evening, when Nehemiah called, there was something else for him to cope with. It started with Nehemiah's blunt assault in a voice that was now lugubrious, though the manner was almost gone.

"He found out who you are!"

It took some minutes for Ben to learn that Castlereagh had discovered he taught at Yale and had pictures in the Gallery, and that Castlereagh now demanded, in the way of sound restaurant business, that Ben put his name to the mural. Ben tried to make it plain to Nehemiah that they both understood from the beginning he would sign nothing he did for him. Nehemiah acknowledged the agreement, but Castlereagh had refused to pay him until Ben would sign, and it was a matter to Nehemiah now of some twelve hundred dollars. Hesitantly, but with an expectancy he could not disguise,

Nehemiah proposed that Ben might drive out to Castlereagh's where Nehemiah would meet him, and explain his position to Castlereagh in a way that would make him understand.

"I suppose by that," Ben countered, "you mean that you don't understand."

Nehemiah returned it quickly. "Oh, no, Ben. I didn't mean that. Listen, about all this I understand everything."

Ben finally agreed to go. Perhaps he sensed something would turn up there that would be a way out of the extra hundred dollars. Perhaps it was the way Nehemiah had intoned *all this*. At least he could challenge him, for only Nehemiah could have informed on him to Castlereagh. But pressed for a final explanation, he would have been uncertain why he went.

"All these goddamned Nehemiahs!" was all he told Maggie when he left.

Neither of them had bargained for what they would get into at Castlereagh's, and even Nehemiah was not up to it. Castlereagh was at the tail end of the day's Scotch, and the scarlet of his cheeks suffused his temples, his jowls. From the beginning, behind the bar, with arms folded across his chest, he was adamant, imperial, angry. He allowed no appropriate time for Ben to confront Nehemiah.

"He puts his bloody name on it or you get the hell out, the two of you!"

Ben, from the moment he arrived, was left with nothing to say because he had come with nothing to defend. And if Nehemiah had planned for something against Ben, he had his own difficulties now. There was nothing he could work off the impervious Castlereagh that would catch Ben, and even when he fished for it, imploring Castlereagh to be calm as he tried to explore with him the differences between what an artist did that was his art and something he did that was something else, Castlereagh simply roared at him.

"I'm only askin' that the sonofabitch put his bloody name to what the sonofabitch did! He signs it or out!"

211

Nehemiah and Ben grew alarmed, and to Ben it was obvious that Nehemiah might panic. He had raised his voice against Castlereagh, but Castlereagh persisted on the same line, roared and puffed and reddened and lost his wind and bugged his eyes behind the rimless glasses. Then the word "Fake!" came out among them, and it was Castlereagh who proclaimed it first, stumbling blindly upon the accusation they could least tolerate. Ben and Nehemiah stood on the other side of the bar from him, between him and the wall of mounted knights. They stood apart, they could not have reached their arms to each other, and yet, the sweep of Castlereagh's arm as he shouted the word—which could have been for them, or for the wall behind them, or for both—wanted to bring them together. And if apart, unable to help each other if they cared to, they were yet together by the way they both stared back at Castlereagh and then at each other. Then Nehemiah did panic. He shouted the word back to Castlereagh, and in a voice hysterical enough to be memorial, he told Castlereagh who Castlereagh was.

"I'm a fake? You call *us* fakers? A Castle*rech* from the Boston Irish! A haberdasher! An alcoholic Irish haberdasher!"

For the barest moment Castlereagh was stunned, but when he regained his voice, the accent, if anything, reaching into a brazen reserve, was more decidedly British.

"You bloody, pryin' sneaky little Hebe!" he shouted.

Ben had to pull Nehemiah away, and with Nehemiah's first movement Castlereagh stumbled out from behind the bar, lunged to the mural and assumed a posture before it, head high, arms across his chest, as if this were the one thing now that remained to be protected: to establish ownership over that very thing for which he only solicited a name. In front of it, regal, challenging, he appeared to have emerged from the grey-brown colors of the castle behind him to deal with the enemies outside, Frenchmen or dragons or Jews.

When Ben pulled at Nehemiah again, he found him limp and quite willing to go. Outside, before his car, Nehemiah trembled. He looked into Ben's face, and Ben thought Nehemiah might cry. Though he did not say it, Ben had it almost on his lips to say that he was sorry, but he did not know what he would be sorry for. Perhaps he felt that Castlereagh had, for the moment anyway, bound him almost by bone to Nehemiah, and he was sorry for that. Having just been impotent and now being trapped, there was nothing else he could do. When Nehemiah shrugged and almost pleaded in his little, "So?" Ben told Nehemiah to get in his car and follow Ben out to his house.

"Yes. Sure. Yes, your house," Nehemiah repeated blankly.

As Ben drove and kept looking in his mirror for the headlights that followed him, he lost whatever sense had been left him of the purposes for which he had come out to Castlereagh's. It seemed to him somehow disastrous that Nehemiah should be coming to his house. He felt, but only numbly, that some sort of arrangement in the restaurant he could not understand had worked for exactly this purpose. He felt it all the more strongly when they entered his living room and he introduced Maggie, and Nehemiah, incredibly, in an instant, lost all sense of the evening and where they had come from. He simply seized Maggie's hand and squeezed her shoulder with his other hand and beamed and sang it out as if he had come to meet a relative at the Cunard pier.

"Ah, it's so good to see you now after all the times we talked on the phone!"

"It's a lovely surprise," Maggie echoed, brushing at her hair, smiling at Nehemiah, at Ben, as though some story long withheld from her would now be pleasantly told.

Aware that it was the furthest thing from Nehemiah's mind now to begin talking of Castlereagh, Ben—astonished, a little abject —went quickly to sit in the Sheraton chair. He had it vaguely in mind that Nehemiah, should he get to the chair first, would damage it in some act of general clumsiness.

"Don't sit down yet," Maggie reprimanded. "Get us something to drink."

Nehemiah smiled, shrugged, pushed his palms. "For me you don't have to bother."

In the kitchen, as he automatically but somehow deliberately mixed martinis, Ben kept before his mind the image of Maggie smiling warmly at the seated Nehemiah, sitting beside him on the sofa, leaning forward, welcoming him with all her earthy indulgence, assuring him as she had so many others, in Spain or Idaho, by a total posture of eagerness, that she would listen, she would learn. And from the kitchen he could hear the pronounced cadence of Nehemiah's incessant voice, the old voice of the court jester, the junk shop lord. It was incredible. There was not a mention of Castlereagh. When he got back to the living room Nehemiah was at the end of some pointless recital about an ancient family in Woodbridge with Yale connections that was involved in some nineteenth century catastrophe of multiple suicides, or murders, Ben couldn't tell which. But Maggie, as Ben scarcely listened, insisted on enthusiastically summarizing what he had missed, and Ben felt some remote alarm when she concluded, singing it out.

"Nehemiah knows where the graves are. We could all drive out some weekend."

Ben had given them their drinks and was in his chair again, sipping at the martini. Nehemiah was on the edge of the sofa, turned toward Maggie, his thighs swelling beneath the pin-striped pants, his face aglow, glancing occasionally at Ben, but absorbing Maggie in his delighted stare. Once he nodded at Ben and then winked when he used a phrase of dialect at which Maggie laughed. He still held the drink well in front of him in the pudgy hand, and with the other hand, in zest, in relief, he rubbed a protruding knee.

"No, not Coney Island. Brighton Beach," he answered Maggie. "Oh, I could tell you stories about things happened there when I was a kid. I mean from high school already when me and Ben knew each other. There was this old lady once . . ."

Then he stopped and swallowed the martini in one enormous gulp so that even Maggie stared. When it went down Nehemiah shivered and unraveled on the edge of the sofa as though a razor had been drawn along his spine. He shook his head and moaned.

"You know, with these things I've tried 'em a few times before but I'll never make the grade."

214

Maggie laughed, and Ben, holding back, still bewildered, at last smiled anyway. Nehemiah saw it and he placed his glass on the floor and he sprawled back into the sofa, and he was off. He left Maggie time only to nod, to say oh yes, or to say oh no, but the sound of her laughter or her smile or the warmth of her eyes above the high cheeks seemed to be the source of all his energy, so intently did Nehemiah stare at her, perform for her.

He spoke of Brighton Beach, and had Maggie ever seen it, and how he went back once a month to the house of his parents and how terrible it was now. He talked of high school and reported Ben as the artist of the school, without once looking at Ben, and did Maggie know how they didn't know what to do with her husband, so much talent he had in high school already. He characterized the Yankee traits he had been living among and before he went on maybe he ought to find out if Maggie was from New England, so then he went on about Detroit and how he had been there once and was so surprised about how close to Canada it was, and did they know a professor at Yale he had once met, a Paulson or Pauling, a fine man who bought his clothes from a good friend of Nehemiah's. And did they have their plans made for the summer because he had this little place on the Cape would be fine for an artist, and the Carps weren't going to use it because they were going to New Hampshire for the boy's asthma. And had they seen *My Fair Lady* when it was at the Schubert and perhaps noticed this one little thing was so skillful someone had done with the stage sets?

Even if Maggie was surprised, she seemed ultimately charmed. But Ben was staggered. He wanted to shout it out: listen, I brought you home to have you cry about Castlereagh, about what he called you, about your money. So cry now, and then get out! But he could think of no way to stop Nehemiah. The man would simply have to unwind, and then, finished, leave them in a vast silence which Maggie would patch with interested questions, with invitations even, and there would be no way of getting back to what happened at Castlereagh's. And without that, there would be no way of ending. Nehemiah hadn't even paused to look around, to be aware of where he was and what was around him, with such fixity did he continue to keep Maggie before his eyes. At last, when it was over, when Nehemiah collapsed against the silence that was heightened by the echo of Maggie's laughter, Ben knew that Nehemiah too had dreaded what lay ahead. Because when Nehemiah began to look around the room now, he had braced himself for it. The walls were covered with Ben's paintings and prints. Nehemiah took them in with a roving, fugitive glance. He bit his lip. He lowered his head and his eyes went up, toward Maggie, toward Ben.

"The way I go on like that. I'm a foolish man. Like an old man. Excuse me."

He got out of the sofa and started walking—almost bravely, Ben thought—toward a wall of pictures. Maggie glanced at Ben and her eyes filled with that blood-love look they exchanged at times when their son might have done or said something in a childish plunge that would arouse their hearts. Ben turned away from her and swallowed what was left of the martini. He wanted to go to the kitchen for another drink, but Nehemiah went for the bookcase and the one picture on top of it that wasn't hung, the spot where Ben always left for a week the latest work he had done. It was the Abraham and Isaac, and Ben remained in the living room and waited. Nehemiah, with his back to them, stared at the print for a long time, and then, at last, he started to turn, but then he turned back again and remained before the print for another long while and Ben was ready to go for the martini anyway. He believed that Maggie, though she smiled at Ben and shrugged, looked too anxiously between himself and Nehemiah. Ben was out of his chair when Nehemiah turned into the room and spoke.

"It takes all kinds to make a world," he said.

"What?" Ben said.

"Kinds of what?" Maggie said, without a smile. Ben sat down again.

"I mean this Castlereagh. What happened to us tonight," Nehemiah said, turning toward Maggie.

Almost incoherently, he summarized some of it for her, but he left out much and Ben waited for the moment to interrupt. He would tell Maggie what Nehemiah had called Castlereagh, and what it was Castlereagh had called him. Then he would confront Nehemiah for having arranged it that way, even to the name-calling, he suspected now. It was done to get into the house and charm Maggie in order to gain through her the Yale he had failed at with Ben. In a month he would have his asthmatic son romping at Dale Baldwin's. And yet Ben could not interrupt him. There was something mournful in Nehemiah's voice that went beyond the manner, something in the stance that was limp even beyond his bonelessness, and in the fleshy face something that was appalled or awed. Suddenly Nehemiah left Maggie and he turned to Ben. "It's something you do is very strange. I mean the picture over there. Even to you it must be a mystery, something that—who can talk about it? 'Abraham Loves Isaac' you wrote on the bottom, and that's also a mystery. Ah, Ben . . ."

"What are you talking about?"

Nehemiah hesitated. "Is it a new piece of work, Ben?"

"Do you mean did I do it on your time?"

"My time! Who cares about my time? English restaurants and stuffed knights. I know what I mean when I ask you if it's a new piece of work."

Vaguely Ben tried to guess at where Nehemiah was leading him now. It should have been easy, but it blurred before the picture they themselves made. Maggie had moved to the edge of the sofa, and with her head cocked inquisitively she looked up at Nehemiah. The nun-like, patient, professionally tolerant manner looped the corners of her mouth. Nehemiah, in his pin-striped suit, stood before the bookcase. In his posture and in his soft face there was a sudden resignation from which Ben wanted to recoil. He thought Nehemiah was going to speak again, but then it seemed he was going first to look around the room. Instead Nehemiah lowered his head, and when he spoke it was as if he addressed only the swelling middle of his vest, or the feet beneath.

"With a plate and a cutting tool you make Abraham and Isaac. So what did you need me for? I mean how could you think I could get something out of you when there was nothing you could get out of me? In all this, there's nothing for me."

He raised his head slowly and took in the room, the pictures he was too far away to see, the old walls Ben and Maggie had painted a pitiless bone-white on their first weekend there, the odd pieces of furniture and the pieces that only served for furniture. Ben was unwilling to endure the pretended heroism and he rose from the chair.

"Look, Nehemiah, back there at Castlereagh's something happened tonight that . . ."

It was Maggie who interrupted. "Let him finish." She turned toward Nehemiah, not smiling, waiting, looking perhaps as though she might learn something now that was not about Nehemiah and that would have little to do with native charms.

"No, I'm finished," Nehemiah protested. "I said how can you talk about it." He pointed with his thumb over his shoulder toward the print. "For my father I go back to Brighton Beach once a month. I bring him this box of cigars. He couldn't afford to smoke one of 'em in a week when I was a kid. I offer to buy him a house out here. I . . ."

"Nem, what the hell are you talking about? And Maggie, you stay out of it now! We started on Castlereagh. I want it straightened out now. Everything."

Nehemiah shouted.

"What Castlereagh? He's a crazy man. You saw. And when I have things to do with him, I'm crazy. And you too. Crazy things you say to me. Yes—you too, Ben! All of us crazy! So what?"

"All right. So what?"

"So I can turn around and look at your picture, that's what, and I can tell you some things aren't crazy. About your father I can tell you. When you call the picture by such a name that . . ."

"My father!" Ben shouted. "You are crazy! If you think . . ."

"Ben!" Maggie pleaded. Ben turned on her.

"If he thinks that's how the hell I make a picture, he's crazy, that's all!" Ben wheeled back on Nehemiah, who looked only at Ben, and hopelessly. "You think you're telling me something now that should flatter me? Well, you listen to me. I'm not a Bible illustrator, but I'm not a family photographer either. When you..."

"Benny, look..."

"Never mind *Benny*! As far as you're concerned I'm very good on castles, and trees also. And when you go tell Castlereagh I teach at Yale to force me to put my name..."

"You're fired, Ben!"

"What? I'm what?"

Even Maggie was helpless. She talked of getting coffee, but they didn't hear, nor would she have gotten up to get it.

"You can't work for me. It makes us crazy, you understand? I will not tolerate it!"

"*You* won't tolerate it?"

"Who's going to tolerate what another faker needs? Look—I don't know. What am I saying? Only look, look at the picture. The picture isn't fake."

Nehemiah, without turning, looking blankly at the wall opposite him, bent his arm backwards and pointed with a finger of it toward the print on the bookcase behind him. Lacking in Castlereagh's bearing, his posture turning him askew, it was, nevertheless, as if Nehemiah too established some protective claim over a work of Ben's. Ben felt this, and he felt strongly the impulse to step toward Nehemiah and smash his arm down, but Ben was still arrested in that awful resignation of the soft man. Then Nehemiah, without turning his head, began slowly to cross the room. His arm fell slowly, limply, but he looked at neither of them and only raised a little the hand that was nearer to Maggie and spread its fingers slightly. It must have been in farewell, because he walked that way to the door before they really knew he was leaving.

Ben didn't move, but at last he shouted after him, after the wound of the heavy feet on the steps, "Fired me! You fire me! From what? From what?" he repeated, turning to Maggie with the question.

But she could only stand numbly at his side, asking him what had

219

really happened at Castlereagh's. He knew he would have to explain it to her now, and for his own sake as well. He guessed already that she would see it all by simply ignoring those things he couldn't explain. She would see it only for what it literally was, and perhaps in that way she would know it exactly. He himself knew only that Nehemiah's renunciations had wanted to make a prophet out of Nehemiah and a faker out of him. More than that, he imagined now that he himself had suspected such a conclusion as soon as Nehemiah had first examined the print. And what if Nehemiah was right? What if it was only the print that could be honest in metaphor, and what if the metaphors by which he lived and Nehemiah lived made them crazy, even fakers? Nehemiah had no right to rush out of the house with such a discovery, to make only of himself the sacrificed lamb. Perhaps even that was calculated as the one final way to win Ben, and Ben knew that if it did win him, it would be the biggest sham of all. And yet it was Nehemiah who had said no one could tolerate another's faking.

In a deepening remorse, in mounting anger, Ben knew what he had to do. He knew also that this would be the final act between them, and the richest piece of faking.

He turned to Maggie and kissed her cheek quickly.

"I'll be back in a little while."

"Good!" she exclaimed as he started for the stairs. "Bring him back! I'll heat a pot of coffee."

Ben stopped at the door and turned to her.

"Bring him back?" he laughed. "I'll fix the bastard. I'm going out there to sign his sonofabitchin' mural!"

DOVISCH IN HIPPYLAND

The name is Dovisch, Simon—Professor. I give it backwards because my name on this first day of class is little more than a clerical proposition. IBM cards call for last name first, first name last. Demonstrate against it as you will, the administrative life of this institution must be served. When a culture loses the real meaning of procedures, not to say manners, it substitutes clerical rigamaroles. Also capital letters: IBM. This is ENG 186 —Individual Authors.

Manners and procedures. Throw in morals, throw in glances at the art of his fiction—there is our course in a cramped summer session. Because our particular author, as announced in the Class Schedule, is Henry James. If you are in the wrong room, leave now. I plan to tell on this first day, at some expense to myself, a private story. Despite what you may have already heard of me, I am not an intimate person. If I reveal something of my private life here, I do so for our common purpose: the course. In my office you'll find me, if not a cold fish, at least reserved. Which is one aspect of the function of manners: to keep essential strangers free of Russian entanglements, Dostoievski-style. So—if you belong here, stay; if you don't, leave. Painfully, through the years, I have found that three units of credit punched on the IBM card draws the line between gossip and education.

I begin with an honest admission. I don't like summer sessions.

As a matter of fact, Henry James is not my cup of tea either. I am teaching this summer because I need to, the reasons personal. You'll find them in the story I shall soon begin. We can at least be grateful that summer sessions in San Francisco take place in a climate which is—as the brochures say—naturally air-conditioned. Other things here also tend toward the cool, but more on that later. About Henry James himself, let's face it. Half of you are here for the laughs. I no sooner put in for the course than it became the night-time telephone conversation of my colleagues. "Did you hear what Dovisch is teaching?" You'd think Kafka had come out of his grave to teach Terry and the Pirates. In short they are suggesting that a man with a size fourteen shoe, and a provincial Bronx syntax, with a habit of hairshirts and rainbows in his literary tastes, that such a man teaching the consummately civilized Henry James is not a proper academic partnership.

To them, through you, I say: unpredictable and uncanny must be the roads we travel toward the instruction which waits for us. For instance, I now know this: Henry James was always fifty years old. So he sits on me now with a particular weight, whether I drink his tea or not.

Enough for the moment on James. Let me sell Dovisch. Henry's books sell him. (What, incidentally, would he have made of our IBM cards, he who had two first names, and, like me, though in a different style, his own passion for his own syntax?) I said *sell* myself. I mean truly by the story I'm going to tell you only to *show* myself. If you are going to come here at this appointed hour every weekday for the next six weeks and behold through my eyes some of the things you'll be reading in James, you have a right to know in whose head those eyes are set. If you have to suffer my digressing observations along the way, know that in my story I am merely character B, primarily there to throw light on character A, my oldest child, son, proverbial first-born, oldest heir now rather than child, for he is sixteen plus. Call it more accurately for myself not even character B but character C. There is a girl for character B. Thus do fathers get pushed ever further down the alphabet of tyrannizing capitals.

Because I am sometimes referred to as a wanderer as well as a maker of rainbows, because my story will appear to travel a little before it comes home, let me, in order to win your interest wheresoever we may stray, throw in now that age-old foreshadowing of things to come. I mean sex. Also love. The love, as always, will be complicated. The sex you can make of what you will. In fact, that is one part of the sum of my story—that you apparently know better than I how to make of it what you will. I throw the subject out now as the hooker in the sales pitch. Should I come to wander, you hang on by the hook. I will get up there with you, eventually. Or down.

Dovisch, Ezra—my son's name. The love in the story I'm going to tell concerns all of us. The sex is mainly his. The possible relevance of his Biblical name for the story, I leave to you. If you are weak in the Old Testament, look it up. Suffice it to say that the naming of him, our first-born, was not a clerical thing. James, who also tried by names to suggest character, would have understood. It comes anyway in my case to nothing but loss. His friends have called him from Junior High School on—I suspect at his insistence—E.Z. More capital letters.

I have used the word *loss*. Before I sail with you into my story, let us explore that word. It has some connection with James, with my story also. Forget for a moment anything you ever heard or read before on the over-worked subject of tragedy-comedy. Except this: we move toward the tragic when the ground on which we stand diminishes; toward the comic when it enlarges. This merely geographical idea assumes a future, for in the actual present the ground on which we actually stand is neither larger nor smaller than itself. In literature the predictable future is understood by the progress of the story's action from the beginning to the end. If protagonist X starts out with his territory all before him and ends six feet under, the diminishment of his ground, his progress toward loss, is what I call toward the tragic. The implied future belongs not to him but to his race, which through him has been exalted to an understanding of the limits of man. Sobering exaltation. If, on the other hand, protagonist Y ends up with his territory all before him, his own implied future has been relieved of the threat of loss. We are toward the comic. But that is only literature.

In life itself the future is not implied. It is being lived through in the present, and all the days of our past shove us through our present and into our unknown but inevitable future. Question: at what point after the initial start of the train is the first car not only pulling the last car but being pushed by it? Take the question into your reading of Henry James. Listen with it to my story. Understand that what pulls my Ezra toward the comic shoves me the other way. What enlarges for him diminishes for me. An old story, generation piled on generation. James always knew it, having always been fifty. That age at which you keep on standing, albeit he wasn't a family man, between the power of the pull and the force of the shove. From that connection, two wires in the same socket, comes his great drama of renunciations. A great piece of Christian engineering. You'll need to fathom it. For James himself, always fifty and always seeing it, the proposition was exhausting. Perhaps it was that which led him to say on his deathbed: "Ah, here it is at last, the great, distinguished thing." As a final statement, I admire it. I aspire to it. For you, who have almost as many years to go as my Ezra, there will naturally be less enthusiasm. James understood that too. "Live! Live all you can! It is a sin not to!" Thus does he make a middle-aged man sing out to a youth in one of the climaxes of one of his novels, *The Ambassadors*.

This my Ezra is doing. He never read the book, but he has the message.

The girl's name is Cynthia. To be perfectly frank, it's a name I don't care for. It seems to me evasive of the profounder impulses which should guide us in names. For a poet like Keats who had a hang-up on the moon, Cynthia had meaning. The parents of this girl I happen to know. He's a psychiatrist. The moon has as much punch for him as the phrase "anal retentive" has for me. I suspect the girl's name was chosen on a certain misguided principle of euphonics. It is designed to take the sting out of her second name. Professional ethics prevents my giving you that name. For all I know one of you could be a patient of her father's. Far be it from

224

me to undermine medical faith. I'll make up an outrageous second name. Let it do for my story and my little revenge. Thus I call him Pimple. Dr. Pimple. In any case, no one calls her Cynthia either. It's Cinder. Listen—for those of you a little uncomfortable that I carry on like this when a Cynthia could be present, rest assured I have checked the class cards. Tell my colleagues that all minds not as fine as James's are not necessarily elephantine.

The girl is fifteen plus. Whatever I think of her name, she herself is something else. From where shall I get the magic touch and the tact to describe her? Teacher, scholar, and my own kind of dabbler in prose, I am not D. H. Lawrence. Not even Nabokov. Think of her as a kind of blooming, a blossom, a sort of permanent spring-time. With remarkable hair, honey hair, Nature's paint. And a sweet face, almost a beautiful face, bright, alert, but not yet to be called intelligent, as though the brightness, alertness, instinctively aware of its, so to speak, residence in so conspicuous a physical embodiment, the blossom, keeps the potential for intelligence as a power in reserve, a faculty temporarily suppressed by the innocent laziness of the conspicuous power—the body itself.

I'm stalling. I look, for the rest of the description, to pluck courage out of propriety itself. But this is the first occasion of my meeting with you. For the time being I deliver my shyness to your imagination. Perhaps as I go on I shall find the way of offering an item or two. This much I can offer now: her skirts are in the current miniscule fashion. What she shows of herself in that pigmy garment is worthy of the impulses which have always led to—art. If I've gone this far, let me add the remainder. Except the shape she brings to her blouses and so forth is not to be understood in the word "remainder." No more so than any other consequence of our California climate and affluent society, especially for psychiatrists. There! Sideways I've sneaked in the whole business.

A few portrait words about my Ezra, then off at last to the story. What we call the description is anyway, you'll learn from James, a part of the story. He also tells us that character is already a kind of plot, while plot is by no means character.

So—he has my big feet, Ezra, but I otherwise make out no

resemblance. In fact, he is short for his age. He suffers from the usual acne of his years, but I fear that in his case the acne is a little bit more and the suffering somewhat less than usual. His hair, which should not be a subject, in the past two years has become one. It has neither the color nor the luster of his girl friend's, but it's almost as long. His vanity for it by no means assumes its upkeep. I have, for instance, pictures of my Russian ancestors whose long beards look as though they had been often in the barley soup. In my son they would recognize a stylistic descendant. I have always taken him to be an intelligent boy, but of late I lack spoken evidence for such a claim. A sentence of five words is long for him. Three sentences in a row of that length is a speech. It usually ends on the word "like," used not as a preposition, adjective, improper conjunction or illiterate adverb, but as an ambiguous climax, a kind of Jamesian "Ah!" And after such oratory he withdraws into another week of Yoga silences, exhausted.

The point of all this, believe me, is not to deprecate my son. I am, for the sake of the course, trying to show a shift in what you would call life-style and James called manners. In my day a blossom like Cynthia was plucked by tall athletic boys in tidy hair. Sometimes by good talkers—liars. The combination of liar and athlete never failed. Fulfilling neither qualification, I drew a lot of blanks. Except for here and there a nervous girl passionate about—and looking as though she should be—working conditions in Kiev or Kharkov. Actually, as a father, I am grateful for the change. I am only academically curious that after twenty centuries of otherwise, the apples should now be given to those who don't reach. Unless you call militant positions against haircuts and bathing a form of willful effort.

All right. Enough portraiture. Go back with me a few months to springtime. San Francisco springtime, something less than that fury of the renewed blood our poets sing about. Here there is no winter to recover from. April then, and Easter holidays. My wife, after years of absence, was back East with the three younger children. Ezra and myself were alone. The prospects were not good. For the past two years we have been something to the left of rainbows. Father and first-born adolescent son. The usual thing. Comes, then, this particular Friday night. Ezra goes out with Cynthia. Another usual thing. Usual, too, is where they are going : a dance. Nevertheless, as an exercise in parental responsibility, I ask him where he's going. When he says, "Dance," I give him the usual long look, but no comment. I mean for him to understand that with good luck I may yet see him go out for such an occasion in a costume I used to associate with dancing. He is in a not very clean T-shirt over which he wears some kind of unbuttoned vest with tassels, purple. Corduroy pants with a barber's razor strop for a belt. Also sandals. The bare toes and heels are not clean. If the point has been to build the outfit around the barley-hair, he is a well organized boy. About his costumes I no longer argue much, fearful of more consequential rebellions. Better that he should look like Crazy Horse than I should add to my burdens the fear of, say, LSD. More capital letters. Plus a kind of blackmail.

"Be back by twelve-thirty," I tell him. Another duty mechanically performed. Ezra nods. What time he returns the girl to her home, I take to be the responsibility of her parents.

"Where's the dance ?" I expect him to name the usual place, a hippy palladium where he has to request of someone over eighteen to take him and the girl in.

"A church," he says.

I stare at him. "*You* are going to a church dance ?"

Ezra nods.

"A costume dance ?"

"Funny," says Ezra.

"You mean to say you are wearing that outfit to go dancing in a church ?"

"It's a Happening—like," he says.

"It's a disgrace !"

"It's all right with the church," says a suddenly ecclesiastical Ezra. "They've gone past Henry James, like."

He has seen me reading for the course. Once, in my presence, he opened one of the novels, read a page, said "Good God!" dropped the book and left the room.

Exit Ezra before I thought to have from him the name and location of the church. My lack of information will figure in the plot. So, too, in addition to the absence of my wife, will the corresponding absence of Cynthia's mother. Some correspondence. She is not with three children visiting her old parents in a cramped apartment in the Bronx. She is in Florence, looking, I presume, at the Madonnas in the Ufizzi while her husband remains at home stamping out mental illness. The other daughter is away at college: Radcliffe. To thicken the plot, let me throw this in now. Unknown to me, the good Dr. Pimple, home alone on a Friday night, is permitting my son the use of his car. You'd think it would occur to this Prince of Progress that if I don't permit my son the use of my car for dates—only for domestic errands—that in donating his convertible Wildcat Buick he is, to say the least, interfering.

So: Ezra out and I alone—utterly. With the exception of Henry James. Henry James and Simon Dovisch in the study of Simon Dovisch, Dovisch in the living body, Henry in the undying books. A study, incidentally, which would have cramped James's style. Under the slanting eaves of the roof-tilt and over the attic floorboards. A table, a chair, a cotbed, a bookcase, a small window looking out on –in this city of noble views—the shingles of the neighbor's slanting roof. Not the most conducive atmosphere in which to read our Henry. I descended on this Friday night to the living room.

By eleven-thirty I was not only still alone, I was lonely. I was again reading, as you will soon enough, *The Ambassadors*. While on the one hand I felt the urge with every miracle of craft and perception on every page to sing out my discoveries to my wife, only to realize all the more how far away she was, I felt, on the other hand, despite these miracles and my discoveries thereof, that James is exactly the kind of writer who, having wounded my awareness of my solitude, could not heal or celebrate it. I went to bed. I fell asleep.

I was awakened out of my darkness into the room's darkness by that noise which haunts our century. The telephone. With your wife and three of your children three thousand miles away, you answer such a noise in the middle of the night with a blood-stopped heart.

"This is Henry," it says.

Henry? You can imagine what raced through my head. This must be the dreaming consequences of an overdose of James. Or some past student, still unreconciled to a justified "F," is putting me on.

"Are the children at your house?" this Henry says.

Let me not make a long thing out of the wrong scene. It was, of course, Dr. Pimple, a man I had previously met once only, and never called him Henry. It was now 2 A.M. and his Cynthia wasn't home. I ran off to check Ezra's room. Nothing. I looked downstairs. No one. I report on the phone. He says he'll have to call the police. When I say I see no need for that, it was then he mentioned he loaned my son the car. He refers to him as E. Z. Not once has it ever occurred to me to call his daughter Cinder. He is worried about an accident. He'll call me right back. I sit at the edge of the bed and wait. In such a crisis I am worth nothing. The doctor calls back and reports there was no accident involving his car.

"So they are still out," I said. "Somewhere in the car. Parked no doubt." By my tone I want him to understand what I think of his charity.

"I hope so," he says.

"You *hope* so?"

"Aside from an accident, what else is there to worry about?"

Do you see, beginning students of Henry James, that this conversation by two contemporary fathers conducted in the middle of the night through the miracle of wires was an involvement of manners? And that the manners themselves were already involved with what you will come to call by the semester's end, issues of the moral imagination. Imagine, then, my humiliation at having to ask the doctor if he knew where the dance was.

"Certainly," he says, his voice wrapped around his opportunity. "I always know where Cinder intends to go." Meaning that my Ezra must already be guilty of having removed her to a place where she

229

didn't intend to be. He names me the church and its location. I tell him I'll drive out there and let him know what I find out. "If it's not going to disturb your sleep," I add. "If you're happy in the knowledge they're parked somewhere, and if you're going back to bed, I wouldn't want to wake you."

It scores more points than I needed. He wants me to pick him up. It's then he tells me his wife's in Italy—a way of announcing he's without a car. Hers is in the garage, also on vacation. I get dressed and drive to his place. I live in the Avenues near Golden Gate Park, he in Pacific Heights—neighborhoods separated by some fifteen minutes of driving. Also by some tens of thousands of dollars. And to pay off on my own house and send my wife to visit aging parents, I teach summer sessions, murdering the scholar's reading time. But while I was driving, my mind was not on such bitter professional differences.

Know first of all that I drive in panic. Ezra has nibbled away before at the time assigned him for returning home, but never to 2 A.M., and never before was he driving a car at night. What if he had taken it into his head to go over the bridge to Marin County and had an accident there on some lonely road in the hills? It might not be reported yet. At such a moment the father tells himself an old tale: let me only find him well and healthy and everything between us will be new again in resumed love. But some unredeemed part of the father knows that one minute after he finds the son alive and well, he will descend into the viciousness of his own relief. He will cry out: "What the hell do you mean by . . ." and so forth. We are imperfect creatures; it enriches our literature.

Know also that as I drove in panic I reviewed in confusion the pictures of my Ezra's presence in my life. The usual pictures. The historic pull. I remembered how, at the age of two, I held him in my arms at the window before bedtime, and he cried for a reason unknown to me. Then he pointed at the dark sky to the first crescent moon he had ever seen and whimpered, "The moon is broke." Before such a universal sympathy worthy of a Shelley, at age two no less, I also nearly cried. And other like memories from ages four and six and eight. Is there a father without a boxful of such recollections? But eight years old becomes ten, and ten becomes thirteen, and thirteen is on its way to sixteen, and who am I to claim that for Simon Dovisch alone the Nature-driven process is to be arrested? Albeit a writer can nail a picture forever within a frame, and none better than James, we are none of us characters in a fiction.

What I am getting to, of course, is the ever-diminishing ground—mine. It gets cut out from under me as surely as I was on that night in the car cutting the distance between my house and the doctor's. Time accumulating constricts space. If it's not a law of physics, it's a condition of fiction. In this case also of life. The built-in hazard of the teaching of my subject lies exactly here. The students are the students, and you are for me always the same age. The texts are the texts, and they are always the same words. Dovisch alone, in this contractual trinity, ages. Can he hand out the lecture of twenty years ago and give it again today when the very composition of his own blood has changed again and again in that stretch of time? And yet there must be a continuity to a man's life, which would be the death of meaning to deny, especially when he has answered to the call of teacher, and is, as you begin to see, within that teacher, a preacher, for whom confession is a part of the craft of sermonizing.

Look—I am also talking about this: sex. You can philosophize this way and analyze that way. You can go up the Platonic ladder or down the Freudian pit. But sooner or later you've got to talk about what you're talking about. I know in advance that it will come to be your biggest complaint about James. You'll say he didn't. But I promise you now you'll say by the end of the semester that he did. Talk about what he was talking about—in his fashion. After all, our fashion had not yet been liberated into what he called "the empire of the sexual sense." I mean that from James's time (1843-1916), through mine, into yours, we have come nearer and nearer to—if you can forgive my putting it this way: our naked subject.

I am indeed talking about what was in my mind during my car ride to the doctor, father to the ever-blossoming Cynthia. It came in the form of pictures, unselected and unsorted. But I am a lecturer in and of English, not the operator of a slide projector. I give it to you in the only public way I can—selected and sorted by indirection in deference to the proprieties.

Know, then, that in my own adolescence I was neither fanatic saint nor frantic entrepreneur in this sex business. Neither is my Ezra, as far as I know, one or the other. Measured by the manners of our own separate times, call us hum-drum. But, ah! How these manners have changed! Those magazines, for instance, that all boys look at. I sneaked looks too. Surprising as it may be to some of you, as it is to my Ezra, they were also available to me. To James, too, no doubt. We were not, after all, Cotton Mather in Salem. The difference for me was one of effort and style. You didn't procure the magazine on any ordinary newsstand. Once procured, you didn't leave it lying around in the living room of your own home. But the atmosphere in my son's home, although not yet that of the psychiatrist's, is nevertheless of our time. Shall his father, a professor of the American scene through its literature, be unenlightened?

All of which left me to fear that Ezra, from excesses of photographic splendor and tricks, when he got old enough to come upon the real thing, would he not think a small mole was nothing less than a running ulcer, a cancer? I could have spared my anxieties for my own problems. He was shortly to grow his long hair, come into his acne, master the art of dirty feet, and behold —Cynthia! Some ulcer.

So picture me in my own household. See me in the two years or so of his magazine phase. Put me in the living room in the evening after supper, reading for class, reading, say—Hawthorne. And a glance away, those magazines. A few strides away and a flip of the wrist, the center-folds. Know for the record I am a satisfied, gratified, and altogether monogamous man—but a man. Am I not right in believing that if Hawthorne's living room had been strewn with such stuff, left there so casually by his thirteen-year-old son Julian, Hawthorne would not have worked himself up into the moral froth out of which came Hester, Pearl, and Scarlet Letters? Who is Dovisch, then, to sit there and brood upon the diminishing Hester when he is in the presence of such enlarged possibilities? And a few years later when Cynthia herself, in the flesh and blood, in my presence, once showed my Ezra a black and blue mark on a part of her body I do better not to name, was I a stone to be without reaction even as I turned away?

I have tried to give you the frame in which to put the pictures that you ought now to be able to imagine were in my mind as I drove in the middle of the night in a silent city to pick up the other father in this affair. In short, was it only plain, green, ugly envy on my part which had spoiled my recent years with Ezra who, whatever the manners, is driven into my heart with the spike of love?

If we must come at last, James too, hedge it as we will, to talk about what we must talk about, is it to be nothing more than my diminishing ground versus his widening territory? Is that what it was when we quarreled about his excessive use of the phone, his poor grades, his friends who plugged in guitars and commenced upon a barbaric yowling that made me think here were the Cossacks again in the last pogrom? Was there, at the bottom of all that yelling and erosion between us, only my envy?

Manners, morals, love and loss. Questions everywhere, symphonic and general, in life as well as in James. Praise be for the specific text, the particular father, and the exact son. For who is there who can deliver the proper answer to the misdirected question? In the car ride, plagued by pictures, I ask myself: if there has been an accident and he is hurt, or the girl is hurt? (That it might be worse than that I dare not ask myself.) Or if they are all right, and I indeed find them parked and in the back seat and . . .? If I am then to be immediately relieved, what am I to be immediately afterwards? Or is the proper question only the guilt of the father? In which case is the guilt general to fathers in the ungenerous nature of the flow of time? Or is it particular to Dovisch? But if Dovisch was also, in the flow of time, a guilty son, when does he get off this joyless carousel? Ah, then, prospective students of the subject before us, do you see what a muddle mere manners can make, infected as it is with psychologies?

In any story you come at last to the what-happened part. Even in a Dovisch story. The doctor was waiting for me in front of his house. I have never been inside it, but I know from my son, as I could tell from its location, the views from inside command more than a neighbor's shingle roof. He got in beside me. I don't remember what I was wearing; I had merely put on clothes. He, however, was in a tweed jacket with suede elbow patches. Also a bow tie—and a pipe. This at 2:30 A.M. Even allowing for the fact that he had not gone to bed, the outfit is nevertheless a signification of his manner. Where other men may aspire by their clothes to be tough, or to be rebellious, or to be negligent of the day and soulfully in touch with the eternal verities, or even to be elegant, Dr. Pimple, my middle-of-the-night ambassadorial companion, aspires only to look comfortably bright. He also wears a beard. To be fair, I do not take the beard to be his way of asking in with your establishment. I am given to understand it was his fashion long before it became yours. A psychiatrist, he grooms it Viennese style, Habsburg Empire.

My slurring remarks, incidentally, are directed against the particular man, not his profession. Some of my best friends, and so forth. What I hold against this man goes back to the one occasion I spent any time with him. At a dinner party at a mutual friend's, we sat across the table from each other. He, not I, started talking about Thomas Wolfe. Observes the good doctor about a writer for whom I keep a lingering sentimental fondness, stroking his beard as he observes, his eyes twinkling with conclusions: "The man is obviously anal retentive. His predominant sense is smell. What he retains of the cities of Europe, for example, is their distinguishing odors. Positively anal retentive."

Paraphrasing our James, I responded: "You should quit reading serious novels. It is not an easy alternative to golf or the bicycle." Whereupon he nailed me with a long look, signifying, I suppose, that he had just come to conclusions about my own dominating aberration.

But now we were linked together in the car, potential ambassadors in that Jamesian sense, off to rescue the younger people from whatever entices and endangers them in their younger world. At least I so thought of myself, and I therefore minced no words as soon as the doctor got in and I drove off.

"Do you object to buses for adolescents? Don't you think I should have at least been consulted about the car?"

His bright answer to that was to insult me. "He drives better than you. If you haven't noticed, you're on the wrong side of the street. I would feel much safer in the car with E.Z."

"My son's name, Dr. Pimple, is Ezra. As for the safe driving, I too would prefer to know he was in the car now with only you. You are not the same kind of distraction your daughter is."

From there on the conversation of our fifteen-minute ride was faltering. He wanted me to know that he came along mainly to reassure me. If, in fact, he spotted the car near the church, that, for the time being, would satisfy him. He wasn't out to make a scene which would humiliate the children. He would talk to his Cinder tomorrow about paying henceforth more attention to the time.

"And if we don't spot the car?" I asked him. "And if we then go into the church and don't find them? And if all things tonight conspire toward calm and equanimity, why did you call to ask me if the children were at my house? Wherever they are, they are. Whatever they do, they're doing. Why the phone call?"

"To be calm rather than frantic," he says, blowing his pipe, "is not to be indifferent."

"Tell me," I said. "What's the worst that could have happened to them?"

"An accident, of course. But as I told you, I called the police. There hasn't been any."

"And if not an accident," I said, "what's the next worse thing?"

"There isn't any," he fires back. "Don't you understand that yet?"

What was I to say? The daughter was his. Mine was the son. But if that was the attitude in his house, on one thing I could now stop speculating. It was foregone. That luxurious home on Pacific

Heights where my son always visits. The permissive parents. The lazy, blossoming girl without a second thought for where the black and blue marks are when she displays them to the world. Bravo Ezra! If I had any lingering doubts, this man of all certainties cleared them up a few minutes later as I circled slowly near the neighborhood of the church while he looked without results for his Wildcat among the parked cars. My mind, clicking off with pictures of mutilated bodies, with that lamentable contingency from which no parent is entirely free who is entirely parent, the wiped out future, the ground not diminishing but shorn entirely away— college, marriage, his children who are my grandchildren, the easing of my envy with my own increase in years, if it was ever envy, giving me in my final years the final satisfaction of a part of the essential job essentially done so that I too, with my wife beside me, could wait naturally for the great, distinguished thing—my mind then filled with the pictures of the catastrophe which might have happened eliminating in one moment the picture of what over the years should have happened, my mind turned murderous toward the man beside me. I blamed him. I parked the car, we walked to the church, and he suddenly said this to me. If I remember, there was even a white smile inside the black bush of his beard.

"I hope you have understood something from the start," he said. "My daughter is on the pill."

My mind, full of disaster, blame, murder, couldn't take it in. I looked at him dumbly. "She's sick?"

He stared at me as though I were the one who had flown in from Mars.

"Oh," I said at last. "Oh! The *pill*." I waited a moment as we walked, then I turned to him. "How old did you say she was?"

"I didn't say. Surely you know. Cinder's going on sixteen."

I responded with a long silence, then I pulled my own tone. "*Cinder*. The pill. Not yet sixteen." Then another long silence, followed by a raise of eyebrows, a nod of the head; and a just plain, ambiguously accented, Jamesian: "Ah!" No more than that, but how much was in that! The power of a syllable with an attitude in reserve. At least for a moment the air of conclusion was mine.

So—into the church in this middle-of-the-night of its ecumenical intentions, enter now the two middle-aged ambassadors, the left out professor and the swinging mental-healer, goose-chasing for offspring. How can I begin to show you what I saw on this night of nights? Am I Emerson to prophesy the national fate through this local happening? Happening they call this too, and Happening it was. If we mean by participial *ing* an event in the present demolishing the future. And Dovisch there, with twenty Western centuries jammed in his head, scraping his heels against being hauled by this now into—nothing. Oh where is Dreiser now with his grubby patience for the murdering details? Surely I lack the heart to give you this picture, but who anymore has such heart? In the past twenty-five years of direct frontal assaults from the murderous living thing—hot wars and cold wars, concentration camps and atom bombs, rockets to the moon and saucers from Mars, assassination and the murder of the assassin—in the face of all this, literature, no less my crippled spoken word, has to crawl in sideways like a rubber-soled thief.

First of all, the noise. Let the clerkish man who still believes it will all end not with a bang but a whimper attend where I attended. If one yowling boy with a plugged in guitar two stories below my study had sounded like a Cossack massacre, consider four of them on the same ground level with me performing simultaneously, all of them plugged in. And if I tried to suggest my Ezra left the house dressed like Crazy Horse, consider what I looked upon in this assemblage when I now suggest that in the lights of their costumes he was decently dressed for the funeral of a parent he honored.

Young men with earrings, young women with boots, but most of them barefoot and everywhere bells on the feet, bells on the wrists, feathers in the hair, bead-bands between the ears. Girls in mini-skirts and boys in mini-shirts; young women dressed like belly dancers from Cairo, and young men dressed like Tom O'Bedlam's from Shakespeare. Girls in tights like Sir Walter Raleigh, boys in collars like Queen Elizabeth. Blankets and ponchos and afghans and burnooses and Gandhi sheets and Woolworth curtains. Everywhere purple and yellow and orange and red, and just plain skin, cadaver hue, much of it. All of them in this large room which must have been the social hall of the church, most of them dancing, some merely wandering, the wanderers in a kind of weightless, expressionless grace, as though they wandered in another body through another universe, and the dancers in convulsions, or in the throes of eczema on backs they couldn't reach. Against the wall, some few merely sit, looking with eyeballs reversed at who-knows-what inside their heads. Above them, on the walls, pictures flash from projectors mounted on ladders and attended by figures with one foot on the ladder and the other in space, moving what looks like dishes on and off the lenses. With such pictures, who needs Dante's skimpy circles? For instance, out of the monstrous ear of a prominent government official, marched squads of soldiers, rumbled files of tanks, soared smoking rockets, all followed by three pigmies with long spears. On every wall blobs of red and blue throbbing like the corpuscles of a gigantic opened heart, perhaps keeping time to the four electrified guitars and the voices which yowled into the microphones an incomprehensible babble in which I could make out only the one phrase I imagined to be "naked in a zeppelin." And to all this, the yowling, the guitars, the throbbing projections, they danced, these costumes on the floor. At least they moved. Moved? Convulsed. Jerked. Jumped. Twisted. Kneeled. Sprawled. But with whom they might be dancing was another mystery. It could have been the Mardi Gras, but I was not in New Orleans. It could have been Halloween, but it was not October.

One thing it absolutely wasn't was a scene from Henry James. If this is what they mean by expanded consciousness, count James out, who, as you will see, gave his life to consciousness, and his will to its expansion. Count out Dovisch too. If this was the public culmination of what I sometimes charged myself for being envious of my son, eliminate the envy. *This* he could have. That this show by-passed my youth in my time was all right with me. It was not my sense of a show. Of time either. Take, for instance, these zeroes and dots projected on the walls and expanding and contracting like the geology of millenniums fulfilling itself in seconds. That too was not for me. Send me visions all the time, but spare for me in them my own sense of time.

So much for generalized first impressions. The main problem was to find Ezra and the girl. In this scene I couldn't share the doctor's concern for making a scene. On the other hand, finding Ezra in all of this was no bright prospect. I turned for helpful suggestions to my ambassadorial partner. He was very ostentatiously nose-puckering. Sniffing. He was making signals to me, but I couldn't decipher. He pulls on my sleeve. He wants me to back out with him. I do so—all the way to the street.

"Incense," he says.

"What?" I say.

"The smell in there, it's incense."

Of all that was to be seen and heard in there, he's worked up about the smell. So much for insights into Thomas Wolfe. It turns out he's allergic. I can go back alone if I want, he'll wait in the car. So be it. I returned to make the effort which would justify our having come. I would try at least once to push my way across that floor. As to hopes of finding two specific youngsters in that maelstrom, I had none. It also occurred to me that no one there had looked as young as the two I looked for.

I went back and pushed and shoved, lugging myself through all that thunderous and sweaty calisthenics, mulling upon, with everything I saw, resumed thoughts of disaster. A simple formula: when I am asked to surrender my sense of shock, I multiply my fears of disaster. For instance: a young man wandered past me dressed in . . . He was not dressed. He was entirely undressed. Well, "entirely" exaggerates. He wore eyeglasses and a string of wooden beads around his neck. Also the hair and beard. Otherwise he was altogether in the carnal pallor of his pathetic skin. And he smoked a cigarette. I no sooner turned the way of my bulging eyes when the dizzying dancers closed behind him. Was it marijuana he smoked? In this building? Did I now have to add that to my sense of the night's woe? Were they in the car somewhere with pot? LSD? I had never specifically warned Ezra against it. But neither had I ever warned him against stealing, specifically. Some things you leave to the mere atmosphere of a home. But how could I have expected my cupful of atmosphere to compete with this? Besides, there was another home. The enlightened doctor's. If he could hand out such a murderous weapon as his car, couldn't he from his own toolbag be giving out pills to Ezra? Didn't he already smugly admit—admit? brag!—that he gave pills to his daughter? Physician and healer, taking Nature by its horns to lead it through its cycles: one kind of pill to provoke, followed by the antidote to forestall. While at my elbow, in the meantime, this far from me and yet centuries away, two of the girls dressed as belly dancers, and belly dancing, were now, also, undressed. Topless.

Ponder with me if you will, in light of the context I have tried to make, how the suffix *less* has always stood us for diminishment. And let the doctor waiting for me in my car ponder a new assumption for his professional work. This great theory of repression serving him for half a century—that, with other things, is also *kaput*.

I turned to the first presentable person. Her back was to me, but at least the back was clothed. She even had a red ribbon binding her pony tail, bouncing as she danced. Almost a farmland sight—a cherished respite. I tapped her on the shoulder. The tap became a rap before she turned. And when she did turn the she became a he. A handlebar mustache, no less, barbershop style. Dovisch in the Happening. Dovisch in the looney-bin. Repeatedly I tried to shout my question. I wanted to know where the younger ones were, the sixteen-year-olds. Was there another room for them? Had they left?

"Curfew!" he roared back, and I lip-read. He kept on dancing, facing me. "Us too," he roared. "They're bustin' us. Blowin' their minds. Calling fuzz."

Linguistics is not my field, but I knew what he-she meant. I have heard you talking, I have read your papers (one last semester on a 3 by 5 card, when I called for twenty pages, brilliantly informing me: "The whale blew Ahab's mind."). So I left. I split. The first thing I put to the doctor when I got to the car was this matter of drugs. When he saw what I was hinting at, he shot me steel.

"What do you take me for?" he said.

A fool, I wanted to say, but lacked the heart. After all, his daughter was also among the missing. When I tried to start the old car—nothing. Dead. This I needed again. Another aspect of my losses shoved at me in old mechanical failures. My bow tie companion performed rescue. With icy superiority, he reminded me: "Ordinarily they start only *after* you've turned the key." A warehouse full of wisdoms. We were getting along as though it were an already accomplished fact: shotgun in-laws. The car underway, we discussed where to. He was for home.

"Are we to run around all night?" he argued. "It's over an hour since I called you. By now they're probably asleep."

Ambiguous observation.

He, on the other hand, was all for reassurance. He insisted on the impossibility of an unreported accident. That Ezra would have taken the car out of the city, also impossible. What I needed, he oiled me, was more faith in the good work I and my wife had already done. He and his wife thought the world of Ezra. The boy was a brilliant conversationalist. And so forth. To tell the truth, for certain kinds of unctuous reassurance, he had the right professional hum. Though I was driving, I see now in retrospect that he was steering. With other words inserted here and there, such as "sweet youngsters," "gentle souls," to describe the little he had seen of Walpurgis Night, he prejudiced the sorting out of my own aftermaths. After all, I said to myself, does the young world have to hold itself accountable to me for its hairstyles? Caesar and Napoleon and Hitler all wore their hair neat. Was that an advantage to us? And those in Salem who judged against witches wore black garments buttoned from toes to Adam's apple. Did it contribute to clarity? I had in fact to admit that never before had I been in a place where so many young people were involved in so much noise and motion while producing for it so little an air of violence. Indeed, wasn't it love they preached against an older world that moralized at them from behind badges and bombs?

I no sooner said love to myself than came the other word: sex. I was about to inform my colleague in paternity of what I had seen there and he had missed, when I stood checked by a second thought. No matter what tone I used to report a naked man and topless women, it would nevertheless be a tone he'd turn back on me. If I said it casually, he'd want to know what I was trying to hide. If I put feeling into it, he'd want to know why such a natural thing excited me. All power to the profession that does the listening. The lecturer and the story teller give themselves away.

Before his house again, the doctor in the bow tie had a bright idea. He would check the garage. He disappeared down the long, dark driveway. He came back to report the car was there. End of bloody nightmares. He assumes Ezra has gone home, but he invites me in for a drink. "Cap off a memorable evening." I remind him it's the morning. I ask him to be good enough to return to the car and tell me that his daughter's there. I'll wait just in case Ezra still is. I wait a long, long time. The more I have to wait, the more I believe Ezra is indeed there. The more I believe that, the more convinced am I of what has been going on. Coming home late, finding the father gone, having to themselves a mansion like that, beds and couches everywhere—and so forth. On the other hand, how long should it have to take Ezra, with his ragbag of clothes, to get decent? Meanwhile, for me: isolation. I sit alone at 3:45 a.m. Everywhere darkness, silence. The city sleeps; Dovisch broods, victim already to the viciousness of a parent's relief. Moments ago eternal gratitude: son alive. Now thoughts of all kinds of hell I will give him once I get him in the car. At last, returning, the doctor—alone.

"He's not there," he reports. I get ready to leave. The solitary ride home will wind me up into a proper anger.

"She's not home either," he adds. "No one's home."

"But the car is here. The buses have stopped running. They wouldn't walk from here to somewhere else."

"Perhaps the car was here when we left?"

"Didn't you check?"

"I saw no need to. If Cinder wasn't home, I assumed the car wasn't either. As a matter of fact, I never checked. They might not have taken it at all. Cinder might..."

Cinder-Shminder! I had had enough. "Dr. Pimple," I declared, "let the sick world give thanks you're not a surgeon. In your work you at least have a chance to try to repair tomorrow what you ruined the day before."

I am not given to motorcycle antics, but I roared off. In the rear view mirror I saw him leaning over the vacancy where a moment ago the car had been. Let him look there for the abyss into which my mind plunged again. Look—the hour flies. There's no time left for all the specifications. Suffice it to say that what I had moments ago to imagine as going on in the doctor's house, I now had to rearrange for its going on in my own. The place where something happens can dictate the point of view. More James. Thus what I had offered myself moments ago as an assuaging gentleness in the midst of all that hippy flummery was now Doomsday ominous. I said to myself: Dovisch, Simon, albeit your heart is pounding, and you have been made the lunatic ambassador, they are the ones acting out the real panic. Why else would they be cluttering up with such a hodge-podge all the territory that lies naturally before them? Cannibal music and Yoga silences; gypsy wrap-arounds and nuthouse nakedness; communions with Nature by way of manufactured drugs which isolate; barley soup beards like the eternal victim, and leather boots like the perpetual murderer; pictures on the wall to expand consciousness, and glazed eyeballs fogging the windows of consciousness. And so forth. In which case, I asked myself, this so forth, this panic—was it at the heart of all comedy? In which case, wasn't it always, generation into generation—the tired older one pulling at and being shoved by the clamoring younger ones—wasn't it forever *the* war right outside one's window? And weren't we all, and haven't we always been, at war out there while we simultaneously watched ourselves from the lonely posts of our own fixed windows?

In which final case, I take my stand. If it's envy boiling in my blood as I drive home with pictures in my head of what is going on in my house, so be it. What of it? I dismiss it as a mere psychology, serviceable in a fiction as bones are in a body, but not yet *the* fiction, not even *the* body. Not even in our James who will appear to build a temple of it.

Then read him this way this semester, and know thereby what this showing of Dovisch has been all about. Watch him put his character at his one window. Watch the character watching himself participate in the war outside. Call the war manners. Call its adversaries what you will, but call them also generations, the young and the old, civilizations as well as people. Call the window consciousness, for which psychology is the mere instrument, a fairy tale. Observe how he who watches goes on to see more and more. Notice how much he loses with the increase of all he sees. Until at the very end he has nothing left but the bare window itself. Which for James is triumph, albeit resignation. The overcoming of panic, having leaped into fifty like a miraculous birth fired into its own future calendar, and there arrested. So that this generation that I myself confront, though it do away with James (and how much else!), cannot do away with his window. For his seeing belonged to his fifty, and sooner or later we all come to stand before that window, whether his discriminating intelligence stands there with us or not. Which is why, incidentally, he is not my cup of tea. Not because I am elephantine and he is fine, but because I was not always fifty. But it's why I have turned to him now. For *your* sake. Because cut the hairstyle how you will, fifty is out there waiting for you.

Forget I said that. I am no Doomsday man. I sign up with James in his plea for you. Live! Live all you can! It's a sin not to. But understand that as I proclaim for your future, I am myself no more than a mere window-washer. For instance, watch me, in this tagged-on conclusion with our time almost gone, see Dovisch see his own window getting rubbed. For that's all that James ever meant. He meant: SEE!

They were indeed in my house, Ezra and his Cynthia, but it took a little looking. I coughed my way through all the downstairs rooms. I hummed tunes and clapped hands before entering bedrooms, even my own. Thus must a father, his spleen full of outrage, advertise his presence in his own house. At all costs avoid trauma, his own included. They were, of course, in my attic study.

I saw the light showing behind the crack of the almost closed door at the head of the stairs. I called his name. No answer. I climbed the steps, pounding my feet. No response. True, I wanted no traumas, but what was I to do with spurts of adrenalin washing out my nobility. Ezra was to hear, perhaps even feel, immediate expressions of my indignation. If it ruined the blossom with him, I resigned myself to that too. I lack the wisdom to be a gardener.

It was not to be.

They were, as the doctor had foreseen, sleeping. And together, as the expression goes, if it can be stretched to mean occupying the same bed in actual sleep. My little cotbed. Each curled like a cat on each end. Each head showing forth from under the blanket, which otherwise entirely covered both of them. Except for the one perfect leg of Cynthia, where the blanket had peeled away. Between them, on the blanket, open but face down, was a book—one of mine. At the side of the bed, on the floor, in a bowl from the kitchen, peels from oranges, cores from apples, stalks from which the grapes had been stripped. That was as far away from the bed as I looked. I went back to them, to their visible faces. The girl first, she being the nearer to me. That honey hair, glowing under the naked rafter bulb, was where it all began. Her cheek also, rose-suffused in living sleep. The lips, still moist from all that devoured fruit, perhaps, were curled at the corners. Call it satisfaction with the dreamstuff going on behind those closed eyes. Possibly. It was, nevertheless, and so it struck me on the spot, the end of my adrenalin, and of all mere bodily subterfuges. It was, plain and simple, the satisfaction of a living thing transported into the innocence of its living self. Maybe.

As for my Ezra, let me face it. Sleep alone could not un-knot his barley hair, nor could it banish the blemishes of his adolescent skin. Process is life, and life is unavoidable. On the other hand, there was something in his sleeping face I had not seen in years, though, to tell the truth, I could not remember when in recent years I had seen him sleep. It was nothing less I looked upon than the two-year-old who, in my arms, at the window, had cried for a broken moon. For it was a face now which, though its eyes were closed, and its mouth half-parted—perhaps mere adenoids, perhaps relief from the tight-lipped wakefulness of our bickering days—a face capable again of crying. If not this time for the broken moon, then surely it would cry, even in sleep, should anything remove the curl of satisfaction from the corners of the mouth of her who was curled in sleep on the cotbed with him.

So Dovisch, the avenger, the moralizing corrective consciousness of another generation's manners—nay, morals—nay, conduct—which, if the square truth be known, still leaves him cold—he tip-toes out. He scrams. He doesn't so much as glance around the room for the evidence of clothes. Not so much as another peep at the exposed leg for the shred of a hope that it might be nothing more than what happens to a leg on a young body sleeping in a mini-skirt. Not even one stride closer to read the title from the spine of the book. Not even a noise to wake them and hear from them that they have perhaps been here for hours, affronted by the mob in the dance hall and carried away into sleep by their reading. Dovisch merely scrams. Let what went on in there be for you as it remains for me one of the permanently undisclosed facts of the story. A technique with James, a necessity for me. The post at the window becomes more important than the war outside.

If you imagine from this, as we draw to an end and you get ready for leaving as I assign you now for tomorrow the first hundred pages of *The American*, if you imagine I have taken you all this way for a fairy tale ending, you haven't picked up, along the way, enough Dovisch clues. And are not yet ready for the endings of James either. For though what I saw through the window of my eyes in my study was described to make you feel it as the triumph of barley hair, nor could it banish the blemishes of his adolescent skin. Process is life, and life is unavoidable. On the other hand, there was something in his sleeping face I had not seen in years, though, to tell the truth, I could not remember when in recent years I had seen him sleep. It was nothing less I looked upon than the two-year-old who, in my arms, at the window, had cried for a broken moon. For it was a face now which, though its eyes were closed, and its mouth half-parted—perhaps mere adenoids, perhaps relief from the tight-lipped wakefulness of our bickering days—a face capable again of crying. If not this time for the broken moon, then surely it would cry, even in sleep, should anything remove the curl of satisfaction from the corners of the mouth of her who was curled in sleep on the cotbed with him.

So Dovisch, the avenger, the moralizing corrective consciousness of another generation's manners—nay, morals—nay, conduct—which, if the square truth be known, still leaves him cold—he tip-toes out. He scrams. He doesn't so much as glance around the room for the evidence of clothes. Not so much as another peep at the exposed leg for the shred of a hope that it might be nothing more than what happens to a leg on a young body sleeping in a mini-skirt. Not even one stride closer to read the title from the spine of the book. Not even a noise to wake them and hear from them that they have perhaps been here for hours, affronted by the mob in the dance hall and carried away into sleep by their reading. Dovisch merely scrams. Let what went on in there be for you as it remains for me one of the permanently undisclosed facts of the story. A technique with James, a necessity for me. The post at the window becomes more important than the war outside.

If you imagine from this, as we draw to an end and you get ready for leaving as I assign you now for tomorrow the first hundred pages of *The American*, if you imagine I have taken you all this way for a fairy tale ending, you haven't picked up, along the way, enough Dovisch clues. And are not yet ready for the endings of James either. For though what I saw through the window of my eyes in my study was described to make you feel it as the triumph of

They were indeed in my house, Ezra and his Cynthia, but it took a little looking. I coughed my way through all the downstairs rooms. I hummed tunes and clapped hands before entering bedrooms, even my own. Thus must a father, his spleen full of outrage, advertise his presence in his own house. At all costs avoid trauma, his own included. They were, of course, in my attic study.

I saw the light showing behind the crack of the almost closed door at the head of the stairs. I called his name. No answer. I climbed the steps, pounding my feet. No response. True, I wanted no traumas, but what was I to do with spurts of adrenalin washing out my nobility. Ezra was to hear, perhaps even feel, immediate expressions of my indignation. If it ruined the blossom with him, I resigned myself to that too. I lack the wisdom to be a gardener.

It was not to be.

They were, as the doctor had foreseen, sleeping. And together, as the expression goes, if it can be stretched to mean occupying the same bed in actual sleep. My little cotbed. Each curled like a cat on each end. Each head showing forth from under the blanket, which otherwise entirely covered both of them. Except for the one perfect leg of Cynthia, where the blanket had peeled away. Between them, on the blanket, open but face down, was a book—one of mine. At the side of the bed, on the floor, in a bowl from the kitchen, peels from oranges, cores from apples, stalks from which the grapes had been stripped. That was as far away from the bed as I looked. I went back to them, to their visible faces. The girl first, she being the nearer to me. That honey hair, glowing under the naked rafter bulb, was where it all began. Her cheek also, rose-suffused in living sleep. The lips, still moist from all that devoured fruit, perhaps, were curled at the corners. Call it satisfaction with the dreamstuff going on behind those closed eyes. Possibly. It was, nevertheless, and so it struck me on the spot, the end of my adrenalin, and of all mere bodily subterfuges. It was, plain and simple, the satisfaction of a living thing transported into the innocence of its living self. Maybe.

As for my Ezra, let me face it. Sleep alone could not un-knot his my seeing, and thus—in this muddled business of manners and morals—my self-assertion through my renunciation, it was also my loss. Emphatically. But also an enormous inch of my resignation toward it. In my own bed, with my wife across the continent, I slept, or tried to sleep, in a somewhat smaller space. And still do today.

But before I went to bed, being a mere imperfect man, I was not above trying to score a small point for myself. I called the doctor.

"Henry, they are here."

Of course he wanted to know more.

So I filled him in. Carefully I chose my words. My clauses and qualifications, my hemming and hawing, all a steal from James. Not one missed opportunity for indirection, for ambiguity, for accuracy. Finally, he could take no more of it. I could visualize the bow tie, sign of brightness, gliding up and down the Adam's apple.

"Will you please in plain English tell me what the hell happened there?"

What I told him you can perhaps already guess. By the end of this short semester you would have known it to a certainty. I took a deep breath and expelled the whole informing insight. I said merely, but entirely, conclusively—and you may all leave now—I said,

"Ah!"